Praise for the County Clare Mysteries

Whispers in the Mist

"Rich, dark, and complex—every aspect of Alber's second novel rises above the commonplace. The mystery's resolution is expertly teased from layers of motive, obligation, attraction and repulsion, all in a memorably atmospheric setting."

> —Sophie Littlefield, bestselling author of *The Guilty One*

"Lisa Alber's mysteries are atmospheric—brooding, complex, and featuring enough twists and turns to keep you guessing about the characters of County Clare."

> —Lori Rader-Day, Anthony Award-winning author of *The Black Hour* and *Little Pretty Things*

Kilmoon

"Brooding, gothic overtones haunt Lisa Alber's polished, atmospheric debut. Romance, mysticism, and the verdant Irish countryside all contribute to making *Kilmoon* a marvelous, suspenseful read."

> —Julia Spencer-Fleming, *New York Times & USA Today* bestselling author of *Through the Evil Days*

*"This first in Alber's new County Clare Mystery series is utterly poetic... The author's prose and lush descriptions of the Irish countryside nicely complement this dark, broody and very intricate mystery."

> —*RT Book Reviews* (four stars)

"In her moody debut, Alber skillfully uses many shades of gray to draw complex characters who discover how cruel love can be."

> —*Kirkus Reviews*

"Newcomer Lisa Alber's stirring debut *Kilmoon*...exudes Irish countryside atmosphere. The murder plot is solved neatly and the door is open for Merrit's further adventures."

—*Library Journal*

"Lisa Alber's assured debut paints Lisfenora, County Clare, at the height of the local matchmaking festival, when the ordinarily sleepy village is crammed with revelers, cadgers, and con men galore. Amid mysteries and mayhem, Alber captures the heartfelt ache in all of us, the deep need for connection, and a true sense of purpose."

—Erin Hart, Anthony and Agatha-nominated author of *The Book of Killowen*

"In this successful debut of a new mystery series, Lisa Alber has set into motion a unique cast of characters, and readers are certainly going to want to know what else she has in store for them."

—BOLO Books

"In the captivating *Kilmoon*, Lisa Alber serves up a haunting tale of Merrit Chase, a woman who travels to Ireland to sift through her family's dark past in search of a future seemingly fated to elude her. With exquisite craft and a striking sense of place, Alber serves up a rich cast of unforgettable characters and an intricate, pull-no-punches plot. Raw with grief and painful honesty, *Kilmoon* is a soulful and beautifully told tale that never lets up, and never lets go."

—Bill Cameron, author of the Spotted Owl Award-winning *County Line*

"Full of surprises...Great Irish setting, compelling characters, and a tale full of passion, hate, and murder, told with style and craft."

—Ann Littlewood, author of the Iris Oakley "zoo-dunnit" mysteries

FIRST EDITION
First Printing, 2016

Book format by Bob Gaul
Cover design by Ellen Lawson
Cover image by iStockphoto.com/18485054©northlightimages
Editing by Nicole Nugent

Midnight Ink, an imprint of Llewellyn Worldwide Ltd.

Library of Congress Cataloging-in-Publication Data
Names: Alber, Lisa, author.
Title: Whispers in the mist / Lisa Alber.
Description: First edition. | Woodbury, Minnesota : Midnight Ink, an imprint
  of Llewellyn Worldwide, Ltd., 2016. | Series: A County Clare mystery ; #2
  | Description based on print version record and CIP data provided by
  publisher; resource not viewed.
Identifiers: LCCN 2016017776 (print) | LCCN 2016007592 (ebook) | ISBN
  9780738749723 () | ISBN 9780738748962
Subjects: LCSH: Teenage boys—Death—Fiction. |
  Murder—Investigation—Fiction. | Mute persons—Fiction. | Family
  secrets—Fiction. | Ireland—Fiction. | Psychological fiction. | GSAFD:
  Mystery fiction.
Classification: LCC PS3601.L3342 (print) | LCC PS3601.L3342 W55 2016 (ebook)
  | DDC 813/.6—dc23
LC record available at https://lccn.loc.gov/2016017776

Midnight Ink
Llewellyn Worldwide Ltd.
2143 Wooddale Drive
Woodbury, MN 55125-2989
www.midnightinkbooks.com

Printed in the United States of Americaw

WHISPERS

IN THE

MIST

A COUNTY CLARE MYSTERY

LISA ALBER

MIDNIGHT INK
WOODBURY, MINNESOTA

ACKNOWLEDGMENTS

I'm honored that I get to thank Terri Bischoff and Jill Marsal. Thank you!

Whispers in the Mist was a long time in coming, and many people provided invaluable feedback along the way. Cheers to you! Michael Bigham, Cindy Brown, Tracy Burkholder, Jeannie Burt, Dawn Caldwell, Debby Dodds, Warren Easley, Sharon Eldridge, Holly Franko, Susan Gloss, Jennifer Goodrick, Wendy Gordon, Alison Jakel, Kassandra Kelly, Becky Kjelstrom, Evan Lewis, Janice Maxson, LeeAnn McLennan, Angela M. Sanders, and Kate Scott.

Thanks to D.P. Lyle and Chris Ginocchio for their medical insights.

I'm indebted to Elizabeth George and the Elizabeth George Foundation for providing me with time.

AUTHOR'S NOTE

I traveled to Ireland for the first time for fiction research in 2001. Since then I've visited the country three more times. With each visit, I become more savvy and better at knowing what questions to ask.

That said, I'm the first to admit that some aspects of Garda Síochána hierarchy confound me. For the series, this means that Division Superintendent Alan Clarkson, Danny's boss, works a position that doesn't exist. What I called garda officers in *Kilmoon* are actually referred to as DOs—detective officers. (In England, the equivalent officers are DCs—detective constables.) I've corrected the latter error for *Whispers in the Mist.*

I'd like to give a special shout-out to my Garda besties, former Detective Sergeant David Sheedy and Detective Sergeant Brian Howard. Thank you, thank you!

As I continue writing and researching, I'll continue to learn—which is one of the fun aspects of writing this series. Meanwhile, literary license covers all breaks with reality, some purposeful, some not. ☺ Thank you.

To Arlene Joyce Alber, my mother,
Who inspired my love of books and reading.
In memory of her memory.

There was always a voice within the fog; from ancient times its wet hiss could cajole, could fool an innocent into Grey Man's grasp. Grey Man brought death, everyone knew that. Locals in Lisfenora village, County Clare, had always known what haunted the fogs that rolled in off the Atlantic.

So it went without saying that on a Wednesday afternoon, mid-September 2009, locals marked the day Grey Man spread its moist shroud over sheep, rock walls, and pocked limestone along the Irish coastline. Local lore about the predatory faerie that oozed its way onto land when the fog rolled in sent children to their mammies' beds in fright for their lives. In the fogs that lay thick over the land, anyone might catch a glimpse of a figure with a cloak made of swirling mists. It might arrive anytime to cling to the land with sinister tendrils, waiting for the right moment to snatch an innocent soul into its gloom.

Later, the most superstitious of the locals claimed to have felt a tingle along their spines and a few hairs risen on their necks.

And later still, all of them would ponder Grey Man within their midst.

Wednesday

There is special providence
in the fall of a sparrow.

William Shakespeare

ONE

A BREEZE BUFFETED DANK mist against Danny Ahern, sinking a chill deep into his bones where regret had already started to calcify. Standing at the threshold of the house into which he had carried his bride and later their wee ones, he wavered, closing his eyes. This, the scene of the slow, corrosive death of his marriage.

On a silent exhalation, he opened his eyes and pushed open the front door to the sound of wailing from one of the bedrooms and screeching from the kitchen. Mandy ran into the living room, her gaze clouded with panic.

"Mam!" She skidded to a halt upon seeing Danny. "Da, you're here!"

"You bet I am. Every day, all the time."

Mandy had called Danny to inform him that her ride to school had cancelled and Petey was acting scared and Ellen had rolled over instead of getting out of bed.

One of Ellen's bad days, in other words. They might both be to blame for the failed marriage, but he was the culprit for Ellen's current mood. He'd moved out a year ago, and he was certain Ellen remembered the exact date as well as he did. September 8, 2008. After two long years of turmoil and waning patience on both their sides, he'd finally admitted that he was the reason she wasn't healing. His very presence rubbed her the wrong way, intensifying her guilt over their youngest daughter's death. Beth had fallen from a jungle gym—an accident—but the extended emotional aftermath had worn out their marriage.

September wasn't a good month for either of them. Beth had died in September.

"I'll drive you to school, sweetie." His son's wailing still echoed from the back of the house. "Why's Petey crying?"

Mandy leaned against him. "He had a nightmare and went to bed with Mam. He won't come out of her room."

Jesus, the look in his daughter's eyes. She was only nine years old, for Christ's sake. Her gaze shouldn't be dulled by worry and fear that she was doing everything wrong. He knew the feeling well, but she must not end up stuck on that sorry path.

"You did everything right," he said. "Just perfect."

Her chin wobbled. Danny knelt and hugged her to his chest, his heart breaking.

"Are you feeling bad?" he said.

She nodded against his shoulder. "My tummy hurts."

"That's no good," he said. "In fact, that's a fat bloody wad of cowshite."

"Da," she sighed, but she smiled as she raised her head. "That didn't even make sense."

Danny carried his daughter back to the kitchen, poured cereal, milk, and orange juice, and told her to brush her hair. He found Petey standing beside the windows in Ellen's bedroom, hiccuping on snotty breath and peeking outside from between the edges of the closed curtains. Ellen sat on the bed with her head resting on raised knees.

5

Danny picked up Petey and carried him out of the room. His initial sadness gave way to worry when he felt Petey's feverish forehead.

"You get to stay home from school today, little man. How do you like that?"

Petey landed on his bed in a jumble of limbs, his hair stuck to the sweat on his forehead. Danny swiped at the reddish-brown hair that his children had inherited from Ellen and tucked Petey's lanky limbs—Danny's contribution to the gene pool—under the covers.

"I'll be safe at home, won't I?" Petey said.

"Of course you will. Mandy said you had a nightmare?"

Petey grabbed his stuffed flamingo. "Because yesterday I saw *him*. You know."

Danny didn't know but he nodded, keeping his expression neutral.

"He came out of the fog right in front of our house. He had a big cape like you see the baddies wear on the telly, and he was dragging someone behind him. Sucking her up. She tried to run away, I saw her, but then he held out his hand and his evil Grey Man powers made her come back to him. But when she came back she was all curled up like her stomach hurt."

Danny sat on the edge of the bed, inhaling the sweet scent of child sweat and trying to come up with a comforting response. Petey, at five, was prone to nightmarish fancies on the best of days—and today wasn't one of those.

Petey gazed up at him, imploring him to believe that he'd seen Grey Man.

"Did you see a swallow?" Danny said. "Swallows always follow Grey Man when he's lurking about."

Petey shook his head. "There was too much mist."

"That's true. Here's what I think. I think that Grey Man passed our house without stopping for a reason, and that reason is that he knows I'm a detective sergeant, and I'll capture him and I'll throw him in jail."

Petey rolled away. "But you don't live here anymore."

Danny rolled him back over and kissed his forehead. "Grey Man knows I'm around, just a few miles away. He knows I protect everyone in this house. Now, how about you think about the great day you'll have doing a bunk from school?"

Petey semi-settled, Danny checked on Mandy in the kitchen, and then returned to Ellen. He exhaled hard in an attempt to dislodge the knot that always affixed itself to his rib cage when it came to his wife. The bedroom smelled fusty, like too many unbathed skin cells settled on every surface. Danny flung back the curtains so that the rings clanged against the curtain rod.

Ellen lifted her head. Dark circles dragged down the skin beneath her eyes. Her hair lay tangled around her shoulders rather than in its usual sleep-braid. "I know," she said.

"Have you been taking your meds?"

She waved a dismissive hand. "Leave it. I had a bad night, that's all. I'm awake now, and I'll see to the kids. I'm fine."

"You're sure? I could—"

"I said"—she tossed a pillow in his direction—"I'm fine."

This was the way of it between them now. Petty jolts of annoyance at every turn.

"I'll take Mandy to school," Danny said, "and I told Petey he could stay home—"

Ellen sighed.

"—and that's not a problem, right?"

Ellen rose and closed the bathroom door behind her with a decided *click*. Not quite a slam, but enough to let Danny know she'd read something in his tone that he should have kept to himself.

"I'll come the usual time tonight," he said through the closed door. Normally, he visited each evening to tuck the children into bed. His favorite time of day, in fact. Reading stories returned them to their sunnier days as a family. He was determined to maintain as many of their old routines as possible.

For now, there was nothing for it but to kiss his son goodbye and bundle Mandy into his ailing Peugeot. The car ground to life with a sputter and a gurgle. Ellen had been better the last three or four months, but her improvement didn't come without relapses.

The fog had thickened in the thirty minutes he'd been inside the house, bringing with it the scent of the ocean. Drystone walls along the side of the road lurked like a monster race of serpents, petrified but ready to return to life. Danny's mother used to tell him all manner of old tales about serpents, changelings, sprites, and especially Grey Man, who festered offshore waiting for its chance to ooze inland, visible to anyone who could see beyond the fog of their limited vision.

Danny turned onto the lane toward Lisfenora and Mandy's school.

"Da?" Mandy tapped his thigh. "I think maybe Petey did see Grey Man. On our lane."

"Believe me, sweetie, Grey Man hasn't come calling. Not to worry."

Five minutes later, Danny's mobile *briiing*ed and Mandy held it up to his ear while he drove. He'd spoken too soon.

TWO

F ROM D ANNY'S HOUSE, DOZENS of lanes wound between hedgerows, whose bare branches disappeared into the mists, and over hillsides dotted with limestone and grazing cows. A few of these lanes meandered into Lisfenora, a village that turned into a tourist attraction each September. Brightly painted shops and pubs with names such as the Plough and Trough Pub welcomed the throngs of visitors who arrived to participate in the annual Matchmaking Festival—or, if not to participate exactly, to join the party atmosphere for a randy weekend.

During the day, Liam the Matchmaker held court in the plaza, a small, cobblestoned square in the village center. Despite flowers well past their bloom and benches in need of new paint jobs, the plaza, and the village in general, held its own when it came to satisfying tourists on the hunt for all things Irish quaint and Irish picturesque.

The matchmaker himself didn't disappoint either. He wore his signature purple topcoat with tails and a fluffy scarf to ward off the chill. He was slender, frail almost, but held himself erect. He wore his advanced age like women wore shawls: casually draped around himself, as if he could shuck off decrepitude with a quick flick of the wrist.

At least, this is what Merrit Chase thought as she wriggled around to get the circulation in her feet going again. She perched next to Liam, the father she'd met for the first time a year ago, on their appointed divan, which the village supplied along with a caravan tent. Merrit supposed she could start thinking of Liam as "Dad" by now, but she didn't. He was "Liam" and would be for a long while to come, maybe even for the next thirty-three years of her life. He was still a little scary to her, a little overwhelming, not to mention a lot worrisome. It had been a challenging year, to say the least.

Distracted by her tingling toes, she half spied a man beelining toward Liam through the crowd that had congregated in the plaza. She didn't think much of him until he halted with a skid of his shoes in front of Liam. His voice practically curdled it sounded so sour.

"You have a death to answer for, Matchmaker," the stranger said.

Merrit froze with one leg stretched out in front of her. Not five minutes previously, she'd felt something lurking besides the mist that had started to creep in from the fields. Foolishness, maybe, but Merrit couldn't help her paranoia. Before leaving for the plaza, she'd discovered the word *slag* painted on her driver's side car door in bold magenta slashes. The graffiti "artist" could be any of the locals who eyed her with skepticism, even suspicion, as she perched next to the celebrity matchmaker at the center of it all. The culprit could even be the man who stood before them now, swaying from one foot to the other with freckles dotting his receding hairline.

"Well?" the man said. "Nothing to say about killing my mother, Matchmaker?"

The man caught Merrit glancing at his shaking hands and shoved them into his pockets. Merrit sat forward, wanting to reach out to him despite his—hopefully—false accusation, but just then Seamus Nagel, who had been waiting for his turn with Liam, stepped up and pushed the freckly man out of the way.

"Bugger off," Seamus said. "Liam chose me next. Been watching his antics for years, and I'll not wait another second for my turn with him."

"We'll chat," the stranger said to Liam. "This needs to end."

"If by 'this,' you mean your rudeness, then yes, I agree," Liam said.

Seamus guffawed and settled next to Liam with an enthusiastic slap of hands on thighs. "Cheeky bastard."

"Indeed," Liam said.

Merrit peered into the crowd where the man had disappeared. That was a little more than *cheeky*. Beneath the man's accusatory tone she'd sensed something more. A kind of desperation.

Liam sat between her and Seamus, unflappable as usual. He nodded at her. *Ready?*

Her lungs spasming with anxiety, Merrit leaned in to whisper in his ear. "What did that man mean?"

"Bugger all if I know."

She wasn't sure she believed him. She knew from firsthand experience that he wasn't an angel beneath his charismatic façade. He had a complicated past and a tendency to sideline the truth when it suited his purposes.

"Promise?" she said. "You don't know what he was talking about?"

"No, and don't you fret. He can find me again, and I'll settle him out. And, before you ask—I doubt that man had anything to do with the message on your car."

She gave up for now. Liam with his unerring instincts had zeroed in on her next question, and shut her down too. His gimpy hand, a result of a long-ago run-in with a rock wall, landed on her arm. "Now focus."

Right. Focus. Merrit inhaled the comforting scent of vindaloo chicken coming off the nearest food kiosk and reached into her coat pocket to touch her inhaler. Its cool and smooth surface grounded her, allowed her lungs to relax. She adjusted Liam's matchmaking ledger on her lap. The book had to weigh twenty pounds with its leather-bound cover and thick stock. It was a monstrosity, but it went with Liam's image. She relaxed her clawed grip on the pen and wrote Seamus's name on a fresh line.

"I'm that ready to meet my second wife," Seamus was saying. "The first one broke Brendan's heart, doing a runner back to Dublin. Years ago now, but I'd eat a dirty nappy before I'd forgive her."

Liam wrapped an arm around the back of the divan. Merrit watched, fascinated, as Seamus reacted to Liam's silent invitation to reveal his innermost thoughts. He shifted his hips toward Liam and reclined so that he almost touched Liam's outstretched arm.

"You already know Merrit," Liam said, "my right-hand woman, learning the ways of the matchmaker because this old gent can't live forever."

"Ay, we all know Merrit by now, don't we?" Seamus said, his tone so neutral he might as well have shouted out his disdain.

Last September news of her kinship with Liam had spread through the village faster than a windswept fire back in her native California. Twelve months hadn't lessened her outsider's status. If anything, the locals had gotten used to disliking her and enjoyed their communal dismissiveness. She knew what her detractors thought. She was a baby to the land, a mewling Yankee pretender to the matchmaking throne who dared to act like a proper Lisfenoran.

If only the locals knew that she walked around the village, with its cobblestones and eighteenth-century storefronts, longing to feel part of the community. No way could she follow in Liam's giant footsteps, but here she sat, in training for a time-honored position. She'd let Liam convince her that she had the talent for matchmaking—he said she was "charmed for it"—but she felt like a fraud. Evidently, the villagers agreed.

Only fourteen more days until the end of September, the festival, and the daily public flaying under the village's critical eye.

Swallowing down her nerves, Merrit readied her pen and prepared herself to learn from Liam's example. She already knew something about Seamus. He was well-known around the village, a man who drifted from job to government dole to job with cheerful ease. He spent most of his free time in the Plough and Trough. He'd moved to the village from Dublin years ago and made himself more local than some born to County Clare.

Merrit grimaced down at the ledger. She hadn't realized she'd absorbed so much gossip. Must be infectious. In any case, she'd often noted him at the center of the other regulars at the Plough, the first to call out a hello to his friends, always the jovial drunk.

"My life is favorable these days, very favorable indeed," Seamus said. "And my son Brendan has proved himself quite the man. I wager I'll be living alone soon enough. I'd say it's the right time to ponder my next stage in life."

Liam waited and Seamus obliged him by filling up the silence.

"Brendan's future—that's what's important. He's doing well at the shop, and I've no doubts he'll be made manager." He waved at a few of his mates in the crowd. Good-natured jeers floated through tendrils of fog in return. "What I've found in the last few months is a bit of relief, and I want to share it with a good woman who knows how to cook. Call me a Neanderthal, but that's what I want."

Merrit's inner antennae quivered. She felt a familiar stirring, an instinct rising to the surface. She'd always experienced these sudden insights but had never paid attention to them until she arrived in Ireland. Liam called it her secret power, this intuition of hers, the best trait for a matchmaker.

"For a chronic bachelor," she blurted, "you're suddenly eager for marriage. What's most on your mind these days? There's something, isn't there?"

Seamus stiffened. "What's most on my mind is my old age, if you must know."

He was telling the truth and lying at the same time. He reminded her of the freckly man. His words hid other thoughts altogether.

Merrit opened her mouth, but Liam intervened. "Seamus, you're a pisser, you know that? I know just the woman you want. You've had too many years just you and the boy. You need a woman who likes home life and is sassy enough to mend your slovenly ways. You need a set of grooves to keep you on track, that's what. You wouldn't mind spending less time in the pubs, now would you?"

Seamus speared Merrit with a gloating little glance. "Bloody psychic, you are. I wouldn't mind someone to help me get this gut off meself, at that. But independent, like—I won't be giving up the pubs altogether."

Merrit stared down at the page, without insight after all, and apologized to Liam after Seamus left. "I shouldn't have spoken out like that. I didn't have a proper handle on him."

"Trust your instinct. You're witchy when you set aside distractions."

"Fat chance today," Merrit said.

"You weren't far off with Seamus anyhow. He's the last person I'd expect to set off on a course of self-improvement. We'll take our time with him. He's jumping the gun on something, possibly about Brendan. That boy never struck me as a go-getter. Seamus is ever hopeful about him, though."

"It's obvious he dotes on his son."

"Oh yes, he'd do just about anything for that boy."

Merrit bent over to write Liam's assessment in the ledger.

Liam blew on his fingers. "Fetch us tea, would you? The damp is burrowing into my bones. And don't you be worrying over me. I'm fine on my own."

"Are you sure?"

"Yes. Go now. I'll take the ledger."

Liam wasn't used to being watched over, and by a daughter at that, so she took her leave, relieved to be away from the shifting crowd. Fog streams that had started to roll in from the fields had thickened. Hazy figures merged with and split from the murk, looming into view and then disappearing again. In the muffling fog, they were closer than they sounded. Merrit spun around, looking for the freckled stranger.

Instead, a girl with a hoodie drawn over her head filtered into view. Masses of curls leaked out the sides of her hood. She twitched away from a group of men and approached Merrit with shoulders hunched and jaw clenched. Quite determined, it seemed, not to mention socially awkward. Plenty of that to go around at the festival, though.

"Hello." Merrit smiled. "Can I help you?"

With unsettling intensity, the girl stared at the moonstone pendant that Merrit always wore, the one she'd inherited from her mom. She raised her hand, signaling something.

"I'm sorry, I don't understand—" Merrit said.

The girl inhaled with a quick hiss and leaned into Merrit. Before Merrit could react, the girl's hand appeared out of the murk and grabbed the pendant. She yanked, and the silver chain dug into Merrit's neck. Another yank, and the girl vanished into the fog along with Merrit's necklace.

THREE

Inside the Plough and Trough, Alan Bressard stood with his back toward his customers and, thus, toward the picture windows that looked onto the crowded plaza. He might have caught a glimpse of a girl darting away from Merrit Chase if he'd been inclined toward window gazing. But he wasn't. Especially in September. He'd long ago lost interest in the Matchmaker's Festival except for what it meant for his cash flow.

He pondered a chalkboard that hung above the cash register. Yes, he was done with this bit of wisdom. He erased a quote by Immanuel Kant: *Out of the crooked timber of humanity no straight thing can ever be made.* On either side of the chalkboard, rows of bottles hung upside down with optics attached to their ends to ensure one-ounce pours. Above them the elite liquors sat ignored and dusty.

"How about something cheery for a change?" one of his regulars said. Before Alan knew it, the old fellas who lined his bar like crows on a telephone line added their shite to the mix. In fact, his regulars called themselves the "crows" and so did everyone else.

"I've got a good one for you from a comedian, can't remember who, though," Mickey said. "*If women ran the world we wouldn't have wars, just intense negotiations every twenty-eight days.*"

"Give me Mae West," said Mackey. "*A hard man is good to find.*"

Mickey and Mackey were brothers, old, garrulous, and forever the bachelor farmers.

"Especially with you lot," Alan said, but his comment got lost amongst the cackles.

There were about a dozen regulars who traded off during the day. Even now, at eleven in the morning, Alan could count on seeing at least two of them slouching on stools closest to the taps. They were the old guard of Irish drinkers with bulbous veined noses and thick accents mixed with middle-aged men following hard on their tracks. The pack leader, Seamus, one of the younger fellas—that is, mid-forties or there-abouts—carried the biggest nose of all. Seamus had just arrived full of news about engaging Liam to find a wife for him.

Seamus to find a wife? Couldn't be true. Not in this lifetime. Alan kept his mouth closed, however, and his ears open, curious despite himself.

"What are you after, going to Liam anyhow, you daft bastard?" Mackey said. "Nothing like a woman to take the wind right out of yer sails."

Exactly, Alan thought.

"I tell you this," Seamus said, "we're in for a sad time of it when Liam passes—God rest his future soul—because that Merrit has all the insight of a mealy potato."

"And a woman," Elder Joe, another crow, snorted. He fiddled with the blue bow tie he always wore, a sure sign that he felt personally af-fronted.

17

Joe Junior, younger than Elder Joe by all of five years, chimed in next. "What's going to become of the festival, I ask ye? That lassie's bad luck, you mark me."

Solemn assents all around.

It was as if twelve days, not twelve months, had passed since Merrit's arrival. The Irish loved to hang on to the past. Just their nature, Alan supposed. In those first weeks after her arrival, Merrit had managed to topple over their complacent village ways. It was like dominoes falling, her arrival and then *bam*—death of a leading citizen, *bam*—tales of bribery, *bam*—revelations about Liam's darkhorse past, *bam*—an arrest no one saw coming. And the last, mightiest *bam*—Merrit as matchmaker-in-training.

As an outsider himself, Alan knew she was in for a massive bollocking for years to come. He'd emigrated from France—he counted back—holy mother of everything, could it be gone twenty years ago now? It seemed so. He'd been an angry young lad, all of sixteen years old, and even this far along in time and maturity he still wasn't considered a proper Lisfenoran.

He shrugged to himself—*c'est la vie*—and blew in the general direction of the top shelf. A mote of dust puffed into the air. It drifted for a second, then dropped as if dejected by its shabby surroundings.

Alan half turned to check the crows' pints and noticed a stranger slouched amongst them, frowning into his coffee cup. Tidy buttondown shirt, but unshaven and puffy-eyed. Yet another tourist after a night of festival-induced randiness. The uptight-looking ones sometimes let it go the most at the festival. Alan had long ago given up on classifying people, except if they were assholes. Male or female, assholes were assholes.

The stranger caught Alan's eye and asked—no mistaking his Dublin accent—about hotel vacancies in the village.

"You might find a family willing to rent out a bedroom," Alan said, "but I wouldn't count on it. Let it go a little late, did you then?"

"Couldn't be helped," came the response. "I didn't know I was coming until the day before yesterday, and I didn't have time to muddle about researching vacancies."

"You might try staying in Corofin or Ballyvaughan."

"I might, indeed, except that my car broke down on top of everything else."

Alan beckoned his junior barman to refill the sorry blighter's coffee cup and turned back to the chalkboard. He'd forgotten what he'd meant to write. Every year, the festival exhausted him. It was one month out of each year that accounted for a hefty chunk of his profits, but by Christ, for that month he lived in the bar. His pub filled to capacity soon after opening, all the way through to closing. He offered the full Irish fry-up seven days a week instead of only on the weekends. Eggs, rashers, sausage, tomatoes, brown bread. The smell of it nauseated him at times, but the extra effort paid off.

Behind him, conversation stuttered to a halt and resumed on a querulous note. Alan surveyed the pub to see who had caught the crows' attention. He couldn't miss the slight girl with darting eyes. If a human could be said to be slinking, then she was, like a cat trying to disappear in plain sight. He understood what bothered the crows; they were old-school enough to question the presence of a girl alone in a pub.

Her eyes grazed over people as she passed them, then caught on Alan. From across the many heads, Alan saw their spark of intelligence, their fathomless brown depths that took in everything around her, and his heart clutched like a fool. *Ah, merde.* Quick as a light switch, he reminded himself that this was the festival talking. Hormones everywhere.

The stranded Dubliner nodded at the girl. Belatedly, Alan realized that the girl's gaze hadn't lingered on his tattered self at all. She signed something to the coffee drinker, who waved his hand in acknowledgment. She continued weaving her way through the crowd. The way she contorted her body to avoid brushing against strangers reminded Alan of a modern dance performance he'd once seen. Odd, but oddly graceful at the same time.

"Not the full shilling, that one," Seamus said.

"I'd wager she's smarter than you," the coffee drinker snapped. With a deep, what looked to be fortifying, breath he raised a hand in quick apology. "She'll find a safe corner. She always does. Best to leave her be until she settles. She's shy, like."

"And who are you now?" Seamus said with a proprietary air that amused Alan. God forbid an outsider trump him in conversation.

"I'm Dermot, her brother." He sipped his coffee. "She's Gemma. And before you say anything else, Gemma functions in society, holds down a job, and pays her bills."

Alan eyed Dermot, comparing his sharp chin and nose against his sister's features. The features looked better than good on Gemma and average on Dermot. He was at least ten years older than she was, and he looked it.

"You're sure about the girl then?" he said.

The man's lips pursed and he straightened. His tone turned frosty. "She's older than she looks. Twenty-six." He sagged as if leaning into a noose he'd never pull free from. "Believe me, I know how it looks, but she's doing well. Fact that she came in at all is a bloody miracle. She avoids crowds if she can."

The girl-woman passed in front of the fireplace and aimed herself toward the back wall.

"Ah, Christ." Alan started forward, but Dermot had risen and held him back with a request to wait and watch.

Bijou, Alan's eighty-pound dog, lounged in a cozy corner to the right of the hall that led to the bathrooms and kitchen. Most strangers sidestepped the dog or ventured a tentative hand toward her for a sniff. This girl-woman, Gemma, however, entered into a crash course straight toward Bijou's throne of a dog bed. She dropped onto the pillow and wiggled herself in between the dog and the wall. Bijou, delighted, pushed her oversized gargoyle head against Gemma's in an ecstasy of licks.

"Gemma's more comfortable with animals than people," Dermot said. "What the hell kind of dog is that, anyhow?"

"That slobbering beast would be the fecking ugliest dog there is," Seamus said. "Uglier than a toad's arse."

"She's a *dogue de Bordeaux*. A rare breed." Alan raised his voice. "Or, a French mastiff to the lot of you *crétins*."

The crows laughed. It was something of a game with them to poke at Alan and for Alan to poke back.

Alan addressed Dermot. "Just so Gemma doesn't feed scraps to my dog. That's forbidden."

"Ay, she'll be fine. Like I said. You can tell her yourself if you want."

"She'll hear me?" Alan said.

"She hears just bloody fine, thank you kindly." He shook his head. "Christ."

Gemma pushed a jumper hood off her head and out bounced a mass of tight curls. She gazed down at her lap, where her hands rubbed over an object Alan couldn't make out.

Remembering the quote he'd meant to write, he returned to the chalkboard. *The meaning of a word is its use in language.* He thought this was true, but whatever their usage, words were meaningless most of the time. Words fooled. Actions did not. He'd learned this lesson long ago, and it was a good one.

"What's that malarkey you've written now?" Elder Joe said.

Alan didn't bother answering as he set about pulling more pints. Outside, the fog pressed against windows and tried to breathe its isolation over the premises, over Alan. Inside, the bar counter shone and firelight cast a cozy glow onto his customers. His realm. The door opened and a slim figure stood silhouetted before Alan made out Merrit Chase. The fog must have been clammier than it appeared from the inside because Merrit made straight for the fireplace. She rotated in a shivery circle while scanning the room.

"She'll not make a matchmaker, that one," Seamus said.

Seamus muttered amongst his brethren as Alan stepped out from behind the bar toward Merrit. She'd cocked her head the way she did sometimes, no doubt aware that her presence always elicited speculation.

"I won't stay long," she said. "I'm looking for someone. Plus Liam asked for tea."

She rubbed at the back of her neck and came away with fingers smudged with blood. A miniscule amount, but it startled Alan, who pulled her toward the peat fire for a closer look. He felt the locals observing them, ready to pass on the word later. On the return run, he might learn that he'd snogged Merrit in full view of his customers.

She pulled her hair to one side and obliged him by leaning into the firelight. She continued to peruse the room, now on tiptoes. "It's nothing," she said. "Just a scratch."

A perfect line of abraded skin rounded the back of Merrit's neck. "Who did this?"

She pointed toward Bijou and Gemma.

"Her?" Alan said.

FOUR

DANNY SETTLED HIS EXPRESSION into a neutral mask. Unflappable. Detached. Objective. Yet inside he felt a squirm clear into his bone marrow. He'd never get used to death. If Danny could, he'd escape into the fog that shrouded the thickets. He'd blend into the murkiness, his own version of Grey Man, he supposed.

Instead, he settled his gaze onto the far edge of the pasture in which he stood, toward a few lingering shops and pubs marked the edge of the village proper. He'd sent one of his men to manage the gawkers who had already started to gather. Detective Officer Simon O'Neil and some of the others strung crime scene tape. Other than that, Danny had the scene to himself and a few minutes to look on his victim as more than a case number.

The boy lay as if he were sunbathing. He looked to be asleep, with an angelic smile and his eyelashes resting on the tender skin below his eyes. His pale skin held memories of life, still waited for his first shave. His chapped lips hadn't started to draw back.

Danny's forensic suit crinkled as he stooped to get a closer look at the boy's head. Blood had dribbled out of his hairline toward his ear, and Danny thought he could make out a lump on the side of the boy's head.

This boy was too far from home, lost. This boy in his skinny black jeans laid out in front of grass bundles that stood almost as tall as Danny's six-plus feet. What was a boy with three silver rings, a pierced eyebrow, and useless city boots doing in Blackie's Pasture?

With a surreptitious glance at his men, Danny peeled off one of his gloves and reached toward the boy's cheek with the back of a finger. The warmth startled him and he jerked back when the boy's eyelids twitched. Heart thumping, Danny placed his hand on the boy's chest and pressed down. Air wheezed out of the boy's mouth. When Danny let up, the boy's chest heaved on an inhalation.

"Jesus and Mary." Danny scrambled for his mobile and dialed. "I need an ambulance."

While he spoke, blue eyes, dulled but aware all the same, blinked up at him. Danny rang off and grabbed one of the boy's hands. He had articulate hands, like an artist with slender fingers, or simply the hands of a sensitive boy.

Danny leaned over the boy, hoping that he found comfort in Danny's presence. Please, let there be comfort.

"You're okay. I'm here. You'll be okay. An ambulance is coming."

The boy continued blinking as if he'd already caught sight of his luminous afterlife. His mouth moved around words that slid past in an undecipherable mumble. His eyes closed but the half smile remained as his hand slipped to the ground.

"No," Danny said. "No, no, no."

He tilted the boy's head back, pinched his nose shut, and blew two breaths into his mouth. The boy's lips were so warm that he must be alive in there somewhere. A rush of chirping and flapping wings sailed over Danny as he proceeded to pump the boy's chest. Birds, yes, call him back with your song. Danny grew lightheaded but he continued breathing and pumping.

Behind him, footsteps approached at a run. "Sir? Benjy the Bagger's here."

"Get him over here." Danny was panting. "Tell him to forget his fecking cigarettes for once."

"Ahern," he heard a moment later, "what the bloody hell are you doing?"

Benjy, the state pathologist, shoved at Danny hard enough that he stumbled as he stood. He moved off, giving Benjy space to resuscitate the boy. Ten minutes later, Benjy checked his watch. "Death confirmed, 10:53 a.m."

Danny watched as a small flock of sparrows hopped and fluttered about on top of the mounds of fodder. In one wave they rose, leaving one to flounder with a droopy wing. It flew a few feet with a lopsided flutter, only to crash-land in the grass next to the boy's shoulder. Its head cocked toward Danny.

"Oh and here we are," Benjy said, "a proper harbinger of death, this one. Sparrows carry the souls of the recently departed."

"And you know this how?"

"Me sainted mother, God rest her soul."

Benjy grinned and made a move toward the bird—a male with a brown head, black bib, and grey belly. Danny waved Benjy away. "Leave him alone. Let him find his wings again."

"True or not, I swear there's a hovering that hangs over some bodies. Sometimes I can feel it in the morgue like a lingering stain. And this victim? Worse than usual, poor soul."

Danny breathed deep. What little dappling effect the sun had over the landscape had disappeared. A grey envelope of cloud passed over them, sealing them into its gloominess. The boy had looked straight at him, right into the murkiest part of his soul. Danny swallowed down a rookie's urge to vomit.

Serious again, Benjy squinted up at him. "Sorry, Dan-o, I suspect there would have been no saving him even if an ambulance had arrived in time."

"I checked his pulse, but I didn't feel anything."

"The carotid is a bigger pulse but it can be harder to find. And it doesn't help that you're wearing gloves. It's not your fault."

Oh, but it was. He should have checked the boy's wrist when he didn't feel a pulse on his carotid. Instead, he'd assumed he was looking at what he'd been told he'd find: a potential suspicious death. He'd let lingering family concerns distract him from his job.

"No identification, no mobile," Benjy said.

Danny gazed down at the victim. Tall and gangly like he, Danny, had been as a youth. And like Petey looked to be growing into.

"He looks seventeen at most." Danny averted his gaze once again. "A boy."

Besides the obvious puzzle of a city boy laid out in the middle of Blackie's Pasture, Danny sensed that the hovering something Benjy had mentioned had already insinuated itself into local life. Into *his* local life.

———

Danny strode away from the silage bundles, noting their expanse of shiny black plastic. There were three of them, and they sat in the pasture like entombed beasts ready to burst out of their shells. He shook the image out of his head. He didn't like his imagination sneaking up on him like this. He'd spent too much time alone in the year since he'd moved out of the house. He had to stick with reality. A boy—a lost boy—had died in his arms.

"Sir," Detective Officer O'Neil called after him. "Crime scene tape all hung now."

"Better get started on the door-to-door," Danny said. "And we'll need a sketch artist too. I'd like a picture for the newspaper."

He continued on toward the other end of the field, nicknamed Blackie's Pasture after a swaybacked gelding that had befriended everyone who cut across his territory. The horse was long gone but the name had stuck. It was only a five-minute walk back to the plaza but this side of the village was sparsely laid out and not well lit at night.

Two men stood next to a harvester that stank of petrol and grease, and Danny imagined it belching its waste into the otherwise crystalline air. He used the image to help him regain his footing: detective sergeant, remote, official.

It didn't work. "Which one of you sorry bastards found the boy?" he said.

The men smoked and stared. The older one performed a quick sign of the cross before nodding askance toward the younger one. Danny knew the look of an old codger who wanted nothing to do with events. He'd seen that flinty gaze and those sucked-in lips dozens of times over the years. Danny turned to the younger man, who extinguished his cigarette with his fingers and tucked it behind an ear.

"That would be me," the man said. He introduced himself as Milo, owner of an operation called Milo's Silos, a for-hire grass harvester. He pointed out the man next to him as the owner of Blackie's Pasture, who had arrived after Milo called him with the sorry news about the death. "I work all through Clare and Galway," Milo said. "Quite the thriving business, I have."

"That's just plummy," Danny said. "Tell me, did you check the boy's pulse?"

"What the hell for? Even I know not to touch a dead body."

Danny gritted his teeth. "The boy was alive. Maybe he could have been saved if you'd called an ambulance when you bloody well found him."

Milo's already buggy eyes went buggier. He stepped back, holding out his palms. "You can't blame me—"

Catching himself, Danny drew in a long breath. Milo may be more stupid than a box of hair, but Danny couldn't blame him. Danny blamed himself instead.

"Fine, let's get on with it." The remnants of a shiner told Danny that this git spent a good portion of his profits in the pubs. "A little late in the season harvesting this field, aren't you?"

The field owner made a spitting noise.

In a subdued voice Milo stated that he'd had a family emergency this week. "I got part of the harvest done last week, and what's today? Wednesday? Grant me leave to take care of me poor ma, will you?"

The owner grunted what sounded like "fecking bollocks."

Upon closer questioning, Milo confirmed that he hadn't visited the pasture since the previous Friday when he'd finished work for the weekend.

"And neither of you had so much as peeked at the pasture since then?" Danny said.

"And why would we?" Milo said. "I had me business, and this bag of bones lives with his cows over toward Doolin."

"So you with your pub mates never take to hauling off to a dark pasture for a business transaction of some sort?" Danny asked.

"Transaction? As in drugs?"

"You tell me," Danny said.

Milo's googly eyes satisfied Danny that the man was as daft as he'd surmised. Still, he took down their names and numbers, and promised that one of his officers would be speaking to them in depth at a later time. Meanwhile, they agreed to wait for the scenes of crime techs to arrive for fingerprinting.

In his notebook, Danny jotted the date and time of their conversation. He'd have to take care with this case because his career wasn't exactly in high gear these days. Last year's disastrous investigation, the one that had caused the rift between him and Merrit, had all but sunk him in the eyes of his superintendent.

Across Blackie's Pasture, a spasm of surprise jerked at the guards now gazing down at Lost Boy. A moment later, the sparrow flew out of the cluster.

"Jaysus," Benjy said when Danny returned. "You missed it. That bird hopped onto the victim's chest, chirped a bit, and then flew away right as rain. Took our Lost Boy's spirit away with it, I've no doubt."

FIVE

In the Plough and Trough, Gemma turned the milky blue stone over. It glowed from within as if it wanted to impart its knowledge to her. The moment she'd caught sight of it out on the plaza, she'd known it was a sign. Why, she wasn't sure, and this was what had frightened her. If she didn't know why, then her impulse to rip it off the woman's neck must stem from the bottomless well. *That* scary place, the place inside Gemma's head where she had long ago stored the bad stuff that bided its time until her memory decided to start working again.

"Excuse me," a woman said, "I'd like my necklace back, please."

Gemma turned toward the wall, still fingering the stone. The comforting mass of the pub dog snuffled and adjusted itself against her back. Unfortunately, she'd have to engage with this woman because answers were required. She hated the inevitable necessity of communication with strangers that set her bones to feeling like glass and her skin to feeling like parchment.

Above and behind her like towering speakers, several voices rose at once. Dermot loudest of all, telling the woman to stand back. Gemma heard the shock in the woman's voice when she said, "You?"

"Back off from Gemma, if you'd please," Dermot said.

"No," the woman said, "I won't. She stole something precious from me, and I want an explanation. From her first, and then from you. How dare you"—she lowered her voice but Gemma's acute hearing caught her words—"walk up to Liam like that, full of accusations?"

Another voice, male, softer and with a slight accent, called the dog. "Bijou, come."

Bijou. Gemma smiled toward the wall so no one could see. Maybe the dog was a sign. A *good* sign. She knew enough French from listening to language tapes to know that the dog's name translated to Gem or Jewel. Someday, she'd open her mouth and speak French; it would come out in a perfect stream. Dermot didn't understand her need to study a foreign language. She'd never explained that someday it might be easier to talk in a new language. To start fresh.

She snapped back to the conversation above her—the inevitable pull of the world.

"Gemma?" Dermot said. "What's that you've got there?"

She concentrated on the pendant that glimmered in her palm, observing how the scant light played ghost games within it. Here she was, causing Dermot problems once again. She could hear it in his voice—the you're-my-burden gruffness.

I wasn't going to keep it, she signed with her hand. *Ask her where she got it.*

Dermot stooped and lowered his voice. He spoke in the careful tone he often used with her. "What's wrong? You don't steal."

She held the necklace up in an open palm toward Dermot, watching his face. He tried to hide his uneasiness beneath nonchalance, but he couldn't stop his skin color from fading to ash. He turned over the pendant, examining the silverwork.

And?

Nothing, he replied in sign language.

Ah. Switching to sign language gave him away. He often signed when he wanted privacy or to hide something. And right this second she could tell by the prissy way Dermot pursed his lips that he was hiding his emotions. He was her dear brother, but he was also a smidge on the stodgy side for a thirty-six-year-old man.

"Oh, okay then," came the soft male voice again. "Go on back if you must. Good dog."

Bijou returned to the pillow. Her tail whapped against the suede, and the scent of cedar rose into the air when her squat body dropped with a huff. Gemma reached back to pet Bijou. The dog's tawny fur tracked smooth over burly shoulders and lean waist. Gemma felt the ripple of skin over ribs before her hand reached well-muscled thighs. This dog was in excellent condition, and Gemma respected the owner's diligence to his caretaking duties.

Dermot stood. "Gemma apologizes. That's not her usual behavior, believe me, right, Gems?"

Because she felt guilty about causing Dermot problems, because the other man was a good dog owner, and because, in the end, she was curious about the woman, she steadied herself and turned around. Her heart accelerated and sweat dribbled out of her armpits, but she congratulated herself for, if not making eye contact, at least letting her gaze rest on the woman's chin.

"Good job," Dermot said. "Like going on stage, right? Worse beforehand, but once you're there, you're fine."

So you say, Gemma signed.

Dermot held up the stone toward one of the sconces and it brightened like an eye. The broken chain dangled below his hand. "This is pretty, Gemma, but if you wanted me to buy you a necklace, why didn't you ask? Of course, I will buy you a new chain for it, Miss—?"

Introductions circled between the three of them standing above her. They hurried through them as if they didn't care to stay acquainted. The dog owner, Alan, was also the pub owner. The woman, Merrit, was American. "And Gemma McNamara meet Alan and Merrit," Dermot said.

Merrit said hello, and Alan reached out to give Bijou a pat. Over by the bar, pint glasses clanked and someone howled with laughter.

Ask her where she got the necklace, Gemma signed.

Dermot returned the broken necklace to Merrit. "She would like to know where you got the necklace."

"Oh, is that all?" Merrit's face brightened when she smiled. Gemma liked her for not treating her like a curiosity and for stooping to answer her. She didn't raise her voice or slow her speech either. Her hair glinted with red highlights even in the shadows, and her light hazel eyes glowed from within like the moonstone, except with a green glow rather than blue.

"I got the necklace from my mom," she said, "who'd gotten it from my father."

"That's the simple version," Alan said. "Most interesting is who Merrit's father is."

"And why," Merrit said, "must I explain when we both know that the minute I leave the whole lot of you locals will rush to confess my many sins to Gemma and Dermot?"

"Come, Bijou," Alan said. "Time for a walk."

Eighty pounds of dog flesh sat up again and leaned against Gemma, then followed Alan's stiff form out of the pub.

"Sorry," Merrit said to Gemma. "Village politics. Long story short, I came to Ireland to meet my biological father and stayed. Or, am staying for the moment." She paused. "My dad is Liam the Matchmaker. I'm the grand usurper and demon seed, especially because his son, Kevin, moved away last year pretty much because of me and hasn't been seen since. He was adopted, and here I arrive, a blood relation—anyhow, I'm suspected of casting him out with a hex, I'm sure, not to mention wrecking a marriage and bringing murder to the village, which of course I didn't. Not really, anyhow. You'd think people would lighten up after a while."

Merrit smiled and shrugged, but Gemma caught the discomfort beneath the nonchalant gesture. "To answer your question, my father the matchmaker gave my mother this necklace as a love gesture back in the 1970s, and I inherited it when she died."

"Excuse me," Dermot said, "did I hear you say that the matchmaker bought this necklace?"

Something in Dermot's tone made Gemma shrink into the invisible shell she carried around with her. She curled back toward the wall. The connection between the matchmaker and the necklace hit too close to home, right where Gemma's bottomless well resided. Out of her mouth came a sound, one of the few she made. The unearthly vocal scratch sounded far away, but it was hers all right. Her skin felt flayed, imagining everyone looking at her and wondering about her awful voice, so unused, so scratchy.

Behind her, Merrit rushed to ask what was wrong.

"We have our own long story." The pillow shifted and Dermot's body warmth replaced Bijou's. Gemma pressed her spine against his side.

"What does my necklace have to do with it?" Merrit said.

I don't know, screamed Gemma inside her head.

Dermot's breath tickled the back of her neck. "You tell your precious matchmaker father that he matched our mother to her murderer, and we need to talk to him."

SIX

ELLEN AHERN STOOD WITH shears in hand, stabbing at the blackberry vines that invaded her garden. She snapped the blades through a skeletal arm that reached for her out of the fog. Most of the time, she missed because tears clouded her vision worse than the fog. After a while, she punched out in any direction until, energy spent, she sagged against the rock wall. She managed a feeble last chop before dropping the shears. Scratches crisscrossed her arms from the blackberry thorns, but she didn't care.

It was no use hacking at the mess this way. She must eradicate the bloody weed by its roots. She'd stared at the blackberry invasion all summer while her marriage continued to flounder, and now that it was too late, she attempted a salvage. She was pathetic. Once in, blackberries took over like chaos itself, overwhelming everything.

She let her head sag toward her chest. The mist muffled sound but not scents. Peat smoke, that comfort; lingering berries like bottled summer; baby shampoo that she'd let Petey rub into her hair during their shower. That last, the smell of innocence.

Without little Petey, she'd not have showered at all today. Couldn't be bothered. But he'd recently started bathing with her again. At five years old, was he too old? She hoped not because that token of time with her son was one thing she could manage. He'd concocted elaborate games to prolong their showers, such as drawing on the tiles with his bath-time crayons and insisting he write the whole alphabet, then his name, then hers on the shower walls. This morning, he'd graduated to older sister Mandy's name.

She almost smiled at that, but felt her lips sag when she realized that Petey was leading her into a conversation. Day after day getting closer to his da's name. Danny. Petey already knew all the letters and sounds; he could spell out the word himself. By the end of the week, he'd ask her how to spell his father's name anyhow, and she'd teach him, and then Danny would be in the shower with them like a steam-ghost.

"Damn you, Danny," she said, turning away from the vines he'd promised to eradicate months ago. Every now and then, blaming her husband helped. She balled her fingers into fists, felt the pressure rub pain into her blisters, and then made for the house, the insides of which were no more cheerful than the outdoors. The gloom sank into rips in the sofa cushions and dulled the shine off the crystal stemware she'd inherited from her mother. Some might say her home was homey, but to her, it looked threadbare and empty.

At first she didn't catch the sound of sobbing, but once she did, her heart wrenched. Petey. Jesus, Petey. She'd spent too long with her self-pity, as usual. She followed the sound of his tears to her bedroom, where he lay with her pillow clutched to his chest.

"Petey, my love," she said. "I thought you were sleeping."

He froze, and then a second later sprang off the bed. Ellen dropped to her knees. Petey patted her cheeks and let loose a series of wails. She picked him up and burrowed the two of them under the comforter.

She inhaled baby shampoo. Between sniffs and little-boy gasps, he said, "I couldn't see you. I looked out every window, but you were gone, and I thought Grey Man got you too."

"Grey Man's not real, I told you that."

Petey shot out his lower lip. "He is too real."

After five minutes trying to reassure Petey, Ellen gave up. She gazed at the snotty smears he had left on the window. She wouldn't survive the day if she had to stay cooped up listening to him munge on about Grey Man.

"I have an idea," she said. "We're going for a walk."

"No."

"Oh yes we are."

"Why? You can't make me."

Oh yes she could. She checked his forehead. Satisfied that he no longer had a temperature, she shooed her protesting son out of bed. She helped him with his sneakers and zipped up a jacket over his pajamas. They set off over the field that backed onto their yard. There hadn't been much rain so the going was easy, none of the usual mud slurry. They walked along the drystone wall that bounded the left side of the field. Officially, they trespassed on neighbor Travis's land, but no one minded such things as long as they left the cows and sheep to their peace. The fog lightened and other rock walls appeared as faint lines that divided the hills into squares and rectangles. Great swathes of heather covered the hillsides in a purplish haze. They'd turned colors overnight, September on the wane.

Little good the peaceful vista did her today. Something lurked, all right, but this could also be her guilty conscience. Failure as a mother. Failure as a lover. Failure as a wife. She just thanked whatever saint was out there that the children hadn't mentioned the babysitter she'd found to sit them last night. Danny would have beetled his eyebrows at her and said "Oh?" in that leading way of his, putting her on the defensive. She deserved a life too.

Such as that went. What a bloody joke on her.

Petey yanked on her arm. "What about Grey Man?"

His whines filled her head but she kept on with shoulders tensed in response to the weight of him, her own sweet boy, dragging her down. Up ahead, an abandoned famine cottage perched on the nearest rise. She called the building their stone folly, and it usually welcomed them to treat it like a playhouse. Today, though, the cottage appeared like a primordial head rising out of the ground. The two windows were sunken eye sockets and the darkened doorway part of a nose. The mouth and chin were below ground, ready to gobble up wayward children. Or wayward parents. She banished the thought from her head.

Make it to the cottage; just that goal, for this moment, for this day. And then they'd turn back.

"That wasn't so bad, was it?" she said when they arrived.

"Yes, it was," Petey said, his tone sulky. "You're mean."

"I guess I am, but you'll have to live with it, won't you?"

His little fist connected with her hip. "I wish Da were here!"

Petey dashed into the cottage, stumbling over the sunken threshold. Ellen followed him but stopped just inside the doorway. The usual abandoned scent of the place had gone missing. Someone's presence had rearranged the dirt on the floor in front of the door and the grit lodged in the rock walls. Petey stood frozen in the center of the room except for the foot he edged toward something bundled on the ground. When it didn't move, he dropped to his hands and knees.

"I'm investigating like Da," he said. "I'm not scared."

On a slow breath Ellen said, "Peter Michael Ahern, come here. Right. This. Instant."

39

"I hear something," Petey whispered.

He crawled toward the far corner of the room, and before Ellen had made it halfway to him, he ran back. "We've got to save these kittens from Grey Man!"

Petey hugged two mewling kittens against his chest. Skinny and matted little things they were, and without thinking Ellen plucked them from her son and set them on the ground. She pulled Petey toward the door.

Petey let out a wail. "But what about the kittens?"

She half carried him over the threshold, and when he resisted, she gave him a get-going swat on the bum. "Off with you, or you'll not be getting dessert tonight."

"I don't care about dessert!" His fist connected with her hip again. He added a second jab before running to the drystone wall. "I hate you!"

Exhausted, Ellen watched him almost disappear into the air itself. Her fingers tingled with unspent adrenaline. Once again, she had handled the situation all wrong, letting the pressures that surrounded her day in and day out—the instability, the loneliness, the isolation, the guilt—turn into a slow burn that lit up at the wrong times.

"Stay where I can see you," she called. "And sing something so I can hear you."

"No!" A few seconds later Petey started in on the ABCs.

Ellen pulled her mobile out of her jacket pocket and dialed Danny's number. But after two rings, she hung up. She couldn't bear the thought of him pooh-poohing her uneasiness, of finding her wanting in some way. Not today.

"Petey!" she called. "I'll be right there. Keep singing."

"I hate you!" His voice, vibrant with outrage and mock bravery, comforted her. Alive and well and sitting atop the wall, waiting to take her hand for the return trek. He continued singing the ABCs.

Ellen stooped back into the cottage and toward the object that Petey had poked with his foot. A sleeping bag. In the far corner she noted a nest of sweaters and a faint smell of cat urine. Someone was feeding the kittens milk with plastic gloves as teats. It didn't look to be going well.

Ah, Christ. Squatters *and* kittens.

She backtracked toward the distressed mewling. Poor, poor mites. Unloved. In need of their share of cuddles too. She picked them up. Under the grime, they looked to be tabbies. She held them against her heart, feeling them settle into her warmth, feeling their fragility, feeling her own like cracked glass.

Something needed to be done, but she didn't know what. Only that she couldn't keep mewling about in ineffectual circles like the kittens she carried against her breast.

SEVEN

THE CROWD WAS STILL going strong at Alan's pub at half eleven when Danny entered. Sleep had eluded him. He couldn't rid himself of the image of Lost Boy's gaze going lifeless, the way his last blink had shuddered to a stop with eyelids half covering his eyes.

So here he stood, surrounded by dozens of visitors to the village, some with arms around their new life-mates. A year ago, he thought, he'd still lived at home, he'd still had Liam and Kevin in his life. He'd *had* a life. Now he had to make do with the pub when his thoughts were too loud to let him sleep.

Danny caught Alan's headshake from above his customers' heads. "Don't bother," he called. "Come around. I'll put you to work."

Danny did as directed. Alan waved Danny to a stool located behind the bar. "Only room there is," he said.

Danny gazed around the pub from his novel position. He'd never noticed the way the firelight and stained glass light fixtures reflected cheerful light baubles across the walls. Or the way the *Sláinte!* sign looked about to fall down. Spilled beer, heated wool sweaters, and peat made for a peculiar but welcoming potpourri. It didn't look half bad and it might not feel half bad to view a sea of smiles every night.

Alan ordered Danny to grab his own Guinness, and while he was at it, to keep on pouring them because he couldn't keep up. Danny was glad enough for the distraction. He lined pints to the right side of the taps to settle and placed the topped-off pints to his left. Quick as lightning they disappeared onto the waitresses' trays or Alan's quick grip.

After fifteen minutes of this, tension brought on by Lost Boy's death settled into a slight tightness in his lower back. The death had felt like watching a premonition take on form. The sparrow hadn't helped his uneasiness. What had Benjy said? Soul-bearers?

Danny gulped a mouthful of Guinness and listened in on the chat. The two Joes, Elder and Junior, were in rare form, soused on gin and mouthing off about the state of Ireland now that peoples from everywhere were moving in, changing their country with their Eastern Bloc "hoorish" ways. Sitting between the two of them, Nathan Tate, a new regular, sipped his beer and dared to disagree with them. "A few Polish girls aren't the problem. The bloody economy is."

The fight was off and running then.

"Most of them can't talk or understand us," Elder Joe bellowed. "They're changing our words the way they misuse them."

Nathan pointed to the chalkboard, where Alan's quote attempted its wisdom. *The meaning of a word is its use in language.*

"Don't give me that shite," Elder Joe said. "You're not even from here, so what do you know?"

"I'm as Irish as you," Nathan said.

"But not from around here. What's your story anyhow?"

Nathan pushed his empty pint toward Danny for a refill. Danny tried to recall what he knew about the man. Originally from one of the *W* counties—Wicklow, Waterford, Wexford, somewhere—but had lived in England for a long while. Nathan didn't speak much, but Seamus had taken him on as one of his crew. He was an artist of some sort. Danny had heard some of the local women liked the looks of him. Goatee and silver rings on his fingers. A bit of early silver at his temples and a wounded air that attracted the lassies.

"I don't have a story," Nathan said.

Elder Joe burped. "The feck you don't."

And so it went. Danny had to wonder how Alan kept his sanity with their voices pounding against him up to the second he tossed them out of the pub for the night. Their leader, Seamus, kept up his own banter with Mickey, something to do with a neighbor's wife who was so mean she'd eat you through a sack. Seamus had the grace to wait for the crowd to thin before bringing up the inevitable.

"Grey Man's after leaving you a present, eh?" he said, more subdued than usual. "No use denying it."

"If you mean, am I starting on a new case, then yes." Danny lifted his empty pint to the tap and filled it halfway. He watched the thick brown liquid swirl, its tan foam rising to the top. A guilty stab reminded him that he'd forgotten to call home to check on the kids. The first twenty-four hours of a major case were always hell. "You know I can't talk about it."

"No matter." Seamus sucked down half his pint in one go. "We've got the nearabouts truth from that eejit Milo of Milo's Silos."

"Brilliant," Danny said. "He loud-mouthing it all over the land?"

"Seems so."

A shiny bald head caught Danny's attention as it leaned into their tight locals' circle around the taps. Malcolm Lynch, owner of Pot o' Gold Gifts. Every time Danny saw the man, he pictured an alien in human drag. The man had no hair, not even eyelashes or eyebrows, not that it mattered. He ran a nice shop, one of the better ones, and always seemed to be smiling.

Malcolm cradled a brandy snifter between his two middle fingers so it rested at a tilt in the palm of his hand. "Gents, top of the lovely coming day to you," he said. "Thought I'd pop in for a nightcap before off to bed."

A series of grunts and waggling fingers greeted Malcolm. His smile widened. "The day I've had." He gazed at them expectantly and when no one responded except for a few more grunts, he continued on a brighter note. "And what's the talk?"

Seamus gulped more beer and swiped at his upper lip with the back of his hand. "And what do you think? Jaysus." Seamus informed Malcolm that they'd been talking about the dead boy in Blackie's Pasture. "You must have heard the news. Grey Man got him, would you say?"

Malcolm let his gaze wander down to Seamus's gut before beaming his smile around the room. "Grey Man indeed."

Annoyed, Danny told them to close their traps about that old superstition. Malcolm sipped from his snifter. A serene smile danced over his face.

"What's got you?" Seamus said.

"It's no wonder I didn't hear the latest news," Malcolm said, "what with my grand day in the shop. I'm telling you it was the dosh all the way around. I'm that lucky I didn't have time to hear the gossip."

Seamus rolled his eyes. "Ay, well, you mind how you treat Brendan, who does all the real work, as we all know."

"The real work—like father, like son—like that?" Malcolm said. "Couldn't be bothered to unlock the shop door if I didn't remind him every day."

Seamus flushed. The two men had puffed themselves up right enough while the rest of the crows jeered them on. Their dynamic intrigued Danny. Malcolm and Seamus were among the smiliest men in the village—Malcolm quick with conversation, Seamus quicker still with jokes. Now, the men considered each other and, while Danny watched, came to a silent understanding. Dance of the alpha male, alive and well in Lisfenora village.

"You mind yourself," Seamus said. "My son, that's what."

"Of course." Malcolm's grin returned. "I'm owing you, is that it?"

Danny pulled more pints. Seamus never talked about it, but he'd almost lost Brendan to meningitis. Danny understood the sorrow of losing a child, the way the sadness burrowed into your heart, dormant but always there. Perhaps Seamus felt the pain of Brendan's near death in the same way. It would be enough to turn anyone into a controlling parent.

Alan came through and lifted his eyebrows at Malcolm. Malcolm declined a second drink. "I've got a trim figure to keep," he said. "Cut a bit of the dash in these suits I buy in Dublin."

"And so you do," Alan said and departed again to maneuver three falling-down drunk Germans out the front door. "Time, gents. Finish your drinks and pay up," he said when he returned.

Alan grabbed up the till and the cash register tape. He told his junior barman to lock the door against newcomers and called Bijou from her corner pillow. The dog followed him into the back office with Danny close behind. Danny could almost hear Alan's ex-athlete's bones creaking and the tendons groaning against his right shoulder from an old hurling injury. By the end of the night, Alan often lurched about his bar like an arthritic bear.

In his office, Alan fell into his chair with a groan. "I need a bloody business partner is what I need," he said. "Here, I count the cash into bundles. You wrap them in rubber bands. Wait, but first."

Alan gathered up the credit card slips into a haphazard stack and shuffled through them. "Tips," he said. "Whatever else you say about Americans, they tip."

He pulled cash out of the till and allocated the tips written onto the credit card receipts into various envelopes for his staff. He then divvied the tips he'd earned amongst the envelopes.

As they worked on either side of Alan's desk, counting and bundling cash, Bijou decided to sniff every inch of Danny's left leg. Satisfied with Danny's odors, the beast leaned against Danny with her head heavy on his thigh. Saliva from her voluptuous jowls soaked through to his skin. Danny fondled the dog's ears, and she blinked up at him drowsily.

"Ay," Alan said, "so what's biting into your sleep tonight?"

"A dead boy's eyes." Danny continued, "To be honest, I still miss Liam's counsel. I'd have gone to him first, but—"

With Liam, Danny wouldn't give much thought to how absurd he'd sound talking about lost boys and sparrows and soul-bearers and hoverings and Grey Man. But then, Liam had a bit of an old-world faerie dusting about him anyhow.

"Fer Christ's sake, visit the man, would you?" Alan said. "Enough already."

Danny nodded, thinking about last year's murder case and Merrit's invasive role in the outcome. In the end, Liam had avoided the consequences of his actions, and Danny couldn't stand his own role in what happened. But fate had a way of exacting its own punishment, didn't it? It had been an excruciating year for Liam, that much was true.

They continued counting and rubber banding in silence, then Alan said, "You should know that on the plaza Seamus overheard a man—his name is Dermot—accuse Liam of somehow causing his mother's death."

Danny sat back and finished off the pint that he'd brought with him, growing more weary by the second. "Was it a serious accusation?"

"Not sure. Seamus wasn't bothered by it anyhow. Thought you should know is all." After a pause, Alan said, "Merrit dropped by the pub."

Danny snapped a rubber band and it broke. "You had to go there. If not Liam, then Merrit."

Alan didn't have to say what they were both thinking about the supposed connection between Merrit's arrival and Danny's separation from Ellen last year. Or, that to some in the village, it was too bloody convenient that Danny had moved into Fox Cottage, Liam's old place located, oh, about 300 yards down the dirt track from Liam's modern home, where Merrit now kipped.

"Merrit came in about that necklace she always wears," Alan said, punching revenue into an adding machine. A tape spooled out the back end with a grind of gears. Alan described Gemma—sister to the Dermot fella—and the case of the stolen necklace. As Alan described Gemma, a guarded expression settled over his face. Danny pretended not to notice.

"Sounds like the situation took care of itself," Danny said.

"Maybe." With more whirring fingers, Alan came up with a final total and compared it against the total registered from the till's tally "*Ah, merde*," he groaned. "I'm twenty euro off. *Putante merde*. Get on with you then, I can't calculate and talk at the same time."

"Cheers then. I have to be in the morgue tomorrow bright and early anyhow."

Thursday

Children, like dogs, have so sharp
and fine a scent that they detect
and hunt out everything—
the bad before all the rest.

Johann Wolfgang von Goethe

EIGHT

DANNY LEANED AGAINST THE wall in the morgue, doing his best to quell the return of the uneasiness that had bothered him the day before at the crime scene. Lost Boy wouldn't have liked the looks of himself now that Benjy had opened up his skull and torso, weighed and measured his internal organs—including his brain—and then bundled everything back inside his abdominal cavity.

Bleary after a sleepless night, Danny had driven to the regional hospital in Galway City with more reluctance than usual. The morgue was an unprepossessing set of rooms located beneath the hospital, and he'd lurched down on the rickety elevator, trying not to think about why he'd insisted on going to this autopsy alone. Normally, he'd have O'Neil with him.

Lost Boy had gotten to him.

Still leaning against the morgue wall, Danny sniffed at the unsettling mix of bleach, stale air, and overripe flesh. The smell seemed worse than usual. He coughed against the cloying taste of death that sat on his tongue.

"What, you squeamish all of a sudden?" Benjy said.

"Bugger off."

"I was after telling you that there's something hovering over this one. You saw Grey Man's sparrow for yourself."

Danny opened his mouth to reply but cut himself off. Benjy was a superstitious and unorthodox old shite, but even he'd scoff at the notion that the boy—far from home, alone, cut down before his first shave—had somehow communicated to Danny. Daft, completely and utterly daft.

"Anything interesting?" Danny said.

Benjy bent over Lost Boy's face. He pushed back his eyelids. "You don't see this too often."

One of the boy's irises had a strip of brown running through the blue. "And?"

"And nothing. You asked for something interesting."

Danny grunted. "You're a right treat first thing in the morning."

"I aim to please."

After another prod from Danny, Benjy got down to business. He estimated that Lost Boy had been lying on chill ground for at least eight hours before his death.

"So he died of?" Danny said.

"Your classic subdural hematoma from a nasty blow to the head. Took him a while to die, poor lad. He had a slow but steady blood leak. It might have happened anywhere and the symptoms caught up to him as he crossed the pasture."

"So we don't know that we have a crime scene."

"True enough."

"Could he have fallen off one of the grass bundles?"

"No other bruises or bumps. He didn't fall off anything."

"Bloody hell, give me something we can use. Is there a crime here or not?"

"Hitting his head this way most likely occurred with the help of another human being. Satisfied?"

"As a drunk in the desert," Danny said.

"Whatever happened, there was some force behind the blow. Did you find anything in the pasture?"

"Not so much as a tree branch." Danny wasn't sure he wanted to know, but he asked anyhow: "Could he have survived if we'd found him earlier?"

"Yes. But the boy might not have understood how serious his head injury was until too late. He'd have had a nasty headache, but that's not enough for some people to see doctors. Sometimes there's a delayed reaction with traumatic brain injuries."

"There was vomit near the bundles."

"If it's his, that's a sure sign he should have gone to the hospital. Poor sod."

Again, Danny coughed against a gluey sensation on his tongue. He tucked the cotton coverlet against the boy's shoulder.

"And see there?" Benjy pointed to Lost Boy's earlobes. "Newly pierced holes by the looks of it. The holes are fresh and they're infected."

"Someone took his earrings as a souvenir?" Danny said more to himself than to Benjy.

His mobile chirruped and he grabbed for it more hastily than usual. There was something about the morgue that made him feel like he was intruding. "Ahern here."

"Might have a Lost Boy sighting in one of the shops," O'Neil said. "A tourist saw the sketch in the paper and called around."

NINE

DURING THEIR HOUR-LONG LUNCH break from festival activities, Merrit excused herself from Liam. She left him with his seafood chowder and in his usual seat amongst the regulars at Alan's pub. She rounded the corner away from the Plough and Trough's handy location on the plaza and onto the noncoastal road that ran through the village. Most of the shops lined this road, and Merrit had it in mind to enter one of them, the most high-end of the shops: Pot o' Gold Gifts.

Bumping along in the crush of tourists, she kept an eye out for the McNamara siblings, Gemma and Dermot. Dermot had offered to pay for a new chain for her necklace, but money was the least of her concerns. She hoped they were the kind to keep their private business to themselves, but she guessed that depended on how bitter they were about their mother's death.

She'd like to protect Liam from a festival scandal if possible. He was still fragile after a year of cancer treatments. She'd had a hell of a time talking him into them in the first place, but in the end she'd dangled the perfect carrot: She couldn't step into his matchmaking shoes without training.

Liam was nothing if not ego-driven to preserve his legacy. She'd bet his will more than the chemo had caused the cancer remission—for the time being, at least.

She reached Pot o' Gold Gifts without seeing Gemma or Dermot, and was surprised by the police officer loitering at the door, smoking a cigarette. Or rather, the Garda officer. Since the Irish National Police were officially called *An Garda Síochána*, she was never sure whether using the term "officer" was correct. She decided to go local, especially because she recognized this man as working under Danny in the detective division.

"Hello, Detective Officer O'Neil."

He smiled, one of the few locals who didn't seem to harbor sideways opinions about her. In fact, O'Neil always appeared to be thinking secret and amusing thoughts, but not necessarily at anyone's expense.

"Filthy habit, this," he said. "One of these years I'll quit."

Merrit caught sight of Danny inside the shop, his lean frame lost in a baggy jacket. Merrit's chest tightened when he caught sight of her. His impassive gaze was worse than a frown—like he couldn't be bothered to acknowledge that he knew her at all.

She plastered a determined smile on her lips as she addressed O'Neil. "Any chance I can talk to the owner about fixing this necklace? I won't be a bother."

O'Neil fingered the broken chain on her palm. "That's it?" he said.

"Since you're here, I'd like to report vandalism. On my car. Like graffiti only worse. Can I give you the details?"

"I'll need to see your car. Give me your phone number, and we'll arrange a time." He grinned. "I'll let DS Ahern know too, shall I?"

On second thought, she took it back about his amusing thoughts at no one's expense.

She jotted down her phone number for O'Neil, and a moment later a signal that Merrit didn't catch transmitted itself from O'Neil to the guards in the gift shop, and from them to Malcolm, who approached from the back of the shop. O'Neil held up Merrit's necklace so the moonstone caught Malcolm's eye through the shop window.

"Merrit Chase," Malcolm said when he opened the shop door, "so good of you to come. It must be all over the village by now that I'm helping the guards with their investigation of that unfortunate lad they found. I expect a journalist from the *Clare Challenger* to drop by, won't he, Detective Officer O'Neil?"

"Only if you called him yourself," O'Neil said. "And I hope you didn't."

Malcolm bowed Merrit into the shop. His excitement was contagious, and Merrit found herself smiling at this man with his strangely eye-catching appearance and buoyant manner. He managed to carry off the hairless thing well.

She held out the broken necklace. With the utmost care, he tipped her hand toward his. The necklace slid onto his palm. "This," he breathed, "is a true vintage piece. Limited quantity, see here?"

Malcolm turned the pendant over. He pointed to letters etched into the silver mount that framed the stone. A curly *F* insignia that could be anything to Merrit's untrained eye. "For Firebird," Malcolm said. "And see the fraction 5/20?"

"I've always wondered."

"It indicates that this was the fifth pendant of this design, meaning the scrollwork around the stone's frame, out of twenty such pendants. Lovely, don't you think?"

He nodded at her with eagerness and Merrit found herself nodding in return.

"And where did you get this, Merrit?"

He said her name with a proprietary intimacy, as if they'd been fast friends for years. Merrit had no doubts that from now on he would consider her a friend. She explained that Liam had bought it for her mother.

"I'm not surprised. Liam's a man with taste. I'm sure it looked as lovely on her as it does on you." Malcolm's eyes shone. "Now. Where were we? Such good luck that you came into my shop, but then I do carry the highest quality jewelry for miles. Let me introduce you to more jewelry by the same designer."

Merrit let Malcolm pull her into the shop with an elbow hooked around her upper arm. "I won't touch anything," she said to O'Neil.

"Bah, don't worry," Malcolm said. "They're done with this area. And here I didn't remember the dead boy was in the shop until Danny appeared. A tourist called in the sighting. Quite fun, I must say. The truth is that as busy as I am, I haven't had a chance to read the newspaper yet. I'm sure I would have called the guards if I had recognized the lad's face on the front page."

The shop carried a fresh mossy scent from a candle lit next to the cash register. Swags of Irish linen brushed against Merrit's arm, and then she was circling around a display of Waterford crystal. Malcolm positioned her in front of a glass cabinet that displayed an engraved wooden sign of a long-necked bird with outspread wings rising out of the words *Firebird Designs*. At Malcolm's prompt, she peered into the cabinet at three tiers of necklaces, bracelets, rings, and earrings.

Malcolm pulled a ring from a plastic finger in the cabinet. "This brushed silver look would be brilliant on you."

"Oh, but I've got to return to the festival. Right now I'm most interested in fixing the chain on my necklace."

Malcolm pursed his lips, and Merrit felt compelled to compliment the jewelry again. She found herself promising to return when she had more time. Malcolm relaxed and said that he'd see her necklace fixed good as the day it was made.

With her stated business complete, Merrit had no excuse to stay. Still, she loitered, picking up the Firebird Designs artist's statement and willing Danny to approach. She had a feeling Malcolm would be insulted if he knew that she was pretending to be interested in the jewelry as a way to talk to Danny about Liam. Malcolm seemed the sensitive type that way.

She read the statement, curious despite herself. Signed "J," the statement professed a need to create jewelry that reflected inner beauty. *Your inner beauty made manifest for all to see.* The picture that accompanied the text showed a man of indeterminate age wearing a brimmed hat and sporting an unruly beard. He hunched over a work surface scattered with gems.

Finally, Danny arrived. "Time to escort Miss Chase outside."

Malcolm called out a promise to have the necklace ready for her on Sunday. Almost to the door, Merrit told Danny under her breath that maybe he could have a word with a couple of tourists named Gemma and Dermot McNamara to tell them to lay off Liam. They claimed that Liam had matched their mother to her murderer.

"I heard," Danny said. "But there's nothing criminal in having a belief."

"So you won't talk to them?"

"No."

Beneath Danny's gruffness, Merrit caught a hint of something else; he wasn't as disinterested as he let on. Liam had always been a surrogate father to him. More importantly, Liam missed Danny's visits. It would be up to Merrit to bridge their gap since she was the one who had caused it in the first place.

"Liam could do without the extra stress," she said. "He's still fragile. Besides, don't you have strict slander laws over here?"

"I think the word you're looking for is *defamation*."

"Whatever. At least they don't know where Liam lives, and no one's going to tell them, right?"

"Let's hope not." Danny handed her off to O'Neil. "No more visitors until we're done."

She grabbed his arm. "You still care for Liam. Don't pretend otherwise."

He shifted backwards a step and spoke as he turned away. "Don't go there. Playing the guilt card on me won't work again."

———————

Bloody Merrit. Of course Danny cared about Liam's welfare, but she'd have to excuse him if he didn't feel like jumping when she called "boo."

"Let's wrap this up," Danny called.

The few partials they'd retrieved might come back with a match. If not, they were back to nothing with Lost Boy.

Danny surveyed the shop, wondering why Lost Boy had entered. To buy an overpriced heraldic name plaque or Irish turf incense? Danny thought not. He approached Malcolm and asked him to go over his interaction with the deceased once again. "Is there anything else that comes to mind?" Danny said.

Malcolm's fingers wandered amongst the pieces of jewelry in his case, twitching them by minute degrees until he was satisfied with their arrangement. "Perhaps if I give Merrit a discount, she'll necklace or bracelet while she works the festival—"

"Malcolm."

Malcolm straightened. His lips puckered up to his nose as if he smelled something bad. "That lad, yes. I have an instinct about people, and this one, he didn't come off right from the second he entered the store. I was onto him, you might say."

"Oh? You didn't mention that before."

"I was trying to keep to the facts, but now that I've thought it through and seen how diligently your men powdered the areas he pawed, I realize that my observations are as important as the facts."

Malcolm had first caught sight of the boy as he'd strolled back and forth outside the shop. He was obvious enough the way he slouched with a mobile over his ear, pretending to have an intense conversation while snatching glimpses of Malcolm's wares in the windows. "At first, I assumed he was a spy for a rival shop owner a few villages over," Malcolm said with a put-upon sigh. "It's amazing the lengths people will go to in an effort to mimic a good thing. I get it often enough."

"Then our victim entered the shop?"

Malcolm perked up at the word *our,* as if he were an honorary member of the investigating team. Danny nodded encouragement.

"He did indeed come into the shop. On Sunday. I had to light a second scented candle because he smelled ripe as curdled milk. But I always give a man a chance, so I called out to him to take his time browsing. He wasn't a bad-looking lad. In fact, a good-looking young fella." He nodded as if satisfied, even pleased, with his opinion on the matter. "Give him a few years and he'd have cut a fine specimen for the women. But still, I could have sworn he was trying to make me out for a shakedown, as they say."

Danny wondered who the "they" were who said "shakedown." Malcolm went on to describe how Lost Boy had pawed merchandise far too rich for him. "Needless to say, I shooed him out," Malcolm said. "It's not good for business, having grubs like that in the store."

The boy's visit had occurred on Sunday afternoon. Benjy's report stated that the boy was attacked on Tuesday evening. Two days. And two days was more than enough time for a person's life to derail. Sometimes all it took was a blink of a moment, the moment you looked away.

"And your shop assistant? It's still Seamus's lad, eh?" Danny said. "I'd like to ask him a few questions."

"Brendan snuck off for lunch even though I'd asked him to start on the inventorying." Malcolm heaved one of his smiles up at the ceiling. "Best done if I do it myself as usual."

"He's working tomorrow?" Danny said.

"If you could call it that, but, yes, he'll be here."

A necklace with a pendant like tree branches caught Danny's attention. The artist had carved in texture that suggested tree bark. The graceful design forked into stylized tines. The work was quite nice, Danny decided.

Years ago he might have bought such a necklace for Ellen. He turned away from the display without examining its wares or his guilt further.

TEN

THE KITTENS WERE NOTICEABLY fatter in twenty-four hours. They couldn't get enough of the warm kitten formula that Ellen fed them through a plastic glove with pinpricks in two of the fingertips. The poor mites were still so fragile, though, mewling like their little hearts would give out when she picked them up. She kept them in a dark and quiet corner of her closet, off limits to the children unless she was present. She still hadn't washed them, not wanting them to catch a chill.

She smiled to herself, enjoying a nostalgic fit of sadness as she remembered her first days breastfeeding Beth, who'd been as ravenous as these two. Plus, later there'd been the constant vigilance, the endless laundry—but she'd loved it all. The kittens weren't far different there either. They had already fallen into a regular feeding cycle, and she already had a pile of soiled towels. As she nudged the dribbling plastic fingers toward their seeking mouths, she thought about kitty litter. So nice to ponder something as innocuous as litter boxes.

She settled herself against the closet wall with legs poking into the bedroom. She had never noticed the mustiness inside the closet or the bedraggled state of her wardrobe. Fallen hems, frayed cuffs, and stains everywhere. She'd been living like this for too long; long before Danny had moved out. It took a fresh perspective from the floor of a closet to bring home to her how far she'd let herself fall since Beth's death. That was three years ago, and perhaps three years was sufficient for the serious grieving.

Tears welled and dripped onto her cheeks. She didn't notice the chronic leaking anymore. With careful maneuvering and much patience, Ellen managed to only lose half the milk to the towels this time. So long as the kittens got enough sustenance to fall back to sleep, she was satisfied.

She changed the damp towel that lined the kittens' box with a fresh one and made her way down the hall toward the kitchen. She tossed a pile of towels and children's underwear into the washing machine. The children would be home from school in an hour, dropped off by one of her neighbors. Ellen browsed the cupboards for an afternoon treat for the three of them. She pulled down pancake mix. Yes, pancakes with Nutella on top. Odd kind of snack, but why not? They'd love it. And so would she, never mind her so-called *flabby* hips.

Just like that, what little energy she had dissipated. She leaned against the counter. For the past day, she'd used kitten care as a pathetic attempt to avoid looking at herself too closely. She'd have one last say. Somehow.

Resolved but not exactly revived, Ellen forced herself back to the task at hand only to hear an engine idling at the front of the house. Danny?

Ellen trotted into the living room and twitched the curtains for a peek outside. The fog had returned, grey enough to leach the bloom out of a rose. No, the engine rumble didn't sound like Danny's Peugeot. This engine sounded troubled in other ways, and it edged along her lane at too slow a pace, fog or not. Ellen doubled back to the laundry alcove, peering along a set of utility shelves. With Danny's old hurling stick in hand, she returned to the living room. Visions of Petey's Grey Man cavorted through her imagination, lurking about on the lane, perhaps in league with the squatters hiding out in the stone folly.

The car had moved on past her house to loiter in front of Mr. Travis's pasture next door. She opened the door and squinted at faint brake lights that faded when the engine grumbled to a stop. The fog's chill penetrated her bones. Footsteps brushed through the grass, loud against the stultifying silence.

"Young Travis, that you?" she called. "How's your father? I hope his back isn't out again."

The footsteps paused, then quickened. She caught a glimpse of a figure heading up the hill along the drystone wall. Ellen surprised herself by breaking into a run toward the parked car. She could at least memorize the plate number. Her troubles with Danny didn't touch on the children. He'd get the owner's name and particulars without questioning her paranoia. Strangers did not loiter within shouting distance of the Ahern children. This was a given.

The car gave her pause: a late-model Volvo. She approached with bat high, more puzzled than suspicious now. She was sure she'd seen this car before. She stopped, listening to the shush within the dark. She eased up to the passenger-side window and glanced into the car's interior. Nice leather interior. Takeaway cartons and—

"Jaysus!" she squealed.

A head appeared in the backseat window. With heartbeat rocketing all around her body, Ellen stumbled backwards and fell into a sprint toward the house. The car door opened and light footsteps followed her. Unfortunately, Ellen was out of shape. She stopped and whirled around, waving the hurling bat in every direction.

"Stand back! Don't come any closer!"

Before Ellen stood a skinny lass somewhere in her twenties, with a mass of tangled curls enveloping her face. Other than a little undernourished and in need of a shower, the girl didn't appear endangered or dangerous. She'd jumped out of the bat's trajectory and now circled around Ellen as if she were the one who needed to take care, not Ellen.

Ellen pointed the bat at the girl and spoke with ragged voice. "Hold your hands in the air. Please. And stand still. Give me a second here."

The girl kept her gaze aimed at the bat while Ellen got her breathing and nerves under control. Now she recognized the vehicle. For two days it had been hugging an embankment about a quarter mile down the lane. Not that she gave a flying shite about that, because the whole thing beggared the question of why this girl and her companion had been cruising her lane in the first place.

"Those wouldn't happen to be your sleeping bags up in the cottage, would they?" she said.

The girl nodded. Her mouth opened and closed while her hands jerked into a graceful dance.

"Are you deaf?" Ellen said.

With a huff of frustration, the girl shook her head.

"Okay then, how about this. Are you here for the matchmaking festival but don't have a hotel? That's a nice chariot you have. I'm guessing that you're not used to sleeping rough."

The girl nodded and stared at the ground.

"Right then." Ellen lowered the bat. "You can relax your guard. I'm not going to pummel you. Bloody Christ, strays everywhere, aren't there?"

The girl stepped forward, her expression intent. She had sharp features softened by large brown eyes that grabbed at Ellen with their expressiveness. The girl reached out a hand, oh so slowly, as if to calm an agitated dog.

Intrigued, Ellen held her ground until she understood the girl's intention. The girl lifted one of Ellen's hands and pressed an index finger against her palm.

"Go on then," Ellen said.

The girl wrote with her fingertip. After a shrug from Ellen, she repeated the gesture across Ellen's palm, harder this time.

"Right," Ellen said. "I understand. Is that a 'k'?"

Exactly, the girl's look seemed to say. She pressed on with the fingertip until Ellen understood. "Kittens?" she said.

The girl pointed to Ellen's house.

"Ah, connection made then. Yes, the kittens are fine. I found them. But you have some explaining to do, young lady."

A nod, cautious like, along with a squint that Ellen took to mean, *Oh, about what?*

"You and your friend about scared my son back into nappies, that's what. That was you two walking down the lane a few days ago?"

Again, the cautious nod.

"The point is that my son thought your friend was Grey Man dragging you into his lair. Come along. I need to show him that there was nothing to fear. He'll be home soon with my daughter."

After another minute of palm-writing *wait*, *car*, and *brother*, Ellen understood that the girl preferred to wait in the car for her friend, who was actually her brother.

"I don't think so. You need nutrients as much as those poor kittens. And don't you want to check on them?" Ellen retraced her steps back to the Volvo with the girl following close behind. "We'll leave your brother a note. You must have writing implements in here somewhere, am I right? What the devil is your name, anyhow?"

The girl burrowed into a knapsack tucked behind the passenger's seat. She pulled out the necessary tools and with a flourish wrote, *Gemma.* Then, *No one talks to me that way—except my brother.*

"I don't know what you mean. How else am I supposed to talk to you?"

Most people talk to me like I'm soft in the head. Like I might break any second.

Weariness sloshed over Ellen in tight waves. She must be an eejit for suggesting what she was about to suggest, but what could she do? Maybe she'd gather all the strays to her side in hopes she'd feel like less of one in her own life.

"See here," she said, "if your brother passes muster and if the children like you, you can lay your sleeping bags out in my daughter Beth's room. It's not so unusual during the festival. I've done it before."

And Danny hadn't liked it then either. But it wasn't like he had a say in whom she befriended. Especially now.

Gemma signaled what Ellen interpreted as an, *Oh no, we couldn't.*

"Yes, you can." On the car window, Ellen drew a broken heart in the condensation left by the fog. "Beth doesn't live there anymore."

ELEVEN

GEMMA TRIED TO IGNORE the glass-like feeling inside her bones. She knew this feeling well—like her anxiety might cause her to shatter any second. On a deep breath she reminded herself that she was the one who had saved the kittens in the first place. Nothing was going to happen to them, and nothing was going to happen to her. She was safe. Ellen was a nice person who meant her no harm. Dermot would return soon.

She sat at the kitchen table with a glass of milk, which Ellen ordered her to drink in a mom-like voice. Gemma obeyed with a troubling sense of déjà vu. This was too close to the childhood home that lurked within the fringes of her mind. Drinking her milk in a steamy kitchen with gauzy curtains over the windows. The memory from the Before time ought to comfort her, but it didn't because it arrived fraught with loss and everything that lurked within the bottomless well.

Gemma's thoughts wandered away as they often did when she was nervous. She wondered if the bar owner's dog came from a shelter, but she thought not. She wouldn't mind going back to that bar again;

she'd bought a box of dog biscuits to help motivate herself in that direction. As she so often did, Gemma practiced being a normal person in her imagination. Her counselor had taught her this exercise, but Gemma wasn't sure it worked. In fact, visualizing herself engaged in everyday activities as her best comfortable self was too daft for words.

Still, while Ellen cooked pancakes, Gemma imagined herself as a spontaneous person who hankered after a pint now and then. She imagined herself surveying the pub for an empty seat, not caring whether people looked at her, not caring about the proximity of so many bodies. She imagined herself with a voice that said "excuse me" as she maneuvered herself toward a stool and leaned over the bar and smiled at Alan. She imagined him returning the smile and herself holding his gaze long enough to notice that he was pleased to see her. "A Guinness, please," Gemma said inside her head, and inside her head her voice sounded easy and fluid. Well-used. Sing-songy and sparkly.

Knocking roused Gemma from her mental exercise. A plate of pancakes sat at her elbow, and she had the sensation that Ellen's voice had been in the background the whole while. "That must be your brother," she said. "I'll fetch him."

Their voices murmured from the living room, and a few minutes later Ellen returned with Dermot. He clutched what Gemma liked to call his Sherlock Holmes cape around him and smiled with thinly disguised relief. The smile didn't reach his eyes.

Dermot spoke with his hands. *Well done. Your counselor will be thrilled you made a new friend.*

Very funny. She has the kittens. I'll visit them after we eat.

Dermot nodded like he usually did when it came to her obsession with animals. Gemma settled into her pancakes, more than content to let Ellen's attentions veer toward Dermot. She didn't let herself slide into Gemma World, though. She kept her ear tuned to their conversation.

After Ellen's initial chastising about the loitering, scaring her half to death when she'd found their sleeping bags, she asked Dermot the natural question: "Why were you cruising my lane?"

Dermot settled a paper napkin on his lap and spread an even coat of butter and Nutella on each pancake in his stack. Hairline wrinkles around his mouth deepened as his expression closed down.

Gemma nudged Dermot with her toe, and he flashed a quick, *What? Settle down,* with his hand.

Yes, why are we here? And don't you dare say for the matchmaking festival. I heard what Merrit said in the pub—that you accused the matchmaker of killing Mam.

"It's strange," Dermot said in his fake ruminating voice. Gemma recognized it from all the times he'd manufactured ways to get Gemma out of the house they lived in together. Like the time he'd "just remembered" that he was supposed to pick up a package, but he was too busy with paperwork and could Gemma manage it on her own?

"Yes, strange," Dermot said, "how you sometimes want to return to the past for no other reason than knowing the past might help you know yourself better."

Gemma rolled her eyes.

"Oh?" Ellen said.

"Your matchmaker matched our mother is what it comes down to."

"Ah," Ellen said, not sounding impressed.

"We'd like to chat with him," Dermot continued, "but of course I forgot about the festival. We arrived on Monday and had a lead on a room somewhere around here but got lost. And our car broke down, to make matters worse. Without transport or a hotel reservation, we've been walking everywhere and we're none too civilized about now."

Ellen plopped more batter onto the skillet as Dermot went on to explain in too much detail that he'd bought sleeping bags off the

McClennan family a few lanes over—and did Ellen know them?—and that morning had finally found a man to tow the car. The spark plugs had needed replacing. They'd waited in the village until their car was fixed and returned to clean out the old cottage. All very innocent, really.

Ellen set a plate of pancakes in the oven. Gemma felt Ellen's skepticism rising off her in waves. She signed toward Dermot. *You need to tell her about me. Then she'll understand.*

Not everything is about you, he signed back. *You aren't supposed to be here, if you remember.*

And confronting the matchmaker doesn't make this trip about me too?

Dermot shook his head, but he couldn't hide the acknowledgment that flashed then receded.

Ellen had turned to watch them. "And what's all that? Secret conversations?"

"It's automatic sometimes. I learned sign language along with Gemma." Dermot poked at his pancakes with his fork. "She refused to learn unless I went with her."

Get on with it, would you?

"You're sure?" he said. At Gemma's headshake, then switch to a nod, Dermot continued. "Gemma has given me permission to tell you about her—disorder—which makes dealing with strangers tough."

Ellen turned toward Gemma as if seeing her with new eyes. Gemma's body responded to the unwanted attention as it always did. Sweat beaded on her forehead. Her heart accelerated. She waved a hand in front of her face in the classic I'm-too-hot gesture and turned toward the wall, signaling for Dermot to continue.

"Gemma's shyness began at an early age," Dermot pontificated much to Gemma's irritation. He had his Gemma-speech down pat by now. "In fact, her shyness was so extreme that in certain social situations—like at school—she wouldn't talk at all. She would take the teacher out of the room to ask her for permission to go to the loo, and even then, she'd whisper. Most children grow out of it, but Gemma didn't get the chance because our mom died and Gemma woke up to reality months later to discover that her brain wouldn't let her talk at all anymore."

Dermot didn't bother relating how much Gemma had improved over the years. No more vomiting at the mere thought of leaving the house. No more leaving the house with a wide-rimmed sunhat tied down along the sides of her face. No more hiding out in the closest Ladies' every chance she got. With a force of will and Dermot's help, she'd come a long way.

"The doctors call her disorder selective mutism," Dermot said, "because she can talk, but she doesn't. Before our mom died, she was your average case. Afterwards, something else entirely: the perfect case study. She's been prodded by the best of them."

Ellen sounded intrigued. "She doesn't talk because she doesn't want to?"

"No, it's more like—" Dermot paused. "Okay, it's like this: You know people who are phobic about snakes? Phobias are irrational and no amount of coaxing is going to get such a person not to lose it at the sight of the smallest snake. There are cases of people dying of fright, crazy as that seems. It's all in their heads, of course, but it's still too real—they can't control the way their bodies react to snakes. The brain is that powerful. It's like that for Gemma with anything she considers public exposure."

"That's tragic."

Gemma wished she could convey the sheer terror that sometimes engulfed her. How could anyone comprehend the sensation of bones turning to glass and skin to paper? It was like at any second she would shatter from the inside out and turn into a puddle of goo. Dermot did his best to describe her disorder, but he never got down to the heart of it, which was that sometimes she thought she was going to die, simply die, if one more person laid another spotlighting and dagger-like gaze on her. Gemma barely remembered what she was like Before, when, according to Dermot, she screamed and cavorted and giggled like a normal child when she was inside their home.

"Our mom's death sent her over the edge," Dermot said, "and I hoped coming back to a place our mom had visited would dislodge some of the anxieties, further her progress."

When did you become such a good liar?

Dermot's grip on his fork tightened. He set it aside with a quiet clink against the wood tabletop. *It's the truth now.*

You think I'll magically start to talk again. Just like that?

We can hope.

No, *he* could hope. He'd never said it in so many words, but she knew he wanted a life of his own—a family with a wife and two kids and a house without Gemma living with them and dragging everyone down. She understood his need for her to make progress, because it was her need too.

But of course, he'd never explain all of this to Ellen. Just like he'd never tell Ellen what he believed, which was that the beginning of the end of their mam's life started with Liam the Matchmaker.

And ended when Gemma witnessed her murder.

Friday

Before mine eyes in opposition
sits Grim Death, my son and foe.

John Milton

TWELVE

IN POT O' GOLD Gifts, Brendan Nagel slapped a price sticker on a hand-carved Celtic cross. These crosses were quite nice, in fact, carved from Connemara marble and standing about eighteen inches high. He'd given one to his dad for his birthday. He'd had to beg Malcolm for an employee discount, the stingy bollocks.

Brendan glanced at the clock. Half ten and Malcolm still hadn't arrived. Except for souvenir-mad customers, Brendan had the shop to himself. Not that he minded. Somehow things went smoother when Malcolm wasn't playing grand host. Not to mention, Brendan didn't like the way his boss sideways glanced at him sometimes. But Brendan's dad had told him to hush his worries about getting fired. Brendan's life was on track and it would remain that way. He'd see to Brendan's welfare, he would, and Brendan trusted his word. Brendan could take over the shop one day, so his dad said. And wouldn't that be a first for a Nagel?

With a smile at the nearest customer, Brendan counted down the hours until he could begin his weekend. At sixteen, his dad had agreed that Brendan was old enough to try his hand at the festival. Brendan squirmed in happy anticipation, imagining breasts, any and all, small and large, older and younger, round or oval. He might not land a shag, but hopefully—luck be with him!—a grope or two. It struck him hilarious that a festival meant for marriage-making attracted plenty of good *craic*. They ought to call it the Shagmaker's Festival, not the Matchmaker's Festival.

He grinned to himself as he lifted the cross, clutching its weight against his chest while he maneuvered toward the shelves along the near wall. He couldn't help the prick of apprehension as he brushed against the fresh-scrubbed shelves that had been covered in fingerprint powder the previous day.

The bell above the front door jingled as Brendan settled the cross in place.

"Brendan Nagel?"

He jumped. "Ay?"

"We need to follow up on a customer who came in on Sunday while you were working," Danny said.

Brendan had never spoken to Danny Ahern while he was on duty, but he didn't seem any different than he was at the pub. A little intense but not in a mean way. Danny leaned against shelves with hands in pockets. Relaxed like that, he didn't seem *all* that keen. Just doing his job.

"Perhaps you heard about the death of a lad about your age?" Danny said. "We've been circulating a description and asking for help in identifying him."

"Ay." Brendan busied himself arranging a display table.

"What can you tell us about the victim?"

"His earrings?" Brendan said.

"Oh?"

"At first I figured him for about the most bent of the bent. Because of the earrings."

"What about them?"

"They were big and blue and girly. He looked like a ponce, is all."

"Anything else?"

Brendan thought back, confused now. He wasn't sure what he was supposed to say. He wasn't a bloody mind reader. "I heard him say—into his mobile, not to me—that he'd found him."

Behind Danny, one of his men stood with pen poised over his notebook, looking too ready, it seemed to Brendan, and he wondered if he'd already talked too much—sounding like a pansy.

Danny reiterated for the sake of the officer taking notes. "You're saying that you heard the victim say that he'd found a man, as if he'd come to Lisfenora *to* find this man?"

"Yes, to find him." Now Brendan was really confused. "But no."

"So which is it?"

"He hadn't found the man yet. He said he had a lead to finding the man. Bloody proud of himself too, I might add. As if he was some kind of Sherlock Holmes."

"And how did you happen to overhear this?"

"Oh." Brendan's thoughts scattered as he tried to remember what was what. "I passed him on my way to the post office to buy stamps for Malcolm. Is that a problem?"

Danny's eyes crinkled in the corners when he smiled. "I don't know, is it?"

A waft of salt-tinged moisture entered the shop as the door opened. Brendan stepped toward the new customers, hoping that Danny would get the hint and leave. He didn't want to talk about the dead anymore. It was too creepy. They were about the same age. *Had been* about the same age.

THIRTEEN

DANNY'S RELAXED DEMEANOR MAY have eased Brendan Nagel into opening up, but it was all show. As soon as Danny stepped out of Pot o' Gold Gifts, his smile dropped. He buttoned his coat against the chill and already wished for spring with its wild riot of violets and primroses. This foggy grey shite could only signal a miserable winter to come.

"Come on," he said to O'Neil. "I need my breakfast, and you can update me."

O'Neil was the most senior of Danny's officers, with a promotion due to him if he were willing to move to a new district. As they walked to the Plough, Danny felt O'Neil organizing his thoughts under his shaggy head of hair. He cultivated a purposeful dishevelment intended to trick the other guards into thinking he was one of them. But this was a man who'd quit Trinity to travel around India, and who counted himself a member of the Grand Masonic Lodge of Ireland. Danny would miss O'Neil if he ever decided to transfer.

Through filaments of moisture Danny caught sight of Liam and Merrit at work in the plaza. The crowd wasn't as thick as usual, and as he opened the pub door, he wondered how Liam was holding up.

Inside the pub, Danny raised a hand in Alan's direction and maneuvered his way between clusters of wingback chairs near the fireplace. Their upholstery carried the genteel-shabby look that came with years of use. He managed to lay siege to a couple of seats just as two young women clomped away with hiking boots trailing a line of dried mud pellets.

A waitress arrived with coffee and a basket of brown bread. She laid silverware, butter, and marmalade on the trestle tray-table at Danny's elbow. As soon as she departed, O'Neil launched into a summary of how little the case had progressed thus far. Danny slouched with coffee cup cradled near his face. He inhaled coffee steam as if it were a serenity incense.

"Nothing came back from the fingerprints we lifted from the shop yesterday, not that we'd expected anything," O'Neil said. "Our boy is still a John Smith. Local inquiries haven't led to any other sightings of the boy around the village, except that old Mickey over there"—he pointed toward the bar where the codger was already seated for the day—"fancies he saw a lad who fits the description at a pub, but he can't remember which pub." He wobbled his head in a fair imitation of Mickey with too many pints under his belt. "The man's too wrecked to know where he is half the time anyhow."

"Keep the questions going out at the pubs—and everywhere else, for that matter."

They lapsed into silence, neither easy nor uneasy, more like primed for the next set of actions. After a few minutes in which Danny spread marmalade on his bread and chewed without tasting, O'Neil said, "Did Brendan Nagel seem a mite jumpy to you?"

Danny had thought the same thing, but the lad's twitchiness could have stemmed from an instinctive aversion to the guards or guilt over a youthful misdeed that had nothing to do with the victim.

"Hard to tell with teenagers," Danny said.

O'Neil grinned. "Shifty, the lot of them, even the good ones. I'm off to see what kind of calls we've received because of the sketch. Probably the usual lunatics. Cheers."

A moment later, Bijou's nails clicked across the floor toward Danny. The pub mascot received pats and cheerful salutations from the regulars, which she accepted with regal poise. Bijou circumnavigated the precarious tray-tables, and once she reached Danny, she flopped her backend down and pushed her head under his hand.

"As if you don't get enough attention," he said.

She knew who her human friends were, did Bijou. She nudged at his thigh. After a quick peek at Alan, Danny laid a chunk of bread on the armrest. A dainty flick of tongue and it was gone. Danny's usefulness finished, Bijou ambled toward her pillow.

Danny heaved himself up and approached the bar. As usual, Alan waved away Danny's money. "My good deed for the day," he said.

Seamus, sitting in his usual spot with his morning Guinness tucked between his hands, snorted. "Business I give Alan, I ought to receive every tenth pint for free." He sat between Mickey and the artist fella, Nathan Tate. They straightened, the better to eavesdrop on what Danny had to say.

"Just came from speaking to Brendan," Danny said to Seamus. "Asked him about the victim."

"Bloody shame it had to happen. And no closer to his name, are ye?"

"No. Brendan might have overheard something, though. Did he mention anything to you?"

Seamus's beaky nose twitched, veins, pores, and all. "What teenager talks to his father? But he's an honest lad, so honest I worry about his future. This world is cruel, cruel indeed to people-pleasers like him." He gulped at his pint. "I'll let you know if he does have something to say."

"Bribe him with a new smartphone," Nathan said. "That'll get him talking."

Seamus cast a half smile toward Danny. "The man speaks. You've met Nathan Tate, haven't you? Moved here last month. Creates clay pots, he does. I plan to see his wares sold in Malcolm's shop."

"Don't bother," Nathan said.

"Malcolm can't like your nose in his business, I'm sure," Danny said to Seamus.

Seamus's bark of a laugh followed Danny out of the pub. "Too bloody bad for him."

FOURTEEN

To MERRIT'S DISMAY, SHE found herself standing in Liam's bedroom with the McNamara siblings. With the help of Danny's wife, they'd found the house and pulled up alongside Merrit as she stood next to her car obsessing about who detested her enough to paint *slag* on the door. Merrit's attempts to shoo them away had failed, and then Liam had surprised her by waving them inside.

And now here they stood. In Liam's bedroom of all places. A leftover whiff of illness tickled Merrit's nose, reminding her that although he was in remission, Liam was far from a healthy specimen. A surgeon had removed a section of his left lung. The good news was that the cancer had been localized. The bad news was that Liam was slow to recover and sometimes had trouble breathing.

"I'm sure you're wondering why we're in my bedroom," he said.

"You could say that," Dermot said.

"Count yourself privileged, laddie." Liam swung an impish smile toward Merrit. "I haven't shown Merrit what's inside this armoire yet."

While Liam used his storytelling blarney to describe the provenance of the armoire—French, Louis XV, 1860s—thereby heightening the suspense, Merrit let her mind wander. Gemma stirred her curiosity, so she took this opportunity to study the girlish woman who stood with eyebrows drawn together and chin tucked.

Whereas Dermot looked like he was about to leak at the seams, Gemma maintained a ramrod straight posture as if girding herself against disaster. A polka-dotted scarf held her curls in check at the nape of her neck, and artfully arranged patches decorated a black skirt that brushed the tops of her coalminer's boots. A vintage Ramones t-shirt layered over a black long-sleeved top completed her ensemble.

And, Merrit told herself, don't ignore a face that could have inspired Botticelli. The constant high color in Gemma's cheeks must have stemmed from her anxiety issues, and the reddened lips from her habit of chewing on them. She did a good job of camouflaging her prettiness with tortured body language and black clothing.

Gemma chose that moment to glance up at her. Her cheeks reddened yet more in response to Merrit's smile, and her eyes darted around the room before settling on the armoire.

"And so," Liam was saying, "it's fitting that I store my history as a matchmaker in this exquisite antique. Look here!" With a flourish, Liam swung open the armoire's doors to reveal shelves stacked with paper.

"Oh, wow," Merrit said, catching on. "These are ledger pages?"

"Exactly. Detailed records of all the matches I've made since I started in the late 1960s." He turned to Dermot, whose expression now registered something other than annoyed forbearance. "When did I allegedly match your mother to your father—"

"*Step*father," Dermot said. "That bastard's no genetic relation to us."

"Of course. My apologies. What did you call him—John McIlvoy?"

"Yes. Matched in 1991."

Liam pointed toward the bottom of a stack on the fourth shelf, and Merrit hurried forward to move pages to Liam's bed. It was heavy going, and Dermot stepped up to help. Liam's matchmaking ledger held 200 pages at a time, bound together with leather ties.

"There," Liam said when the dates "1990 to 1992" surfaced on a piece of cardboard, one of many that separated the sheaves from one another.

Their solemn procession returned to the living room, where the group arrayed themselves around Liam at the end of the dining room table. As soon as Liam sat and began turning the pages, Merrit pulled a chair closer and perched with elbows on the table. Dermot did so as well while Gemma propped herself on the arm of his chair. The pages grabbed at each other with a shushing noise before they parted.

"I can't believe you haven't shown me these before," Merrit said.

"And scare you back to the States? I thought not."

True. Most of the time, she felt like she still had one foot facing back toward California. This was especially true now that Liam's health had improved, and she had time to take stock of what her life might be like in Ireland, living in the shadow of Liam's beloved status.

And now to see all of these records from Liam's matchmaking career. Mind-boggling and scary at the same time. Liam had created thousands of joined lives, and thus thousands of new generations, and even if a rare couple ended badly, they all began as members of an elite club. Merrit knew this because she'd seen it in the pubs by night when Liam introduced chosen men to chosen women. She'd watched the chosen accept their destiny with the kind of faith Merrit had never known.

In these ledger pages, decades' worth of tradition stared her in the face. The impact hit her full force: the decades of *her* life stretching out in front of her. She wasn't sure she could make that commitment. She wasn't sure she *should* make that commitment. She felt inadequate to the task, plain and simple. In the end, her decision to stay in Ireland after Liam's eventual death couldn't just be about becoming match-maker. She needed her own reason, apart from Liam's plans for her.

She hadn't found that reason yet.

Liam watched her with forehead crinkled in concern. He opened his mouth to say something, but, thankfully, Dermot chose that moment to push his agenda.

"My mom, where is she?" he said.

Halfway through the ledger they came upon a page marked *1991*, and thereafter a list of names for that year, plus descriptions and various annotations in the margins. Liam pushed the sheaf toward Merrit. "You do the honors. Your eyes will be faster."

"Her name was Siobhan." Dermot's voice strained against some emotion he barely held in check. "Siobhan McNamara."

He spelled out the name for Merrit. Pronounced *Shiv-awn*, she'd never have recognized the word in written form. She felt the weight of their gazes following her finger down the list of names, past the descriptions and simple codes that Liam used to track each person. His writing had changed over the years, and she tried not to suc-cumb to sadness at the sight of the firm and flowing hand that was so at odds with his current crabbed script.

Siobhan McNamara appeared at the bottom of the third page. "Here," she said.

Glancing up, Merrit caught Gemma's headshake and fluttering hands. Before they had a chance to read Siobhan's ledger entry, Gemma had retreated to the fireplace, where she tucked herself into a ball on one of the armchairs and fiddled with one end of her hair scarf.

"She's bloody petrified now that we might learn something," Dermot said. "Give me a second."

Dermot retreated toward Gemma.

Liam angled the ledger page toward himself, read the entry, and sighed with a long whoosh that ended with a cough. "Thank Christ."

Merrit shifted closer. "You okay?"

"I should be asking you that question, but never mind that for the moment." He tapped the page. "I wasn't sure, you see. Still, maybe I could have prevented her death."

"Don't say that—"

He waved her into silence and turned his attention toward the fireplace, where Dermot stooped next to Gemma. He whispered in her ear while she twisted her fingers together and shook her head. The troubled tableau stung Merrit into asking if anyone wanted tea. No one answered.

Dermot jumped to with renewed determination shiny as the sweat gleam across his forehead. He stood over Liam's shoulder and read aloud a portion of Liam's comments about his mother.

"*Widowed and still in love with deceased husband. Hopeful will find love again. Vulnerable with the need. Her truth: it's too early. She needs more time, but she seems determined.*

"That doesn't make sense," he continued. "And this ledger is dusty too. You haven't looked at this thing in years."

"What are you talking about?" Merrit said. "Face facts. You were wrong. Liam had nothing to do with what happened to your mom."

Liam tapped the null sign beside Siobhan's name. "This means that I never saw her again. Sometimes people change their minds or, for other reasons, leave Lisfenora without word to me. You can see that I didn't plan on matching her anyhow. She wasn't ready."

"No, that can't be." Color flared on Dermot's cheeks. "Not after all this. The answer lies with you. It has to. How can it be otherwise?"

"I'm sorry," Liam said, "but at the same time I'm relieved. That's a burden I don't need."

"You're sorry. That's it?"

"Sometimes," Liam said, "people match themselves and they let me know. Your mother didn't."

"Maybe you don't remember. If you could try harder to remember—"

"No," Liam said. "The null sign says it all. She left. I use an 'x' when people leave but contact me about their decision. Most do let me know, and I note down their reason. They might leave a message at the Information Booth or with one of the pub owners. Your mother didn't. I never saw her again—"

"Didn't you think to follow up? My God, man, you state right here that she was vulnerable."

Liam hesitated. "I'm sure I wondered. I'm good at filtering out the people who are only testing the idea of using me. If they leave then I don't think anything of it. But your mother—"

"So you did think it odd."

Merrit stepped between the two men. "Out. Now. Liam didn't match your mom to your stepdad."

"What about John McIlvoy?" Dermot said.

Dermot almost tore a ledger page as he hauled the stack toward himself. Merrit tried to push him away, but Dermot responded by elbowing her right back.

"Let him look," Liam said. "No harm done."

Dermot traced down the list of names for 1991. And then again. "He has to be here," he muttered.

"Time to go," Merrit said. "They met on their own. You'll have to find your answers elsewhere."

Without word, Dermot grabbed up his cloak and left. Outside, his car engine revved, and he honked the horn.

Gemma roused herself and pulled a notebook and pen out of her rucksack. When she'd finished writing, she tore the sheet out, rose, and placed the note on the chair seat. Staring at the ground, she hurried out without looking back.

Liam stared after her. "She needs help."

Merrit touched her throat where her mom's necklace had hung. "I know, and I'm going to help her whether or not anyone likes me in this bloody village. *Slag* be damned."

"I think you're confusing your issues with hers." He tidied the pile of ledger pages. "But no matter. Time to hit tonight's pub. I have some lucky souls to match up. What does her note say?"

Unsettled by his remark about her confused issues, Merrit picked up Gemma's note. "It says, *Please excuse Dermot. He hasn't been himself since we got here.*"

"Ah," Liam said. "Not an imbecile, that girl. Why would he care how dusty my old ledgers are, anyhow?"

FIFTEEN

DANNY EASED THE FRONT door closed and paused to clear the work-day out of his head as best as he could. Lost Boy was still lost, and so far canvassing hadn't turned up anything more about his activities in Lisfenora.

But never mind that for now. Danny's children awaited him for their daily wind-down: teeth brushing and stories and lights out. Ellen never interrupted his visits. She preferred to retreat to the bedroom until he left. Whatever their difficulties, she understood that the children missed their father and that he'd always been better at putting them down, anyhow.

He hesitated to call out, not wanting to disturb the peacefulness in the house. Perhaps Ellen had gotten them into bed herself. It could be. He hoped this was the case. He peered out a rear window to check Ellen's parking space.

No car in sight. She must have larked off with the children then. To visit her estranged father up in Ballyvaughan? He shook his head at such an unlikely fantasy. The day Ellen Tully Ahern brought her kids to see Marcus was the day Danny believed in the Grey Man shite bantering its way back and forth across the village.

Danny swung open the kitchen door, expecting the usual mess of dishes in the sink and discarded outdoor gear next to the back door. He flipped on the overheads.

The kitchen sparkled, and he caught a whiff of cleaning fluids with lemony fresh scents. Danny picked up a coffeepot that no longer contained years' worth of brownish film. "Could it be?"

Perhaps his wife had returned to the woman he'd married, a woman who wasn't weighed down by depression and bitterness. Ready to take on household management with her previous zeal. And maybe she *was* off on an adventure with the children. It was a Friday night, after all. He remembered with the suddenness of a bee sting how, when the children couldn't or wouldn't fall asleep, they'd drive until they spied a place—a ruin, a craggy beach, a churchyard—that they could explore by torch. The little ones had loved playing at detective like their pappy.

It could be that Ellen had remembered these jaunts also, that they were out this minute scrambling across a limestone-strewn headland.

Danny checked a window again. His hope waned. The fog was still too thick. Ellen wouldn't endanger the children driving along the twisting coastal road carved into the cliffside. She could still be out with the children, true, but nevertheless an immaculate overnight change in her behavior didn't feel right. Worry replaced his initial hope.

Returning to the living room, he plucked the top off a wicker basket to find toys that were usually strewn about the room. In the children's bedroom, someone had made the beds, but toys still covered most of the floor. Relieved at this sign of normalcy, Danny moved on to the one uninhabited room in the house. Little Beth's.

The quietude felt loaded, whispery and primed. Danny hesitated at Beth's door with prickles mounting the back of his neck. He couldn't help thinking about Petey's fear of Grey Man—that dark faerie that stole people into its mists.

On the count of three he pushed open the door and turned on the light. The boxes he'd set out to sort Beth's belongings still stood against the wall, and they still contained headless dolls and early drawings. A year's worth of dust coated them. He hadn't had a chance to finish clearing out her room before moving out, and Ellen wasn't prepared to delve into the sadness on her own.

The room was the same as ever, except for the two shiny sleeping bags laid out as if for a pretend camping trip. Danny thought back to the last time he'd entered this room—this Sunday past. No sleeping bags then.

Lost Boy's final slow blink flashed through his mind. Danny jerked toward the master bedroom, fearing what he might find on the other side of the closed door. He thought of Petey, he thought of the uneasiness he'd felt since viewing Lost Boy's body. That sense of *proximity*, for lack of a better word, as if whatever lurked around Lost Boy also circled his family.

Gathering himself, Danny approached the bedroom and opened the door. The bedside radio whispered to an empty room. Ah, right. Ellen often left it on. He stepped into the room. The cleaning genie hadn't made it here either. The bed sat under its usual mound of tangled blankets, and the chair in the corner hulked like a hunchback under discarded jumpers and jeans.

Danny wasn't comfortable with change in this house while he wasn't living under its roof. He would have preferred to see the usual messy kitchen and no sleeping bags in Beth's room. The only explanation that made sense was that Ellen had visitors in for the festival that she had forgotten to tell him about. Typical.

Still uneasy but now also annoyed, Danny rooted through Ellen's bedside hutch. He wasn't sure what he was looking for. Anything that might give a clue to Ellen's state of mind and activities.

He didn't find anything but random receipts, leftover antidepressants, a romance novel, and a journal with dated pages. She wasn't much of a scribbler, so he browsed it quickly, telling himself that he was only checking to verify that this hadn't changed either. He caught sight of a few shopping lists and the odd sad comment about Beth. He was about to set the journal aside, disgusted with himself, when he arrived at the first filled page. He flipped pages, not reading—no, not that—but catching phrases that hinted at Ellen's inner turmoil. *What can I do to get him to notice me again?* Near the end, one sentence screamed across a page in large letters: *What is wrong with me that I care?*

He clapped the journal closed and placed it where he'd found it beneath the romance novel. The book's cover featured an image of a half-naked man bending a busty damsel backwards over his arm in a pose that looked bloody painful. Danny had never known Ellen to read romances.

Passing the dresser his eye caught on the simple wooden box that Ellen used to store her jewelry. He lifted the lid. The upper tier held delicate gold baubles that Ellen had inherited from her mother. The pieces looked old-fashioned, fussy even, but they suited Ellen. Danny lifted out the top tray and found his wedding band on the lower tier. He pushed the ring onto his finger. Looser than ever now. He'd taken it off years ago when it slipped off at a crime scene and had never gotten around to having it adjusted. Danny wondered if Ellen would notice or care if he reclaimed it.

A small black gift box tucked into the corner of the jewelry box looked new. He picked it up, cradling it in his palm. A mewling sound startled Danny. A second later, two dervishes—his own little dervishes—rushed him from out of the closet, pushing at him until he fell backwards onto the bed. Petey climbed up beside Danny. His hair was still damp from the bath, as was Mandy's. She vaulted onto his lap and burrowed into his chest.

Danny wrapped his arms around them and kept his tone light. "You scared the living bejaysus out of me. I see you're fit for bed. Has your mother left you alone to run a quick errand?"

"Don't be silly," Mandy said. "We're too young to be on our own yet."

Thank Christ for that. "Where's your mom?"

"It's like this, Da," Mandy said, turning serious. Her hair was starting to reveal henna-like reddish highlights similar to Ellen's. She brushed strands away from her face with an annoyed grunt. "We could hear you very well, you know, and even though we knew it was you, we decided to stay very quiet. It was hard, especially for Petey." She shrugged with an exaggerated movement. "We were in the closet anyhow, see. We wanted to play a trick on you. But Gemma got scared. She's our sitter, but she's shy."

"Gemma?" He'd heard that name recently. From Alan and then from Merrit, right. Gemma was the odd girl who had stolen her necklace. With the brother who had an accusation against Liam. "Now wait a minute—"

"Da!" Petey piped up. "Look what we got. Come look and see. But shh, we have to be quiet."

Following his children's lead, Danny dropped to all fours and crawled toward the closet, where two kittens blinked against the light.

"We need to keep the door shut for now." Mandy poked her head into the closet, and Danny followed suit, looking at the woman crammed in at the other end. So this was Gemma, necklace stealer. The woman's knees were drawn up under her chin, and she stared at a pair of Ellen's summer sandals.

"They're still getting their strength back," Mandy said. "They need quiet, right, Gemma?"

Getting no response, Mandy shooed them backwards again and eased the closet door closed. "We just fed them. They need to go to bed now."

"They're our new kittens," Petey said. "One for me, one for Mandy. Mam said it was okay."

"So," Danny said, "Mam invited Gemma and someone else—her brother?—to sleep over?"

The children grinned like it was the world's best slumber party.

"For how long?"

"Hopefully forever!" Petey said.

Ellen must have lost her mind. Kittens Danny could handle. But not a couple of siblings with murky agendas.

"Kidlings," he said, striving for a light tone, "fetch Gemma out, please. Tell her that as your da I need to be officially introduced to her and to her brother. Where is he?"

"He went to the pub," Mandy said. "Gemma said he's upset about something, so it's better for him to be alone."

"She didn't really say anything," Petey said. "She writes everything."

Bloody brilliant. An odd girl who refused to talk, and a brother who drank his problems away. "And where's your mom?"

"Don't know. Just out for a while."

Just out. There was no *just* about it.

"Go on then, coax Gemma out," Danny said. "Tell her I don't bite."

Mandy swatted his arm. "You're funny. Of course you don't bite."

They shut the closet door against him and began their quiet entreaties to Gemma.

Danny still held the jewelry gift box, but now with the full force of his aching fingers. Sweat matted the black velvet. He raised the lid. A pair of earrings blinked up at him with an iridescent blue sheen. He was no expert, but he guessed opals—and nice ones too. No way would Ellen buy these for herself, so the question was, who gave them to her? And where was Ellen now, leaving their children in the care of a woman who refused to talk? Now he wished he'd read his wife's journal while he had the chance.

Danny replaced the box in its compartment, then slipped off his wedding band and replaced it also.

SIXTEEN

ALAN HANDED OFF A whiskey and soda and continued on down the bar, picking up empty glasses. He moved fast, trying to keep up with the festival crowd. He was essentially a servant, his presence forgotten until his customers needed a drink, so forgotten that they didn't bother lowering their voices when he was in the vicinity.

"—and you are too eager to please." Seamus sat with Brendan at the end of the bar where it curved toward the wall, away from the rest of the regulars. "I swear to Christ you need to—"

Every night it was like this, catching bits of conversation that were none of Alan's business. He set the dirties in a bin for later washing and turned on the taps to rinse his hands. The noise drowned out Brendan's response to Seamus. They looked alike, those two, with their beaky noses and fair skin. Brendan didn't have his father's outgoing temperament, so whereas Seamus took the measure of you in a direct manner, his son engaged in glances. They had the kind of relationship that Alan used to hope he could foster with his father back in France. But that was before his father turned out to be a right prick.

Alan dried his hands as he scanned his customers. Off in a corner, Malcolm sat at a cozy two-top table with a woman Alan didn't recognize. Malcolm leaned forward on his elbows, listening to her. He nodded and responded, apparently asking her a question, because she smiled and continued her end of the conversation.

Unlike Alan, Malcolm never seemed to have trouble attracting women. Gentlemanly manners and charm worked wonders, apparently—even for a man as unusual-looking as Malcolm. Alan could use some charm lessons.

A raised glass beckoned Alan back to his duties. Dermot, the poor sod. His erect posture but bowed head, the way he clenched his glass yet let his lower lip hang, told Alan that the man was on his last edge. It was as if his body wanted to simultaneously erupt and melt.

"You ever hate yourself?" Dermot lifted his head like it already hurt from a hangover. "Never mind. I'll take a double."

Alan pushed the glass up against the Scotch optic to dispense one shot, paused, and then pushed up again to release the second shot. He set the glass in front of Dermot and wiped the already clean counter with a bar rag. "Gemma okay?"

Dermot swallowed a large gulp and wiped his mouth with the back of his hand. "We have a place to sleep now, anyhow. A woman named Ellen Ahern lent us a room. Kind of her."

"Careful there, mate," Alan said. "Her husband's Gardaí. Still married even if they're not living together."

"Police? Fan-fecking-tastic." A spasm contorted Dermot's face. "We should have been here and gone already—back to Dublin."

Dermot looked so pained that Alan rolled up the left sleeve of his hurling jersey. He pointed to a tattoo that encircled his forearm. It swirled in a vibrant smoke of imagery around his arm, one illustration feeding into the other in waves of blue. "The design's called 'A Man's Ruin,'" he said.

Alan rotated his arm to show off the overall theme. Booze bottles, dice, fags, pills, a small Catholic cross, and in the center of it all a blonde woman with a snake covering her pornographic bits.

Dermot caught Alan's wrist and rotated it underside up. "What's that supposed to mean, the shamrock?"

"It means that depending on luck can ruin a man as well as anything else."

Dermot almost threw Alan's arm back into his face. "But you forgot a few things, didn't you? You forgot family. Family can hang you up like nothing else."

Without word, Alan pointed to the snake entwined around both the Celtic cross and the blond woman.

"And there's secrets also. Where's secrets on your arm? They'll eat you alive."

"Yes," Alan said. "But I didn't think of that at the time."

Nathan Tate squeezed in beside Dermot and ordered a Black and Tan. Alan once again caught himself up in the swirl of customer satisfaction. He kept an eye on Dermot, who drank steadily without talking to anyone. Alan was aware of Seamus returning to his usual spot amongst the crows with Brendan at his side, and the subsequent debate about who had first coined the term "crows" to describe themselves.

The vocal blur washed over Alan. He kept half an ear attuned to the crowd while his thoughts gravitated back to Gemma. She had to figure heavily in Dermot's preoccupations with family and secrets. He slapped his bar rag against the counter.

Stop. Gemma was none of his business. He maneuvered his way around one of his waitresses and almost bumped into Bijou. She pawed at the ground, her signal for a bathroom break. Every night at 11:00, more timely than the wall clock. Alan assessed the teeming room and the wave of newcomers pressing in from the front door. He pulled Bijou's lead out from behind the cash register.

"Brendan," he said. "It's time."

With a ready smile, Brendan held out his hand for the dangling lead.

"Your pint will be waiting." Alan tucked a plastic bag into Brendan's hand. "And don't be forgetting this. Fitz will talk me a new piehole if he finds one of her piles. That man can smell dog shit in his sleep."

Brendan laughed. Over the summer he'd filled out and his acne had faded. Alan had watched Brendan grow up in the bar, sipping sodas alongside his da until this year when he'd graduated to sneaking sips of Guinness from Seamus that Alan pretended not to notice. Brendan enjoyed his status as the youngest crow and often looked on his father with pride. It embarrassed Alan to see his doting expression. His adulation wouldn't last; it never did. Seamus would betray him at some point.

"Off with you then," Alan said.

The crowd parted for boy and dog. Alan pulled down his sleeve to cover a man's ruin.

Saturday

Children are very nice observers,
and they will often perceive your slightest
defects. In general, those who govern
children forgive nothing in them,
but everything in themselves.

François de Salignac de la Mothe-Fénelon

SEVENTEEN

Danny pulled up in front of Alan's pub, hoping that Alan's call was a false alarm. The Plough's lights cast an ominous glow through the fog. Given the hour, the plaza was otherwise enshrouded in the peaceful hibernation of night. He rubbed his eyes, exhausted at the start of this new day. Ellen had returned to the house thirty minutes ago, at around 2:30 a.m., and she hadn't been thrilled to see him waiting up for her. By then, Dermot had arrived drunk and, with barely a how-do-you-do, had weaved his way to his sleeping bag, apologizing the whole way.

At least his wife's maternal instincts hadn't completely abandoned her. Gemma McNamara appeared to be a responsible and caring person. His evening with her and the children had passed quietly enough once the woman ventured out of the closet. After a tortured session of sign language, inept translations, and finally, the written language, Danny understood that his wife had offered the McNamaras free accommodations in return for help around the house.

All the better for Ellen to engage in nocturnal adventures outside of their home.

He hadn't mentioned the opal earrings, but he had plenty to say about inviting strangers into their house without consulting him first. Thankfully, Alan's call had interrupted his whispered argument with Ellen. He couldn't get away from the house fast enough after that.

Inside the pub, wall sconces cast pools of light onto upturned chairs. Their legs pointed toward the ceiling, stiff as rats in rigor mortis. Alan pressed an ice pack against Bijou's ribs. Seamus slouched on one of the wingback chairs beside the hearth. A half-empty bottle of Jameson sat on the floor beside him.

"Brendan's missing," Alan said.

"I'm after telling you," Seamus mumbled, "that you're wrong."

Alan adjusted the ice pack on Bijou's ribs. "Brendan and I have an agreement during the festival. Every night at eleven he takes Bijou for her constitutional, only tonight, Bijou returned dragging her lead."

Seamus's voice wobbled. "Brendan's first festival as a man. Letting his rod point the way." His face crumpled. "No, Grey Man along and grabbed Brendan into the mists."

"He's been talking to himself like that for the past hour," Alan said.

First Lost Boy, now Brendan. Boys about the same age, just starting to come into their own. Danny wished Seamus hadn't mentioned Grey Man, even in jest.

Whining, Bijou pulled away from Alan and planted herself next to the door.

"He's got sunshine for shit where Brendan's concerned," Alan said, "but dogs don't lie—to themselves or others. I'd trust her over anyone."

"You two have been sitting vigil for Brendan's return since closing?" Danny said.

Alan pointed to the Jameson bottle. "Seamus didn't mind, but now it's gone almost four hours, so I called you."

Alan kneeled beside Bijou and beckoned Danny closer. "It's okay, girl. Down. Play dead."

Bijou obeyed her master but now panted with anxiety. Danny knelt by her head, let her sniff his hand, and cooed a few soothing words. Short-haired, lean, and now stretched out long, it was obvious where a foot had connected to Bijou's side. The swelling hid the ribby waves beneath it.

"Bruised but not broken. I'll take her to the vet tomorrow to be sure." Alan's voice tightened. "Some bastard did this to her."

"But I don't understand," Seamus slurred. "Where's Brendan?"

"That's the point, you sodden fool." Alan swiped up the Jameson and poured what remained of the whiskey into the fire. The fire flared. "Get your head out of your arse."

By firelight, Alan's skin looked glazed and semi-hardened, like he'd been removed from a kiln too early. He stared down at the bottle, at the warped orange glints caught in the glass, then tossed it up in the air. Catching it by the neck, he considered it again, hefting it, then with a grunt smashed it against the stone hearth, leaving a jagged weapon still fisted in his hand.

"No one harms me or mine," he said. "That's the given. I thought everyone in the village knew this about me."

Danny eased the broken bottle out of Alan's white-knuckled grip. "Give me that."

Alan's hardening yielded. "Right. Come with me then."

They left Seamus almost passed out by the dying fire.

"He's not going anywhere," Alan said.

A few minutes later, torches lighting the way and Bijou unleashed but keeping close, the men turned right out of the plaza and made for the church. Danny kept his mouth shut while Alan ruminated aloud that, given the right circumstances, Bijou might consider herself the alpha. Perhaps she'd lunged at someone who'd made threatening moves toward Brendan.

The dog led a slower than usual pace toward the church grounds. They entered the parking area and circled around three clergy flats and onto a little green located at the back of the property. A rock wall more ornamental than protective, and with a wrought iron grille atop it, hid them from view of the buildings on the next street over.

"This is where Brendan takes her," Alan said.

Alan's feet shushed over the grass accompanied by Bijou's pants. Other than this, Danny heard nothing, not even a rustle from within the clipped junipers that lined one wall.

Alan waved to him, and Danny caught up. A damp dog pile sat in the middle of the grass.

"That's hers, all right." Alan pulled a plastic baggie from his pocket, and with a guilt-ridden glance at Fitz's flat, bent to clean up Bijou's mess. "We know they made it this far."

"No, leave it for now," Danny said. "We shouldn't touch anything—even that."

Alan grimaced. "If you say so, but Fitz'll have me for dinner when he finds it."

Bijou sniffed the pile and, uninterested, wandered away.

"Could she track Brendan?" Danny said. "Seamus can give us a personal item for her to smell."

"She couldn't track her way out of a doghouse."

The light from their torches stretched Bijou's shadow toward the corner of the enclosed green. They followed her to a recessed portion of the wall, where a wrought iron gate hung open. The passage deposited them onto a lane of mixed shops and homes. A faint glow from behind a few second-story curtains exacerbated rather than relieved the dank sensation lurking about in the dark.

"We could knock on doors," Alan said.

"I'll get my men on it. You go home."

Alan stooped beside Bijou. He pulled a treat out of his pocket and she licked it up in her dainty way. "Home to an ice pack and aspirin for the dog."

Danny caught a movement from within misty tendrils. Lost Boy, he thought, and half expected a sparrow to glide out from under the eaves. He waved the torch to dispel the figments and turned away from dark windows that winked back at him, seemingly in on the joke of his haunting.

"What's got you?" Alan said.

"An overactive imagination."

EIGHTEEN

Lisfenora was just starting to wake up when Danny received a call on his mobile from a fretful Malcolm. "This is urgent," he said. "I need you at my shop. Please."

As luck would have it, Danny was just down the street waiting for O'Neil in front of the church. They were set to question Father Dooley and Archdeacon Fitzgerald about late-night foot traffic in the church green. Brendan still hadn't returned and, with sinking hope, Danny suspected that the randy lad wasn't sleeping off a drunk in some randy lassie's bed.

Now Danny stood in front of Malcolm's shop staring at lines of paint marring one of his windows. More graffiti, which was an annoyance but not exactly urgent. The words announced *limp dic* with the missing *k* nothing but a downstroke that veered off to the right, undone.

"This is outrageous," Malcolm said.

Nathan Tate slouched into view with hands in his pockets. "Someone doesn't like you."

"Which makes no sense at all, and not just because I work perfectly well in *that* department." Malcolm smiled, looking as if he was trying to force a good mood on over his irritation. "I can't think of who dislikes me. It must be a mistake, or a prank, wouldn't you say, Danny?"

But Danny was thinking about the graffiti on Merrit's car.

"Ridiculous, isn't it," Malcolm continued, "the way some people need attention?"

"Indeed, some people crave it and don't even know it." With a wave, Nathan sauntered toward the pub. "Cheers."

Malcolm eyed Nathan's retreating form. "His pottery isn't even that good, did you know? Seamus is the one after me to take on his sloppy work, but he wouldn't know quality if it poured itself into his pint." Something lit within him. His skin flushed. "Seamus."

"What about Seamus?" Danny asked.

"Nothing."

Malcolm tapped his lower lip with a finger, lost in thought. He was thinking something, all right, but he must not have heard about the *slag* painted on Merrit's car. Seamus wasn't a likely suspect for that bit of vandalism. Danny waited.

"Fine then," Malcolm said. "It's not nothing, but if this is what I think it is, then I can take care of it myself. Nothing but an intimidation tactic, and after the way Seamus has taken advantage of my generous nature too. Taking on Brendan, when what I really need is a shop employee with initiative, organizational skills, customer savvy—"

Danny held up a hand. "Stop. Brendan Nagel is missing. You saw him yesterday, correct?"

"Missing? Oh, dear." Malcolm blinked. "I saw him yesterday, as usual, in the shop. He closed for the day on his own, and I suppose he went on his merry way to the pub after that."

"If you think of anything else, don't hesitate to call again. I must go now."

Malcolm nodded as he turned away to study his marred shop front. "Look at this. I try so hard to create a pretty façade for my customers. I insist that you question Seamus about my window, yes?"

Danny felt a sigh ascending from his diaphragm. The intimate nature of village life never failed to aggravate petty annoyances. That said, the next time Danny saw Seamus and Malcolm, they would be drinking together with the rest of the crows, right as a couple of pigs in muck.

───────

Ten minutes later, Danny sipped Earl Grey from a porcelain teacup that felt fragile as old parchment in his hands. He sat in Father Dooley's flat along with Deacon Fitzgerald, whose girth overwhelmed the antique chair upon which he perched. Everything about this room, from the tea set to the chair, bespoke an old lady with a Victoriana fetish rather than a celibate who kept a flask filled with the best cognac.

"Last night?" Father Dooley said. "Might as well be in a cloistered order for all I heard. And you, Fitz?"

The rear window of the flat provided a view of the green. A flutter of wings shot past the window, startling Danny. He set his cup aside and wiped errant tea drips off the back of his hand, trying not to show his sudden sense of urgency.

The deacon's chair squealed when he shifted. He tilted his head so he looked at Danny from between teetering eyeglasses and furrowed forehead. "I didn't hear a thing. Something about this incessant drippy greyness has me sleeping harder than usual. Too early in the season for it, I tell you."

"You're used to Brendan coming around with Bijou then," Danny said.

"Can't miss them, though he only does it under cover of night."

"No harm in it," Father Dooley said. "A little fertilizer doesn't hurt anything, does it?" He grinned in response to Fitz's scowl.

"How often did Brendan bring Bijou around?" Danny asked.

"Every night since the festival started," Fitz said. "Patrick here is too lenient by half, letting that brute empty herself on our grounds. At least Alan taught Brendan to clean up the mess. This may or may not be helpful, but he always arrived a little after eleven."

"Did he ever meet anyone or bring a friend along?"

The clergymen shook their heads in unison. "Here and gone in under five minutes, thank Christ," Fitz said. "I don't know how many times I've shooed kids from our grounds over the years. I don't know what they hope to accomplish back there—I can only imagine—"

"You'd best be only imagining," Father Dooley said. "And you might want to confess some of those thoughts, also."

Fitz's voice rose; he was not to be sidetracked. "Last week a couple of lurkers decided our green was just the place for an—interlude—and they woke me clear out of a sound sleep. I knocked on the window to warn them off."

Father Dooley's tone turned thoughtful. "Brendan Nagel. Did you know that he about wore a path on the grass using our back gate for a shortcut? He lives a few streets over, and he'd run through with a wave every morning on his way to classes. Since starting at the shop, I've seen less of him. I suppose he lets himself in at Malcolm's back door rather than circle to the front through our gate. I always thought him a good lad. Not a genius by any means, but well-meaning."

With a nod and thanks, Danny let himself out, leaving the clerics to continue their ruminations without him. He'd already had the same discussion with himself. According to Alan, this was the second year Brendan had helped out with Bijou during the festival.

"Detective Sergeant?"

Dermot McNamara stood in the parking lot in front of the clergy flats. The fog had thinned, begrudging them a smudge of yellow sun, just enough to spotlight Dermot's bloodshot eyes and sallow skin.

"I don't have time now," Danny said. "I'll find you later. You'd best not have been drinking in front of my children."

Dermot staggered and caught himself with a hand on the wall. "If you'll listen, I can explain about last night—"

"Stumbling into my home dead drunk?" Danny retorted. "Mad, with children in the house. And here you are ossified once again."

"I can explain." Dermot sucked in his cheeks. His next words came in a cloud of beer breath. "I saw the newspaper last night. Your victim, the boy in the police sketch. I can identify him."

NINETEEN

"SEE?" MERRIT SAID.

Detective Officer O'Neil perused her driver's side door. In the States, vandalism like this didn't rate a house call, so she was glad to see him pull out his mobile to snap some pictures. Afterwards, he pressed a few buttons and held his mobile up alongside the *slag*. On the tiny monitor, Merrit caught a glimpse of a shop window with *limp dick* arrayed in big, sloppy magenta letters. The same color paint, no doubt about it, and the same loopy letter *l*.

"I'm not the only one then," she said.

"You sound relieved."

"Maybe I am." Merrit hadn't realized how paranoid she'd become. "But this makes it even more weird, don't you think?"

"I'm not sure. No offense to you, but I wasn't worried about your grievance, only now we've got Malcolm in the mix, and he's a right local citizen—a right *mouthy* local citizen."

"What? I don't count?"

"Not entirely." O'Neil smiled to lessen the sting.

He was a handsome guy. Like most Americans, Merrit was fussy

110

about good teeth, which he had—but she suspected that he was highly aware of what he could get away with because of his looks.

He scraped paint into a little plastic bag. "Any idea what you could have in common with Malcolm?"

"You mean besides rubbing some mysterious person the wrong way?"

O'Neil grinned. "Ay, that wouldn't be hard. Could be anyone. Wouldn't take much—look at a person sideways like."

Before Merrit could think of a witty comeback, O'Neil was on the move, trotting back to his car. "Twisted day. I'll let you know if I find out anything." He paused beside his open door. "Where were you and Liam last night?"

"In the Thistle and Burr, matchmaking as usual. Why?"

"I assume you know by now that Brendan Nagel is missing." She nodded. "Did you see him? Hear anything about him?"

"Sorry, no."

With a wave, O'Neil accelerated away, leaving Merrit to ponder Seamus Nagel, who'd been so proud of his boy and ready for a wife. Unsettled, Merrit taped a large garbage bag over the graffiti to preserve it for a few more days.

Leaning against the car, she breathed in the moist scent of all things green. She imagined moss and peat on the breeze, and let the gentle touch of Ireland soothe her nerves. Beyond Liam's plot of land, the hills rolled away from her, losing themselves in a peaceful mist like a faerie-tale place.

Her disquiet wasn't just about Brendan's disappearance, she realized. Even if O'Neil had been joking, she should have stuck up for herself. So why hadn't she? She had as much right to protection against vandals as Malcolm did.

With a last look at the lovely land, she walked to Liam's car for the return drive to the plaza and the festival.

TWENTY

ALAN SAT IN THE vet's waiting area. Owners of arthritic retrievers and yowling cats came and went according to their regularly scheduled appointments. For some reason, Gemma's presence calmed Alan even though the fact of it—her, here, with him, alone—still struck him as odd. Not because he took issue with her presence but because of the way Dermot had foisted her off on him earlier that morning. He hadn't expected to see Dermot in the pub again so soon. He'd arrived at opening with Gemma in tow and a look of pained resolution on his face.

Straight away, Dermot had started sucking down a breakfast pint. With bloodshot blinks aimed at a row of whiskey optics opposite his barstool, he'd announced his intention to see to some personal business later in the morning, and asked Alan whether he minded Gemma's presence for a few hours. When Alan mentioned going to the vet, Dermot said, "Brilliant. Take her along. Gemma, you want to go, right?"

Gemma signed something, and it was obvious from her expression that she questioned his "personal business" and why she was excluded. He'd brushed her off with a universal enough flick of his fingers.

Now, Alan watched this strange woman's hand stroke over Bijou's gargoyle face, kneading the folds of skin with her thin and expressive fingers. A prick of jealousy surprised him at the sight of her hands smoothing themselves over Bijou's fur. He imagined they communicated a secret sign language he didn't know how to translate. He didn't want to go there, but he felt the first stirrings of the watchfulness that he'd sunk into with Camille back in France. Yet another pathetic tale of unrequited love, but with a twist, and oh what a twist that had been—as swift and painful as the kick to the ribs that had landed on his dog.

He grimaced, and Gemma, who'd just glanced up at him, ducked her head. A blush seeped into her cheeks, and she dragged fingers through her hair. When she let go, the curls popped right back into place. Camille, on the other hand, had worn her hair short, in a modish pixie cut, and her hands had been almost masculine in their sturdiness. She'd brush at her hair with a smile that issued a dare: *Come get me.* Later, Camille's raking hand had communicated her contempt for him and his romantic notions. "What did you think?" she'd said. "That we'd get married and live happily ever after?"

Since then, he hadn't let himself fall into the love trap again. He didn't like himself when he fell in love, not that it mattered in this case. Gemma was too traumatized and too vulnerable. It felt sleazy somehow. *He* felt sleazy.

"Bijou needs the loo," he said. "Back in a minute."

Outside, Alan inhaled a breeze laden with the coming winter, a chill just this side of the shivers, a hint of decaying leaves and sheep wool. Low-slung clouds drifted under a grey globe of a sky. For the first time in days, he could see the horizon blending its greenish haze into the sky.

Behind him, the door opened. Bijou rose from her pee crouch and wagged her tail. He turned to see Gemma beckoning Bijou toward her. Bijou understood a dozen hand signals. On the ride over,

Gemma had grown animated when he'd mentioned what he called *doggy sign language*, or DSL. While she practiced, she'd even smiled enough to show a dimple. Alan had caught his breath at this, his first sighting of her with self-consciousness all but forgotten. Her contented shine brought out the caramel hues in her skin and eyes.

Gemma signaled *come*, and Bijou approached without hesitation.

"Some loyalty." Alan caught Gemma's quick smile as she turned away. "And you hear too well, by the way," he said.

She signalled something back at him before pointing toward the reception desk, where the tech assistant, Lizzie, stood.

"You're in luck," she said. "We had a no-show but all you've got is me today. Dr. Evans is that swamped. Let's see you in then, Mr. Bressard." She peered down at Bijou. "Poor dear. Been in an accident, has she?"

"If you call a brush up against a man's boot an accident."

"People. Like to make me weep sometimes."

They entered a room with a sliding door at the far end. The place was as airy and cavernous as an indoor riding ring, and in its center sat an enormous x-ray contraption. The stainless steel table stood in its vertical position, ready for a horse to be shackled to it. Lizzie pushed a button and the slab shifted into a tabletop position with a well-oiled whirr of hydraulic cogs.

Lizzie gestured beyond Alan, puzzled. "Your friend?"

Friend? Not quite, but Alan returned to the hallway where Gemma hovered, looking sheepish as she stuffed a piece of paper into her pocket. She stood before a bulletin board filled with community notices and flushed so scarlet that Alan decided not to comment.

"You want to watch?" he said.

Gemma waited for him to enter ahead of her. Once inside the room, she positioned herself against the wall next to the door, staring around the room with evident fascination.

114

With Lizzie's help, Alan lifted Bijou onto the table. Lizzie strapped Bijou down and maneuvered the x-ray apparatus into position, then shooed them into a glass cubicle. She fiddled with a few knobs, made adjustments, and then pressed a button. A pristine image appeared on the computer monitor.

"Wow," Alan said. "High-tech."

"Gotta be. Racehorse owners are picky that way, and they're the backbone of our business. We're the only facility like this for three counties."

"Ay, my local vet said as much."

Alan noticed Gemma shining again as she gazed at the machinery and monitors, but he refrained from addressing her for fear that she'd retreat.

Lizzie pointed out hairline fractures in two of Bijou's ribs. "Not much different from cracked ribs on humans," she said, "and the patient care is the same: don't overexert, get lots of rest, and alleviate the inflammation. Also, I'll have Dr. Evans sign over a prescription for painkillers." Back in the x-ray room, she lowered her face into Bijou's. "Stoic thing, but you'll feel better soon."

They began the hour-long drive back to Lisfenora with Bijou relaxed under the influence of a pain pill. Alan drove without speaking, aware that Gemma had bestowed on him the rare gift of sitting in front with him rather than in the back with Bijou.

TWENTY-ONE

DANNY HELD HIS BREATH against Dermot's alcoholic stink and led him into the St. Patrick shrine. St. Patrick gazed down at them with kindliness that didn't inspire Danny to a higher road. He surveyed the central nave, where several groups of tourists stared above the altar at Jesus on the cross. Here and there vigil candles flared in the shadowy, whispery space, highlighting the profiles of penitents praying to their favorite saints within other shrines. The officious Mrs. O'Brien, local matriarch, paused on her way to the front of the church to glare at Danny as if he were to blame for Dermot's unseemly sniffling and groaning.

A clanking noise brought Danny's attention back to Dermot. Dermot stood against the far side of the shrine with hand braced against the wall, dropping coins into a wooden box that hung below a sign that read, PLEASE PLACE ALL CANDLE OFFERINGS IN THE SLOT BELOW.

"How many candles do you think you need?"

"All of them and then some."

Danny escorted Dermot toward the collection of candles that stood in tiered rows in front of dear old St. Patrick in his green robe, with four-leaf clovers and a dying snake at his feet. Dermot lit his first candle. The flame glowed within red votive glass.

"You have information about Lost Boy?" Danny said.

"Toby. That's his name. Toby Grealy."

Danny picked up a lit votive and turned it this way and that, watching the flame, letting Lost Boy's name settle. Toby Grealy. His relief was so palpable it had a taste, sweet and sour at the same time. "And you know his name how?"

"I meant to fetch Toby back to my aunt before he got into trouble. He's my cousin." Dermot lit a second candle from the flame of the first. "I don't understand. How could he have died? How did he die?"

Danny refused to get into the details of Toby's death until Dermot sobered up. "We're looking at it as a suspicious death."

"Suspicious?" Dermot's hand trembled as he continued lighting candles. "If only—"

"If only what?" Danny said.

"It's Gemma. She needs help and protection. I've let her down."

Danny leaned in to catch his mumbles.

"Look at me, I'm bloody pathetic. I've become a man I don't know anymore." Dermot turned to Danny, wobbling a little, and Danny felt the pent-up tension in the hands that clutched at his upper arms, trying to shake him but too drunk to move anything but Danny's sympathy. "You've got to understand."

"Does any of this have to do with the search for your mother's murderer?"

"You know about that?"

"Let's say that people inform me when someone accuses our matchmaker of getting someone killed."

Dermot's voice descended into a drunken series of slipping vowels and sliding consonants. "That was my frustration talking. Was just, I don't know, trying to retrace Toby's steps to McIlvoy. Liam was supposed to know something. I was sure of it. Sure that Toby would have talked to him first thing, but it seems he didn't visit Liam at all."

"And who is McIlvoy?"

"John McIlvoy. Her killer, of course. Toby said he'd all but found him."

Ah, Danny thought, this explains the mobile conversation Brendan had overheard. Perhaps Toby had found him, after all.

Dermot kicked at nothing. He was starting to cave again, his burst of tension engulfed by grief and perhaps guilt. Danny understood both. When it came to family there was plenty of both to go around.

Dermot waved a hand, almost slapping Danny in the process. "Toby didn't need to be mucking about in our family's past. If only he'd talked to me before he left. Anyhow, my aunt was hysterical that he'd actually find that McIlvoy, so I came to fetch him away. Gemma wasn't supposed to be here. That was the kicker—Gemma is always the kicker—"

Dermot wobbled again. He tried to catch himself with a hand on Danny's shoulder but missed and landed on the stone floor with a thud and a groan.

"Bloody hell," Danny said. "That'll be it for today."

He beckoned one of the volunteers who worked as docents during the festival. A few minutes later she returned with Fitz. A small crowd gathered around their hushed conference. Fitz agreed to let Dermot sleep off the pints on his couch.

"It's all right," Fitz said to the gawkers. "One of our own in the depths of grief."

Dermot roused with a rough shake.

Danny threw one of Dermot's arms around his shoulders, and on an exhale, stood with Dermot hanging off him. He'd be in a proper sorry state tomorrow. With Fitz's help, they retreated from St. Patrick's commiserating gaze and the lit vigil candles, four up and three across in a letter *T* for Toby.

"I need to be strong for Gemma—always," Dermot mumbled. "I'm so bloody tired."

"Lucky you, time for sleep," Danny said. "We need you sober so you can make a statement."

"Mmm, no." Dermot's head weaved in a figure eight. "Gemma doesn't know Toby's gone. She doesn't know I came to fetch him back. She can't know until she's ready. A bit complicated, I hope you understand. I'm supposed to protect her ..."

His words trailed off as he slumped against Danny.

Danny didn't understand a thing, least of all why Dermot would keep Toby's presence in Lisfenora a secret from Gemma.

At least he knew Lost Boy's name now. Toby Grealy, far from home, seeking an alleged murderer for some reason. Danny pictured the boy's deep blue gaze, a gaze already lost to the beyond. He'd tried to communicate his last message with a host of sparrows chorusing above them. Benjy had called them harbingers of death. Perhaps they'd accompanied Toby Grealy on his last journey. Or maybe they were Grey Man's minions.

With Dermot sleeping it off inside Fitz's flat, Danny said his good-byes to Fitz and stepped outside. A grey flutter froze him in mid-step. A sparrow perched on a dangling birdfeeder, its keen black gaze aimed at Danny. It found its song in a fluting *chirrup* and then went silent.

"Did Toby find a murderer?" Danny asked.

The bird twittered a high-pitched *tsip-tsip-tsip* and flew away. Danny took that as a yes.

TWENTY-TWO

TALL HEDGEROWS HELD THE mists within their branches. They towered over the drystone walls and scraped the side of Alan's car. He rolled down the window to catch the stir of wind speaking through the leaves. The scent of murky, mossy green stuff reminded him of autumn in the south of France. Not just any autumn, but the autumn he turned sixteen and fell into an aching, tortured love with his father's hothouse employee. Sexy Camille with her worker's hands and practical haircut. Worldly Camille who called him a pretty little schoolboy before seducing him.

Earlier that year, his mother had moved back to her hometown in County Kilkenny, taking Alan's two younger sisters with her. He'd had no sense of women, of their needs that were too complex for naïve Alan. His mother would have noticed his lovestruck idiocy, would have steered him down a safer path.

Instead, he took to watching Camille from afar when he was supposed to be studying. He'd follow her on his bicycle while she ran errands, as if the act of observing her would allow him to possess her heart. His obsession led him to wear a path through a wall of lavender bushes, back aching, knees muddied, so that he could spy on her in the hothouse.

The hothouse on one particular misted morning had glowed with beckoning warmth. He'd sniffed at the mess of dirt and dew surrounding him and imagined the sweetness that infused the hothouse. The orchids, yes; the begonias, yes; but also intoxicating Camille, who tended the blooms with a tenderness that she never showed him.

Today at the vet, Gemma's hands stroking Bijou's ears had reminded him of those moments of longing.

Alan pulled his car onto an embankment. He slid out and inhaled deep, hoping to rid himself of France and the feeling that he was once again stepping into emotional quicksand. This scent was pure Ireland, a land of softer loam and greener greens. Not like France at all, he told himself. But the memories didn't banish themselves as easily as all that. In fact, they were brighter than reality as Alan continued toward Danny's house on foot.

He'd dropped Gemma off after the vet appointment, and without thinking about it had turned his car right back around a mile later. Self-loathing was beside the point.

If memory lent the scent of that long-ago pre-dawn the pungency of his undoing, then it also lent Camille a breathtaking beauty. She was all the adolescent clichés: ripe, full-breasted, and flushed, whistling to herself and every once in a while tousling back her hair with dirt-encrusted fingers. He'd known the heady stink of her after the hothouse: fresh dirt and green tea soap and garden chemicals.

He should have heeded her toxicity, those chemicals, but he hadn't until that last morning when she threw a smile over her shoulder and with a come-get-me thrust of hand through hair, turned toward an unseen someone.

His father.

The shame of it, his inability to walk away from the peep show of his own making. Their frantic jabs at their clothes, their hasty but altogether passionate coming together. A tangle of twisting limbs and then Camille's blink in Alan's direction.

No surprise in her gaze. Almost as if she'd planned the peep show to rid herself of her little lap doggy once and for all. His still-married father had only shrugged in response to something she said and pulled her to the ground and out of view.

The worst of it: That he'd crouched there until they rose again, smiled into each other's eyes, and pulled their clothes back on, as languid as they'd formerly been frenzied. They must have known he still watched. After that morning, autumn seemed like nothing more than the decay of deadened fields and the sham of artificially grown flowers. Alan had moved across the Channel to live with his mother and joined a national hurling team, first with Kilkenny before moving to Clare, letting his bitterness burn out his throwing shoulder over the next six years, yet helping his teams take the Liam McCarthy Cup four times.

Alan stopped walking when he reached Danny's house. Fists clenched, he stood behind a tall hedgerow just as he'd stood behind bushes to watch Camille. He told himself this was different; he was curious about Gemma, was all.

Alan had planned to stay in France forever, take over the fields and hothouses that his sisters now tended. Strange, that they'd switched countries. He'd vowed never to return, and, so, when their father died, the two daughters returned to oversee the family flower business instead of Alan. He'd sold them his third so he could buy the pub. With that, his ties cut, he'd hoped for liberation that had yet to come.

Mandy's voice startled him out of his reverie. Then Petey's. Gemma appeared a moment later. She sat on the porch's top step and watched the children's show-offy play-acting. In contrast to her utter stillness, they were a couple of human-sized muscle spasms, jerking all over the place.

Alan rubbed at his tattoo while watching Mandy pull Gemma to her feet with the order that Gemma play tag with them. "You're Grey Man, and you have to catch us."

Petey appeared uncertain, glancing this way and that along the hedge. "He's already here," he said in a spooky voice. "I can *feel* him watching us."

"No!" Mandy mock-screeched. "Come get me, Gemma. You're Grey Man's sister! Hide and seek!"

They disappeared around the house in a hail of high-pitched screaming laughter. Gemma stood. She faced him, head cocked. As ever, his gaze wandered to the most expressive part of her: her hands. As she approached the hedge, they moved as if they had brains of their own, signing in doggy sign language. His DSL, as taught to her while driving to the vet clinic.

Imbécile. If he could see her then she could see him.

Her hands were delicate yet robust as bird's wings. She repeated two gestures. The first: a pacifying signal, as if Gemma patted an invisible dog's head. The second: a stop palm. *It's okay,* Gemma signaled, stay. *It's okay, stay. It's okay, stay.*

Over and over. Still frozen, Alan watched Gemma's small hands fill his tunnel vision until she was standing three feet from him on the other side of the hedge. He turned away, unable for the living hell of himself to meet her eye through the branches. So this is what it's like to be her, he thought. This petrified feeling. Shame engulfed him, that green-scented shame and disgrace all around him.

Gemma's palm lifted in a quick *away* gesture, which was his off-leash signal for Bijou: go on then, but stay close. She retreated in a leafy mosaic of maroon tights and black dress, leaving Alan breathless.

TWENTY-THREE

GEMMA PRESSED HER HANDS against her stomach as she walked around the Aherns' house. She hadn't spoken aloud, but she felt as if she'd tried. Sweat trickled down her ribs, and she shook so hard she felt it clear into her heart. But she'd done it. She'd approached Alan. Of her own volition, she'd spoken to him in his language.

Catching sight of him from inside the house before he stepped behind the hedgerow, she'd been struck by his bewildered expression. That had been the real Alan, the private Alan, the Alan who needed his safe place also. Now, as she chased Mandy and Petey over a rock wall and into the adjacent sheep field, it occurred to her that Alan might be selectively mute too. People can be mute to many things. To their needs and desires. To their potential for happiness. To their delusions. To their prejudices.

She'd thought about muteness a lot—too much perhaps. Perhaps she saw selective mutism in others as a way to feel better about herself. She thought this was, in fact, the truth, but she didn't care. Sometimes she was right.

Gemma clapped her hands, one, two, three, and beckoned the children to follow her back to the house. The abandoned cottage that Ellen called their folly looked down on them. It longed for inhabitants. Everything and everyone longed for something. The kittens, for protection and food. These wee children, for a sense of security. Ellen, thrashed by her own internal winds, for love. Everyone stuffed something away.

No, she admonished herself, not *everyone* stuffed. This was about her own self, not to be confused with anyone else. This was about what *she* stuffed away. Not just the tragedy of her mom's death, but that other thing she also avoided but saw in every abandoned pet at the animal shelter where she worked, deep within their eyes, like deep within Alan's—a longing for a safe and secure connection.

The children tumbled into the house ahead of Gemma. That week's *Clare Challenger* rested on a pile of unread circulars and catalogs. She grabbed it up and headed toward Ellen's closet. When she opened the door, the kittens blinked up at her sleepily. Their disconsolate cries had lessened. Now they trusted their warm and well-fed existence, and had started to explore the bedroom.

Gemma eased them aside and checked the new litter box. The kittens were using it, so that was good, but now they were getting litter everywhere. She spread a sheet of newspaper on the floor, and as she did so, she caught the headline from a few days ago. Her skin prickled at the sight of the drawing, and too soon she'd shrunken into herself so small that nothing existed except the comforting sound of tiny kitten breaths.

Toby, oh Toby.

TWENTY-FOUR

ELLEN LAY ON HER bed with the kittens on her stomach. She buried her fingers into the kittens' thickening fur over rounding bellies. They purred more with each passing day, and she tried to take comfort from their cozy warmth against her palms.

Mandy appeared at her door. "Can we eat now? I checked and there's sausage and leftover fried potatoes. That will be easy, won't it, Mam? Not hard to cook, right?" She turned away without looking at Ellen. "We don't mind refried potatoes."

Ellen rolled onto her side, shifting the kittens onto the bed. "All right then. Take over the kittens, will you? I just fed them."

With adult-like relief that saddened Ellen, her daughter bustled over and retrieved the kittens. In a chirpy voice she explained that the tabbies now had names. "Petey's kitten is the grey one called *Ashe* with an 'e' on the end. And mine's the orange one, and he's called *Flame*. That word already has an 'e' on the end." She stooped to settle Ashe and Flame in the closet but didn't close the door all the way. "Do you like their names?"

"Lovely, pet, lovely." Ellen heaved herself into a sitting position. "I'll be right there, sweet pea. Why don't you and Petey gather the food onto the counter for me?"

Ellen closed her eyes against an image of ashes and flames that became a phoenix rising out of the embers of loss, betrayal—a living death. The gall of it, to hope that last night she could have risen renewed and whole again like some mythological creature. Instead, she'd arrived home from the village feeling worse than before the outing. And to find Danny here too. She'd all but confessed her sins right there and then.

Ellen shifted to the end of the bed, where the opened jewelry box sat upon its plain of dusty dresser, its lid still upright in a mock salute. The sign of Danny's passage through territory that she'd assumed no longer interested him. Feet leaden beneath her, she stood and set aside the top tray to once again peruse the lower one. He'd dropped his wedding band into the wrong compartment, and the gift box—the infernal box with the earrings she should have flushed down the bloody toilet—sat askew in its slot.

She slammed down the jewelry box's lid and heard an echo of it from beyond her bedroom. The front door. Mandy called out—now truly relieved and not bothering to hide it—that Gemma had returned. Earlier in the afternoon, Ellen had arrived home to find Gemma in the closet, rocking like a disturbed person. Her alarm had turned to surprise when Gemma roused herself and bolted out of the house.

Now, Gemma knocked and entered the bedroom. Her eyes were red-rimmed and puffy, and she held herself tight as if afraid she'd shatter any second. She held out a note.

I'm all right now. I needed to get out of the house and walk it off.

"You don't look all right." Ellen continued when Gemma didn't respond. "Well then, why don't you lie down awhile. I'll call you when dinner's ready."

Gemma pulled out her pad and pen. After writing, she held out a new note, her expression shuttered.

Dermot hasn't been here? I haven't seen him since this morning when he dropped me off at Alan's pub.

"My husband called earlier. He wanted you to know that Dermot's in the proper langers and is sleeping it off on our deacon's sofa. You won't see him until tomorrow."

Gemma switched her gaze to the ground. Something flickered there, like she wasn't surprised. She continued writing.

Poor Bijou. Someone kicked her in the ribs last night.

"Ohh," Ellen groaned. "Bijou, yes."

She'd heard a yelp, hadn't she, as she'd stood there on the street, hidden by fog? The noise ricocheting out of the silence like that, hushed yet too loud, had startled her into scuttling back to her car.

Ellen opened the jewelry box again, unable to stop herself from picking at the wound she'd dealt to no one but herself. She pulled out the gift box. Smashing the earrings with a meat mallet might do the trick, but no, the earrings could give pleasure elsewhere. She wouldn't begrudge anyone their beauty. She could at least show this much maturity. "You might like these."

Gemma pointed in the direction of the children's bedrooms, where Mandy's voice could be heard ordering Petey to pass the orange crayon. Ellen convulsed at the thought of passing these earrings on to her daughter. "I have plenty of time to collect for Mandy," she said. "Take them, please."

Shy but pleased, Gemma signed *thank you* and popped open the box. Her smile froze into something more closely resembling a rictus. The box tilted down her slackening hand.

"Gemma?"

In a slow slide, the box tipped off Gemma's fingers and somersaulted toward the carpet. Her pained gurgling, so scratchy and feeble, was nevertheless the most shocking noise Ellen had ever heard. The girl stared down at the carpet where the scattered stones blinked like animal eyes out of the dark. Ellen snatched up the accursed things. Gemma had felt their taint, no doubt about it. Ellen could have torn her hair out over the misstep, and just when the girl was feeling at home with her.

"Never mind," she said. "I'll flush them right now, away they go forever, never to be seen again. Forget you ever saw them."

If anything, Gemma's pinched and stricken expression intensified. With taut fortitude, she pulled Ellen's hands toward her. Her clammy fingers stumbled over Ellen's. She continued gurgling, her skin flushing with the effort.

Finally, with a stamp of foot, she scrawled another note and shoved it at Ellen. The jagged letters yelled their desperation, their frantic need.

Where did you get these?

Sunday

Becoming a father isn't difficult,
But it's very difficult to be a father.

Wilhelm Busch

TWENTY-FIVE

DANNY SAT IN THE incident room with his men, trying to lead by example with what he hoped was a cooperative expression. In front of the chalkboard with its lists of assignments and follow-up tasks stood Superintendent Clarkson. They'd already wasted an hour debriefing.

"In other words, you have nothing," Clarkson said.

Danny explained that now that they'd almost confirmed the victim's identity, maybe they could move forward.

"It's a confused family story. I don't understand the half of it yet, but I'll be running the victim's cousin Dermot McNamara through the wringer as soon as we're finished here. He's been puking his guts out since last night, but I expect he's right enough now to answer questions and make his ID official. Other than this, we've found few people who spoke to the victim, and those who did notice him didn't mark him as anything other than a lad in for a festival shag. We'll continue asking around the pubs, though." Danny paused. "One shop owner, Malcolm Lynch, seemed to think the victim might be a petty thief."

"Right then," Clarkson said. "What about the missing boy, Brendan Nagel?"

Danny outlined the incident with Bijou late Friday night. Once again, nothing on forensics and no witnesses except for the dog.

"No way Brendan larked off to make his fortune in the big city or even to follow a lassie," O'Neil added. "He'd ask old Seamus—that's his father—for permission to shite before he'd make a decision like that on his own."

Clarkson nodded, looking pleased with O'Neil. "We'll proceed as if they're separate cases until we get indications otherwise. On with you then. We're done here for now."

"We haven't discussed Malcolm's complaint," Danny said. "Yesterday, he opened his shop to find *limp dick* painted across his windows."

"Go on."

"Malcolm blamed Seamus Nagel for the mischief. There's tension between them about Seamus's son, the missing Brendan, who works at Malcolm's shop. In any case, whoever wrote the message was no artist."

"And then there's Merrit's car," O'Neil said. "Someone also painted the word *slag* on Merrit Chase's car in a color I'd describe as magenta, the same color as *limp dick* on Malcolm's shop window."

"And Merrit Chase—wasn't she the one from last year, the American?"

"Oh ay, that would be her, all right," O'Neil said.

Danny ignored the sideways looks the rest of the men aimed at him.

"How does she connect to Malcolm and the rest of it?" Clarkson said.

Good question. She'd better not connect. "She shouldn't connect," Danny said.

"Except that she went to Malcolm to repair her necklace," O'Neil said.

A few men wandered out of the room, Clarkson on their heels. "A phantom graffiti artist isn't our priority—unless the messages are related to the murders, of course."

"What a ponce," one of the men muttered after Clarkson exited the room.

"A ponce who fancies O'Neil," said another.

Danny stood to the sound of kissy noises aimed at O'Neil. "Off to the morgue to confirm the ID on our lost boy."

As he left, Danny thought about the color magenta, and what kind of temperament you'd need to use that color for graffiti. Creative, perhaps? Nathan Tate popped into his head. The newcomer artist with the haunted look around his eyes, the artist who Seamus had boasted was good enough to get into Malcolm's shop, where Brendan had worked and where Lost Boy had loitered.

TWENTY-SIX

DANNY STOOD NEXT TO Dermot in the morgue. The scent of decay held in momentary abeyance coated his tongue. Next to him, Dermot covered his mouth and gagged with a dry, hacking noise.

Witnesses arrived with preconceived notions about the vessel called the human body. Danny knew from past experience that most of them imagined that a soulful essence remained just under the skin. Danny was used to the flash of disillusionment that crossed most of their faces before despair engulfed them. He expected the same out of Dermot.

Lost Boy's physical form lay under a pristine cotton sheet, as snowy white as baptismal linen. To Danny, the sheet always appeared innocent of its function and out of place, like it should be lifted with a flourish—*voilà*—to reveal nothing. But, alas, Benjy pulled back the sheet and Lost Boy's head appeared.

Instead of the usual disillusionment, Dermot raised his bloodshot gaze toward the ceiling. He tracked along the darkest shadows to the darkest corners with lips pressed together. Danny had seen that too—the fight to keep the howls inside. "I don't understand," he said. "How did he die?"

"A blow to the head."

Dermot covered his mouth again and rushed out of the room. The door swung shut against the sound of retching. Danny waited in silence while Benjy searched his pockets for a cigarette. When the retching stopped, Danny poked his head out the swing doors.

Dermot leaned against the walls with eyes shut. "John McIlvoy. That bastard. He snapped, I think, when he killed our mom. You'd have to be crazy for that to happen, wouldn't you?"

"Momentary insanity doesn't change his guilt. Do you want more time with Toby?"

Dermot pushed himself off the wall and followed Danny back into the viewing room. He spoke through ragged breaths. "For the longest time, Toby insisted he was psychic. He believed in ghosts. He said his totem—*totem*, I ask you—was the sparrow."

Benjy fingered an unlit cigarette, his silence loud as he nodded at Danny. *You see?* He moved to cover Toby, but Dermot pushed his hand away.

"*I watch*," Dermot said, more to himself than Danny, "*and am as a sparrow alone upon the house top.* Our granny, she loved nothing better than to wash her hair nets in the kitchen sink while Toby sat on the counter watching her. She'd quote that psalm like it meant something, and maybe it did."

Dermot reached out as if to pat Toby's head but dropped his hand. "She used to call Toby 'sparrow,' and I used to get jealous because she said it with such pride. But then one day a sparrow entered her house and perched on the piano, staring around until it flew at Toby's head. Later I heard Gran tell Aunt Tara that when a sparrow

135

enters a house, a death shall come. She was an eerie old thing with her lores and fables."

He choked a little but continued. "That day, the day the sparrow swooped at Toby's head, Granny said, 'There is special providence in the fall of a sparrow,' and never spoke of sparrows again. Maybe she knew Toby's fate."

"From Shakespeare," Benjy said. "That quote."

Danny stepped away from the rolling cart upon which Toby lay. Toby, in the air, in his imagination—it didn't matter—seemed to hover around them. He resisted the urge to check the room for fluttering feathers. Don't be daft, he told himself. There wasn't even a window.

"Do you confirm that this is Toby Grealy?" Benjy said to Dermot.

Dermot nodded and stumbled out of the room.

"Didn't I tell you this was a strange one?" Benjy said.

———

Danny led the way along various corridors until they reached the hospital's staff lounge. They sat in the quietest corner away from the vending machines. The artificial glow from the overhead lights leached the color from Dermot's already green complexion.

Danny left him sagged over the table and returned with tea. "Let's talk about Toby. You weren't what I'd call coherent yesterday."

After a few forced swallows, Dermot said, "I can't remember what I told you."

"Start with the reason he came to Lisfenora."

Dermot groaned.

"Okay," Danny said, "start with your mother then, Siobhan. She was widowed, divorced—?"

"Widowed."

"And then?"

Dermot spoke in a robotic voice. "She married John McIlvoy, but don't get excited. I went through all this with your lot back in Dublin. They couldn't find anything on him, and what family he had didn't want anything to do with him. He fell off the Earth after he killed my mother. The investigators figured him for crossing into Northern Ireland and then who knows where."

Dermot shoved his teacup aside. The brown liquid sloshed over the edges.

"Go on," Danny said.

"What do you want to know? My mother was the trusting sort, and lonely and overworked and susceptible. She didn't need any man's money, not that McIlvoy had any. He was a rough sort, looking for his ticket to the good life. After my father died—heart attack—my mother became sole proprietor of a high-end tourist shop on Wicklow Street, just off Grafton."

Danny nodded his understanding, Grafton Street being the prime pedestrian thoroughfare between Trinity College and St. Stephens Green. Excellent hotels and restaurants and shops jammed the warren of lanes off Grafton Street, as Danny well remembered from his honeymoon, that joyous time in his marriage.

"Give me the timeline," Danny said. "What year was this? How old were you? How old was Gemma?"

"My dad died in 1990 when I was seventeen and Gemma was seven. I hate to say this about my mother—God rest her—but she didn't fare well without a husband. I tried to help, but she wouldn't hear of me not going to university. I had my heart set on business, hoping to get out of being just a shopkeeper." He fiddled with the teacup, sloshing more liquid over the sides. "I had dreams and plans.

Maybe I still do—sometimes I can't tell anymore. It's been difficult to grow my life what with Gemma—not that I regret it, not at all."

But he did. Danny caught a whiff of resentment and conflicted loyalties.

"Your mother was lonely," Danny said.

"Utterly. She ended up at the matchmaking festival in 1991. She was determined that I not worry about her or the shop while I completed my education. She returned with McIlvoy in tow, as jolly and beer-laden as you please." He shuddered. "But he didn't seemed bad at first. By then I was away at the UCD School of Business, my first year, living on campus and quite the little man. I managed to get through most of that school year without laying eyes on McIlvoy, except for Christmas, but the bastard still seemed okay then, or maybe he was on good behavior while I was home. In fact, I know he was, because Gemma has since told me this was the case."

While Danny listened, Dermot related how it became obvious once his mother had died that she'd been protecting Dermot from the true McIlvoy, whose opportunistic nature became apparent over time.

"Mom and Gemma would take to coming up with day trips or Sunday brunches rather than have me visit the house. Mom didn't like to worry others, you see, and Gemma is that way also." Dermot stuck his finger in the tea and flicked out a few droplets. "Are we done now?"

"No." Danny's mobile vibrated in his pocket. He forwarded it to voicemail with a quick click. "How was your mother killed?"

"By rage. McIlvoy had her by the neck." He stopped to take a deep breath. "He banged her head against the kitchen counter as he was choking her."

Danny waited until Dermot nodded the okay before continuing with the next question. "Fast forward many years and Toby arrives in Lisfenora. What day was this?"

138

"Saturday. And then Gemma and I arrived Monday. I thought he'd spoken to Liam. The story had always been that he matched McIlvoy to my mom." He slumped in his chair. "At least, that's the happy story my mom told."

Danny nodded, thoughtful. Toby landed in Lisfenora without knowing a soul and four days later he was dead, perhaps by the mysterious McIlvoy. If Toby had found McIlvoy without Liam's help, then they were missing the link between Toby and McIlvoy.

"And where is McIlvoy, I ask you?" Dermot said. "He must live in the area."

"Why must he?"

Dermot grimaced at the cup as if he wanted to pitch it against the wall. "Because Toby as much as said so."

"Why did Toby take it upon himself to find McIlvoy?" Danny said.

"The crux of it, that."

Danny's phone vibrated again and stopped. "Go on."

"Toby was—"

The mobile started up again. "Oh, bloody hell. You hold that thought right there. Ahern here. Make it fast."

"Call came in to the station," O'Neil said. "We've got Brendan Nagel."

Danny sagged with relief. "At the station? I'm on my way."

"No, face-up in Blackie's Pasture. The same as Toby Grealy."

TWENTY-SEVEN

GEMMA SIPPED HER PINT and let Dermot's words flow over her. In front of her, beef stew glistened in brown sauce. Onions and potatoes sat like spongy lumps between mounds of meat.

You could have told me that you were coming to fetch Toby back, she signaled.

"I wouldn't have to lie, if you'd just—" Dermot stopped himself before saying the obvious out loud.

If only she could live on her own. If only she weren't dependent on him. If only her mind would unlock itself so she'd start talking again. Dermot had had a few girlfriends through the years, but they never lasted long after they met Gemma. In fact, she would have believed Dermot's initial lie about attending the matchmaking festival except for one thing: no way would he lark off at the last minute without a hotel reservation. Dermot was a planner. He'd have made reservations months in advance and he'd have discussed his trip with her.

So something had happened, something to do with their mom's murderer. John McIlvoy. The man she should remember, but didn't.

The man who had changed everything. Seemed her instinct had been correct.

I deserve to know what's going on too.

Dermot clanked down his steak knife. "I don't know if I can bear too much more of this—you need to just—"

She raised her eyebrows at him.

"Don't look at me like that. It's more important than ever that you get better."

Dermot bowed his head. That's right, feel like a toad, Gemma thought. About everything, down to contriving lunch in a public space so she couldn't throw a silent tantrum, so she'd feel trapped in place by the humanity pressed in around them, so she'd have to listen to him turn everything around on her—as if Toby's death were her fault, which she knew somehow that it was—and so she'd have to stuff down her grief to a soft spot beside her heart.

At least Dermot had had the grace to tell her that he'd identified Toby earlier in the morning. That, yes, the sketch she'd seen in Ellen's newspaper was their dear, sensitive, headstrong cousin.

She forced down a swallow, thinking about Toby. She couldn't stand herself sometimes, the way her head worked. She was too aware of the stringy contour of the beef in her bowl and the way bits of parsley stuck to the potatoes like mold, yet after the initial shock of seeing Toby's picture in the paper, she no longer felt the reality of his passing. It felt like a continuation of the bad dream that lived inside her bottomless well. Something to be consigned below surface reflections.

And there sat Dermot, trying to act strong when he wasn't, while around them a happy crowd ignored them in favor of listening to a traditional band playing in the corner of the room. The band members used their violins, tin whistles, and accordion to rousing effect.

For once, she was glad for the ruckus, which gave her a chance to gather her thoughts.

She pushed aside her soup bowl. *I know you want your own life. I want mine too. That's why I followed you—at least in part. I need to face the truth about our mom's death, whatever it is. But now Toby is dead too.*

Back in Dublin, she'd begged a ride from a friend who worked at the shelter with her. He was on his way to Galway for an Animal Rights Action Network protest against the fox fur trade. Once she'd arrived in Lisfenora and texted Dermot, he'd had no choice but to pick her up. Too bad his car had broken down right afterwards.

"I'll make arrangements for you to get back to Dublin," Dermot said. "Can you handle the train?"

Damn him. First he wanted her to get better faster. Now he wanted her gone. Her dear brother was going mental on her.

She stood. *If you're staying, I'm staying. I'll find my own answers.*

Pulling her hoodie up as a makeshift blinder, she hurried out of the restaurant toward Alan's pub on the other side of the plaza, where Bijou would greet her like an old friend. Petty though it may be, she decided not to tell Dermot about the opal earrings that Ellen had given her and that reminded her of those their mother used to wear. She felt the shock of memories wanting to emerge whenever she touched the box she kept in her pocket.

TWENTY-EIGHT

CHIRPS AND FLUTTERS FOLLOWED Danny across Blackie's Pasture.
He imagined a feathered messenger cocking its head back and forth
as it tried to watch them out of one side of its head, then the other.
Mad though it may be, the hovering presence wouldn't let Danny go.

Toby's sparrow. And maybe now Brendan's sparrow too.

Brendan Nagel lay not far from where Toby had died. Unlike
Toby, however, his peacefulness was already marred by the smell of
decay. Danny tried not to associate this shell with the Brendan he'd
known. Sorry hapless lad. He'd gotten caught up in something, all
right, and what did he get for his troubles but slug trails across his
face and eyeballs already half eaten away?

"Neck broken. He died quickly, unlike our Lost Boy," Benjy said.
"Also, the wallet and mobile are still on him. Our man didn't give a
rat's arse about this one's identity."

Benjy pulled a battered cigarette out of his shirt pocket and
rolled it between his fingers. "I predict one killer. You've got your
very own Grey Man."

143

"Grey Man," seconded several of Danny's men at once.

Not the name Danny would have chosen for their unknown subject, but it was too late to change it now.

Wind off the Atlantic gusted. Through thinning fog, rock walls appeared beyond the edge of the village, undulating toward the ocean. Closer still, the plastic-wrapped grass bundles that stood sentry over the field rose out of the dissipating murk. Danny squinted, catching sight of a color that shouldn't be there, and walked part way around one of the bundles to get a better look at it.

Scrawled across the black plastic, magenta words appeared as if lit in neon: *come home.*

A sparrow glided low over them and landed on top of the bundle. Feeling an uncustomary need to vacate a crime scene, Danny pointed out the words to O'Neil, told him to check it out against the other graffiti, and announced he'd best notify Seamus Nagel about his son's death. He turned away from the sparrow's mournful presence and the sight of another boy who couldn't go home.

———————

Thirty minutes later, Danny sat at Alan's bar. Nathan Tate had notified him that Seamus had wandered out of the pub but was sure to return soon because he'd left his pint behind. Danny didn't mind the wait. He'd already sucked down one pint fast. He signaled Alan for a second one while reassuring himself that someone had to notify next of kin. Before leaving the scene, Superintendent Clarkson had arrived and in his usual fashion sidelined Danny anyhow.

Alan handed him a Guinness. Danny swallowed half of it in one go. Good man Alan walked away without asking; he knew when to stay silent.

Pint cradled between his palms, Danny watched Alan change the chalkboard quote while the crows hectored him. *Man is a rope stretched between the animal and the superman—a rope over an abyss.*

Nietzsche. Lovely. Just the philosopher to brighten their day. Elder Joe echoed Danny's thought: "Ay and you're a font of sunshine, aren't you? It's enough to send me tits up."

Alan's expression remained closed, but his gaze swept over Gemma, who sat on Bijou's pillow, reading.

Danny beckoned Alan over and in a low voice revealed the latest news.

"Ah Christ." Alan's mouth drooped. "Brendan was a good lad."

"Have you heard anything interesting from behind the bar?"

Alan rubbed chalk dust off the back of his hand. "Only the usual shite. Malcolm slagging him for forgetting to shake out the welcome mat and Seamus lobbing the shite right back, telling him he'd best leave off Brendan. Brendan sometimes fled to O'Leary's Pub to get away from them."

"The O'Leary girl works behind their bar now. Grown to a fine thing, I hear."

"Got all the lads quivering, that one."

Alan pushed off from his elbow-stoop on the counter with a grunt. A moment later Seamus entered with a book under his arm and without his usual boisterous hello to the crows. His mates tried to rouse him, but he only responded to the prods with a wan smile. Drunk but not completely ossified, and Danny was grateful for that as he slipped into the cheeky flock and excused both himself and Seamus out of the pub.

"I need to take a look at Brendan's bedroom," Danny said.

Seamus bumped along beside him like a half-deflated wheel. He held up a novel, *The Three Musketeers.* He was after borrowing it for Brendan, he said, who was quite a reader, like his mother. Danny didn't interrupt Seamus as he explained that he didn't put much store in reading books himself, but so it went—his son liked his adventure stories and had lately moved on to what some called the classics.

"Deacon Fitz offered up the lending and best to grab him on a Sunday, isn't it?" he said. "I kept meaning to get around to the borrowing. Promised Brendan, I did."

They were cutting through the church green's back gate as Seamus said this last. He saluted Fitz's windows. "Fusty bloke but generous."

Danny let Seamus natter on about Brendan's start at reading the Bobbsey Twins tales, his absurd tendency to read through the night, his stabs at writing adventure stories of his own. "He's smarter than Malcolm gives him credit for."

He voiced his hope through a veil of hopelessness. At Seamus's house, Danny stepped into the comfortable habitat of a couple of bachelors with shoddy domestic habits. A pile of newspapers sat next to a leather lounger. The matching sofa stored a collection of glasses and plates and magazines with buxom girls on the covers. Danny imagined Seamus on his lounger and Brendan on the sofa, telly's glow bright in a dark room. They ate on their laps, no doubt, and muted the sound on commercials to flip through their respective reading material.

"Seamus, I'm sorry to inform you we've found Brendan, deceased."

Seamus staggered out of the room and up a flight of stairs to Brendan's bedroom, where he collapsed onto his son's bed. After settling *The Three Musketeers* on the nightstand, ready for no one now, he pulled the covers over himself. "It was inevitable," he said.

"How so?"

"Just when I think I've got life figured out for the both of us. Overstepped meself and God punished me." A bitter snarl transformed his face before melting back into misery. "Ah, Danny, you didn't need to tell me." He tapped his chest over his heart. "I feel it here."

He closed his eyes. Within a minute, Seamus had slipped out of his bereaved reality. Danny set about prying into Brendan's young life while Seamus's hitched breaths filled the room. The leftover hand of a mom's presence was evident in the ruffled curtains and color-coordinated bedding; otherwise the room was all boy, down to the smelly trainers tossed into the corner.

The room yielded nothing except for a stash of handwritten pages. Brendan had made serious attempts at writing adventure stories, more so than he'd probably admitted to his father. Danny sat at the desk and browsed a tale about a boy going off to sea on a haunted pirate's galleon. The pages oozed with secret yearnings. Perhaps Brendan had attempted a real-life adventure that betrayed him in the end.

Danny replaced the pages in the bottom desk drawer and hovered over Seamus, who slept with a frown and spittle soaking into the pillow. Danny pulled off the man's old boots.

He prodded Seamus awake. "Did Brendan know Lost Boy? His name was Toby Grealy."

Seamus shook his head. He blinked with sorrow fathoms deep and let his eyes drift shut. Danny unfolded a wool blanket from the end of the bed and spread it over him. A tear leaked out of one of Seamus's eyes.

Danny sat on the edge of the bed. Now he could absorb what he'd learned today, and not just about Brendan's death.

Toby Grealy. Somehow his arrival in the village had unleashed their very own Grey Man as Benjy had said. Somehow Brendan got swept up in the darkness at the heart of the McNamara family's past. On the return drive from the morgue, Dermot had managed to quell his tears right up to the moment he'd blurted, "Toby is—was—our brother. Gemma doesn't know yet. She can't. Not until she can handle it."

Half brother, Dermot had meant to say, with John McIlvoy as father.

TWENTY-NINE

MERRIT HELD OUT GEMMA'S polka-dotted scarf and tried to ignore the buzz that assaulted her from all directions. Alan's pub was busier than ever. Merrit felt more than a few curious stares from the locals aimed at her back as she stood before Gemma, who seemed oblivious as she read *Love in the Time of Cholera*. Bijou lay with her head on Gemma's lap. Her tail whapped the suede dog bed in greeting.

"I found your scarf on our porch. Must have slipped off the other day." Gemma continued reading, so Merrit placed the scarf on the pillow near Bijou's stomach. "Gemma, listen."

But Merrit didn't know what to say next. As usual, Gemma barricaded herself within her hoodie and curls. Her face was visible in profile, expressionless in that mystifying way of hers. Today, though, red puffiness rimmed her eyes.

"I don't know what's going on," Merrit said, "but I'd like to help. If I can."

Still, no response from Gemma. Giving up, Merrit turned to find Ellen Ahern waiting with her two children holding either hand. She said nothing, but her squint caused Merrit to excuse herself. She wanted to apologize for her very existence and assure Ellen that the *slag* painted on her car meant nothing despite what tongue-waggers might say about her and Danny. Instead, she retreated backwards until she backed into Alan.

"Ellen knows Gemma?" Merrit said.

His gaze wandered toward Gemma, then away again. "She and Dermot are staying at the house."

With that, he walked away. On her own and feeling it, Merrit watched Gemma light up as Ellen's children climbed onto the pillow with her and Bijou. Ellen spoke, and Gemma tilted her chin down in some kind of agreement. After a few more words, Ellen beckoned the children and left without acknowledging Merrit.

Shrugging off her discomfort, Merrit returned to Gemma. Again, Gemma ignored her.

"I'm at loose ends today because it's Liam's day off from the festival. He didn't use to do that, but with his health—"

Merrit waited. Gemma turned a page in her novel. "Okay then. I'll see you around. I'm going to pick up my necklace now. The owner of the gift shop around the corner should have it fixed good as new. You can come with me if you want." She paused. Still nothing. "Right. I'll let you know how much it costs. Not that I care, but Dermot insisted that he wanted to pay for the repair."

At long last Gemma responded by grabbing her rucksack and pulling out a pad and pen. *No,* she wrote. *I broke it. I'll pay for it.*

A few minutes later, they stood in front of Pot o' Gold Gifts. Gemma's force of will had been evident in every tortured step they took away from the pub. Squaring her shoulders, Gemma raised her chin enough to blink at Merrit's neck. Her nostrils flared like a shying horse. If only Merrit knew what was going on inside the woman's head.

Inside the shop, a harassed-looking blond girl stood behind the counter poking at a monitor. She peered at the screen as if trying to decipher Egyptian hieroglyphics. At the sound of the entrance bell, she hollered for Malcolm. He appeared, looking dapper as usual and with a bright smile aimed over the head of his grumbling employee.

"Merrit! Top of the day to you," he said. "And a wonderful day it is. I have your necklace right here, better than new if I may say so."

"I'm glad it wasn't a problem," Merrit said. "I miss wearing it."

"Of course you do. Who wouldn't?" He aimed his satisfied smile at Gemma lagging behind Merrit. "And who's this?" He twisted to catch a glimpse of her. If anything, his voice ratcheted up a notch, and his wide smile returned fresher than ever. "A new customer, perhaps?"

Gemma leaned away from Malcolm's enthusiastic attempts to engage her. Poor Gemma, thought Merrit. She must get this kind of crap all the time.

"She's along for the ride, that's all," Merrit said.

Malcolm's shoulders stiffened.

"Thanks so much for fixing my necklace. You don't know how grateful I am, and I know your time is valuable."

Relaxing again, Malcolm led the way past marble crosses and local pottery. "Valuable indeed. And I must say that it's amazing that I function as well as I do sometimes. Believe me when I say that owning a shop isn't for the faint of heart."

Behind her, Gemma grabbed Merrit's arm, then let go. When Merrit turned, Gemma shook her head as if saying, *I'm fine, I'm fine.*

Gemma hadn't looked up since she'd entered the store. It could be too much: the tourists bumping against them; Malcolm's big presence; the prospect of seeing a necklace that had disturbed her the first time she saw it. Merrit found herself brightening her tone to match Malcolm's.

"Gemma liked my necklace," she said. "Maybe she can check out the rest of your jewelry."

"Of course, of course, but you'll have to excuse me. Busy day today. You take your time." Malcolm stooped behind the counter and rose with Merrit's beloved keepsake dangling from his fingertips. "That will be twenty euros."

Gemma fumbled with her pocketbook and dropped a bundle of euros onto the floor in her haste to pay. Malcolm didn't seem to notice as he placed the necklace in a box and the box in a bag, saying what a pleasure it was to see Merrit. Finally, Gemma pushed four fivers in Malcolm's direction and stepped back.

"Very good, and a good day to you." Malcolm moved down the counter to help another customer.

"Come," Merrit said. "I'll show you jewelry by the same designer as my necklace."

At the Firebird Designs display, Gemma stared, mesmerized, as she trailed her fingers over the glass cabinet. Her other hand dug into her jacket pocket. With the same shell-shocked gaze that had animated her face right before she snitched the necklace, Gemma pulled out a small black box and snapped it open. She held it up against the glass near other semiprecious earrings with silverwork borders.

Merrit leaned in for a closer look. "Were these your mom's?"

Gemma shook her head as she continued to compare them against Malcolm's current stock. Merrit held out her moonstone necklace. All from the same designer, no doubt about that.

"Where did you get these earrings if not from your mom?" Merrit said.

Gemma wrote that Ellen Ahern had given them to her, that they'd been a gift. Merrit didn't know what to make of this except that it didn't bode well for Danny's marriage if his wife was giving away his presents. But that was neither here nor there. Merrit's only concern was Gemma and the distress that etched the first faintest lines around her eyes.

"I think I understand." She aimed for a low and easy tone. "Your mom had jewelry like this."

Gemma's blink told Merrit she was correct. *A matching set*, she wrote. *I just remembered it.*

"My necklace is a moonstone, and your earrings are opals. Do you know what kind of stone your mom owned?"

Gemma shook her head.

"Maybe this Firebird man keeps records. Maybe we can contact him to see who bought a matching set of opals or moonstones or some other blue stone back then."

Gemma's head shaking grew more agitated. She was about to write something when Malcolm reappeared.

"My new salesgirl needs to learn the trade, and what better way than straight into the fire? Most people aren't as quick to catch on as I was at that age, I'll admit, but still there's no use for it because otherwise I'd run myself ragged with this business. In fact, I already do. Ah, well, what's a man to do? May I show you a ring, or perhaps a pretty bracelet?"

Gemma still held the box against the glass case. She'd frozen in place at Malcolm's breezy interruption.

"My goodness." He plucked the earrings out of Gemma's hand, surprise evident. "What do we have here?" He lingered over them and handed them back. "One of his better designs, I must say." A customer approached him. "Oh, excuse me again."

To Merrit's relief, Malcolm escorted the customer to the other side of the shop. Gemma snapped the box closed and tucked it into her jacket pocket. For many minutes, she studied the Firebird baubles. No, not studied, Merrit corrected herself. The opposite, in fact. Her eyes had landed on them but her focus had turned inward with such intensity that Merrit almost passed her hand in front of Gemma's face to see if she would respond.

"Gemma?"

She surfaced with a blink and picked up the framed artist's statement that stood beside the display. Her hands trembled as she stared at an image of the artist himself, caught in profile and half obscured by a floppy hat as he bent over his work. His scraggly beard fit the image of a recluse.

Gemma set the statement down so that it faced away from her. She scribbled on her pad.

The man who killed my mom was a jewelry maker. Back then, he didn't have a special name for himself, though. She tapped the jewelry case and continued writing. *This is him. Firebird Designs is John McIlvoy.*

THIRTY

Danny arrived at his house more than ready for the children's nightly ritual. They were his wee antidotes. He couldn't get Seamus's devastation out of his mind, the way he'd accepted Brendan's death as if it were a fate he deserved.

Ellen retreated ahead of him to her bedroom with the comment that Dermot was already asleep. No surprise there. He had to be nursing a bugger of a hangover. Gemma didn't look up as he crossed the living room. She huddled on the sofa with a book on her lap, picking at nap on the sofa cushion.

The house felt weighty, like any second something was about to erupt. Along with Seamus's grief, he kept seeing Toby, the way his soul-bearing light had faded out, and his daughter Beth, whose light had also faded. All he wanted to do was squash Petey and Mandy against himself so they'd sink into his skin and he could carry them around with him everywhere.

Three hours later and playtime, dinner, baths, and reading ticked off, Danny sat in the children's darkened room watching the shifting moon shadows through the fog. A breeze churned it into alternating thinner and thicker wisps. His children's faces brightened then faded, their sleep smiles doing much to relieve his generalized distress.

Petey's hand rose from the covers. Danny knew what was coming, the pleas not to leave yet, and preempted the request by sliding onto the bed next to his boy. Petey burrowed himself against his hip, like the warm wee kitten he was, and his hand dropped onto Danny's stomach, relaxed, open, trusting.

He could hold his children tight, tight, tight against him, but this hadn't helped Seamus with Brendan.

"Da?" Petey whispered.

"Hmm?"

"When will you move back home?"

"That's a difficult question."

"No, it's not. You can talk to Mom after I go to sleep and then move back in tomorrow."

"It's not that simple."

"Why not?"

Why not, indeed? "My turn for a question: When you saw the Grey Man outside our house, did he see you?"

"No, that's not right." Petey sighed in imitation of Mandy, who imitated her mom. "It was only Dermot with Gemma walking up the lane because their car broke down. Gemma found the kittens in Mr. Travis's field."

"Right, that's good then. No Grey Man."

"Yes, Grey Man. He's still out there."

Danny pressed a goodnight kiss against Petey's forehead and eased out of the room. He opened the door to the master bedroom without his usual knock. Ellen set aside her diary as he closed the door behind him.

"I'm uncomfortable with Dermot and Gemma in the house. I'd like them to leave."

Ellen frowned. "You don't live here anymore. You don't have a say."

"I do have a say," Danny said. "My income pays for their food, for everything around here. More importantly, they're connected to my current investigation."

"I like them here and the kids like them here."

"I understand that, but this isn't negotiable. I'll pick up the children for a sleepover tomorrow night and drop them off at school on Tuesday morning. This will give Dermot and Gemma a day to sort out a new place to stay."

Her watchful gaze irked Danny, as if *she* had cause to worry over *his* behavior. He opened the jewelry box and pulled out the top tier, but the box with the earrings was missing. "Gone," he said. "And now it's all okay, I suppose."

"I gave them to Gemma."

He could care less about that. "Who gave them to you?"

"Danny, don't. It's done. It doesn't matter. I was a fool. Besides, you think people haven't poked their noses into our business, wondering about the coincidence that you happen to be staying in Fox Cottage with Merrit just down the track in Liam's house?"

"Nothing happened. Nothing is happening."

"So you say."

"I shouldn't have to say anything about her to you, or anyone. She was a witness and victim in my last investigation. You imagine some attraction between us, so that makes it bright and bonny for you to shag someone else, fine. That's your delusion." He slammed the jewelry box shut. "Don't forget. I'm picking up the children tomorrow night."

"Fine." She shoved the diary into her robe pocket. "You'd know who gave me the earrings if you'd bother to observe, detect, put two and two together—do what you do so well with your work."

Touché.

Monday

The gods visit the sins of
the fathers upon the children.

Euripides

THIRTY-ONE

MERRIT PUSHED AWAY HER seafood chowder, for once having eaten less than Liam. "Almost time to get back to the plaza," she said.

Liam sat with the matchmaking ledger in front of him. He jotted a note beside one of the names, but most of his gaze was aimed at a woman who sat next to the fireplace. Merrit remembered her. A music teacher from Cork. Unlike some of the festival participants, she'd seemed at ease with the process, ready to be pleased rather than disappointed. A man pulled up a chair next to her. They leaned toward each other, laughing over a private joke. "I put the bug in his ear to talk to her." Liam eased the book closed. "Sometimes they don't need me at all."

Merrit smiled, but her thoughts were on Gemma, who sat curled up beside Bijou as usual. She noted how Gemma tensed when the door opened or when a customer made a sudden move. Yet her vigilance softened when Alan came into view or when his voice rose above the general chatter and clink inside the pub.

"Now," Liam said, "please enlighten me about what's troubling you." He glanced at Gemma. "And never mind sorting out the vandalism or Gemma. Those are nice preoccupations, but not the heart of it."

Dang him. He wasn't going to let it go. Merrit could tell by the way he gazed at her, that penetrating look he used on the lovelorn during the festival.

"What's bothering me is that we need to find John McIlvoy," Merrit said.

The day before, Merrit had managed to lead trembling Gemma back to the comforts of Bijou after their foray into Pot o' Gold Gifts. Other than letting herself be led, she hadn't responded to Merrit's appeals for more information about the man behind Firebird Designs. John McIlvoy, her mother's killer, if Dermot was to be believed.

"*We* do not need to find McIlvoy," Liam said. "Talk to Danny. You ought to mend those fences anyhow." Liam waved at someone behind her. "Speaking of. Danny-boyo," he called.

Merrit sighed. Village life. She still wasn't used to the closeness of it.

Danny approached from the entrance, bringing the scent of fog with him. He wore a jacket and tie under a black trench, all of which fit him on the loose side. Ellen must have bought the suit because its dark chocolate hue mimicked the depths of Danny's eyes. He didn't seem the type to care about that kind of thing.

"Fancy this good timing." Liam patted the chair beside him. "Sit down."

Merrit sipped her coffee, all too aware of the not-so-furtive glances coming from the locals in the room. Even Alan had paused to take in their threesome.

Danny sat where Liam indicated. "Old troll."

Liam acknowledged his son Kevin's nickname for him with a nod. His smile dimmed but the crinkles remained around his eyes.

Danny swung his glance toward Merrit and then out the window. "I need to follow up on the graffiti."

"O'Neil got the details already," Merrit said. "He didn't seem too worried about it." Her nonchalance was a sham, and she knew that Danny knew it. She continued before he could reply. "I found out something that might interest you. About Dermot and Gemma."

"Of course you did."

Merrit ploughed on. "According to Gemma, the man who killed her mom also made my necklace. John McIlvoy—"

"Yes, I have heard of him."

"—and he's a jewelry maker. Firebird Designs, to be exact. The jewelry in Malcolm's store." Merrit felt for her moonstone's comforting smoothness. "Malcolm must know McIlvoy's details, so maybe you could help Dermot and Gemma resolve their mom's death."

"That's a helpful fact," Danny said, "but I need you to quit meddling in Dermot and Gemma's affairs."

"Why?" Merrit said. "They came to us—or rather to Liam."

"How about because their affairs are Garda business, not yours." Danny addressed Liam. "Do you remember buying Merrit's necklace from McIlvoy? Any insights into the man would be welcome at this point."

Something else was going on related to McIlvoy, Merrit realized, something that had Danny jumpy. She could see it in the way his gaze kept twitching toward a bird that flew back and forth under the eave.

"I remember the man well enough," Liam said, "but I have no idea what he was called or what became of him. He lived out of his van like a bloody traveller. We're sure he's the same man who married Siobhan McNamara?"

"According to Gemma, yes," Merrit said.

Liam ruminated aloud about the jewelry maker who appeared each year for the festival, with his long hair and paisley shirts. This was the 1970s, after all.

"How old would he be now?" Danny said.

"Late fifties?"

"And twenty years later, when Gemma's mom arrived for the festival he was still living out of his van? That's a long time to be on the road."

"I don't have a clear memory of him after the early 1970s. The further back in time, the clearer my vision."

"I can ask Gemma if she remembers a van," Merrit said.

Danny leaned forward, his voice unequivocal and stern. "You need to stop. Right now."

"Oh, is that right?" Merrit clenched her hands together on her lap. "I've taken an interest in Gemma, and I mean to help her. There's something about her, struggling with her anxieties the way she does. Anyhow, it's something I can do."

She didn't need to remind him about her panic attacks. Comprehension flickered before he looked out the window again. "My mom used to say that bad luck came like the Morrigan triple goddess—in threes. True to the old ways or not, I don't know, but she also used to say the Morrigan was a purveyor of death, and once she took root there'd be more to come."

He shifted forward to the edge of his chair, close enough that Merrit smelled mint on his breath. "Back to the graffiti. I didn't come over to talk to you about the McNamaras. Something's still undone, and that something could pertain to the graffiti on your car. So far, three public declarations, and so far, two people confirmed dead. I need to know what you might have to do with these events."

Danny's grim certainty settled over Merrit like a caul that she pictured enshrouding the Morrigan, or Grey Man, or both together, the best of friends spreading death in their wakes.

"If Gemma hadn't ripped off my necklace, I wouldn't know anything except through the newspaper and gossip like everyone else."

"Still, there's no ignoring the graffiti pattern. Malcolm's shop, where Brendan worked. A grass field, where the victims died. And before everything, your car. The only thing that comes to mind is that you work with Liam, whom Dermot accused of killing his mother."

"That seems a bit hazy."

"Indeed." His unsettled gaze followed another bird in flight. He stood, checking his watch. "Do me a favor and stick to matchmaking."

His abrupt leave-taking left Merrit so deflated that she longed to join Gemma on the dog pillow. The pub's chatter and clink pressed at her from all sides. In her corner, Gemma's usual stillness showed signs of wear. She twitched about on the pillow, causing Bijou to sit up.

"Would you mind if I took a couple hours off right now?" Merrit said.

"I keep telling you I'm fine." Liam gazed out the window at Danny's disappearing form. "The boyo's perturbed. You mark him, Merrit—whatever he's sensing is close by. Take care with yourself."

"I will."

"And I'll not forget you never explained what's troubling you."

"I'll figure it out." She squeezed his hand goodbye and approached Gemma. "Want to come along on another errand? I've got some questions about paint."

THIRTY-TWO

MALCOLM'S NEW SHOP GIRL blinked back and forth between Danny and O'Neil. She wore a dozen sparkly clips in her hair and a confused expression. Merrit had looked much the same by the time Danny had left the pub. If scaring her kept her from meddling further, all the better. He couldn't outstep his uneasiness even as he'd gathered up O'Neil and headed to Malcolm's shop to follow up on Merrit's helpful fact about Firebird Designs. Every bird flutter brought Toby Grealy back to mind, blinking up at him, pleading with him to see the connections. But which connections?

"Never mind," he said to the hapless girl. "We can find our way upstairs on our own."

"But Malcolm's after telling me that I'm not allowed to let anyone up to his flat," she said. "That's a way to get me arse canned."

"Ah, but then we're the guards," O'Neil said. "You can't be expecting us to obey Malcolm's rules."

The girl wavered, then shrugged. "Right then. Good luck to you."

Danny led the way to the back of the shop, where Waterford crystal gleamed within glass cases. "You're so full of shite your skin'll turn brown."

"Aw, now, don't be jealous because I've got a way with the lassies."

In the back corner of the shop a door opened onto a corridor with a rear exit and a staircase at the opposite end. Danny led O'Neil along a Turkish runner in bright greens and yellows. Shop sounds faded, allowing them to hear footsteps creaking overhead. A door opened and murmuring voices approached.

"And now," Malcolm said, "we have nothing but equality between us. We all know this makes for a fit and lasting friendship."

Whoever he spoke to responded and two sets of feet descended the stairs. Malcolm appeared first. Seamus stepped down behind him.

"Danny!" Malcolm said. "Today's the day for guests, I must say. Before I know it my new girl will be letting anyone through unannounced. I train them with care, you know, and these young pups never fail to take advantage of my good nature."

Seamus clenched his jaw in response to Malcolm's remark. In the last twenty-four hours Seamus had aged a decade. Deep creases divided his forehead and punctuated his mouth. He hadn't shaved and a sickly yellow film coated his skin. By comparison, Malcolm looked like he'd emerged from a germ-free bubble, bright-eyed and wrinkle-free.

Danny addressed Seamus. "Can you excuse Malcolm and us?"

Seamus steadied himself and pushed through them without acknowledging Danny or saying goodbye to Malcolm. He stank of mildew, like damp clothes left in the washer for days.

"Odd," O'Neil said. "Him with no questions about our progress."

"He can hardly walk, much less talk," Malcolm said.

"What was that you were saying about equality?" Danny said.

"My goodness, pub politics. He seems to think I'm out to usurp his place as lead crow. Why that should be important at this juncture, I don't know." Malcolm clapped his hands together in an *isn't this fun?* fashion. "Now how can I help you today? Jewelry for your wife, perhaps?"

"Let's sit down. Easier for O'Neil here to take notes."

Without word, Malcolm led the way up to a cozy flat. They entered in the kitchen area with scrubbed hardwood floors and ceramic spice containers lining shelves above the sink. Beyond, the living and bedroom areas overlooked Lisfenora's main street.

"Nice place," Danny said.

Malcolm aimed his smile around the flat. With the finesse of a magician demonstrating that his disappearing box was indeed solid, no tricks here, he swung open a second door to display a room crowded with storage shelves, file cabinets, and pristine work counters. "The inner sanctum, where I keep the expensive inventory. The Waterford, the Lenox, the jewelry." He picked up an etched crystal champagne flute and sighed. "Everyone should surround themselves with beauty."

O'Neil motioned Malcolm to be seated.

"I hope you have news on the vandal who defiled my window?" Malcolm directed his question to Danny as he locked up the room behind them.

"Not yet. We have many questions about Friday night, believe me, and we're hoping you can help us with anything you observed."

Malcolm pinched at the crease in his dress pants. "About that boy, you mean? It's amazing how much I manage to retain despite being run ragged by my employees and the general public. He had the most grubby fingernails, for example." He shuddered. "Encrusted and black."

O'Neil coughed into his hand. His cough sounded like a smirk.

"No," Danny said, "this would be this past Friday night or early Saturday morning when Brendan disappeared. Your front windows overlook the street. Did you see or hear anything unusual?"

"No, I can't say that I did. I last saw him at the shop, as I mentioned before. I went to bed early. Weekends are still the workweek for me. If I take a weekend at all, it's on Tuesdays and Wednesdays, but never mind this month. September is never ending, isn't it? I don't know how I get through sometimes. I have to eat extra to keep the weight on." He skimmed his hand down his flat stomach, ending in a happy pat. "I'm sorry I can't be more help with Brendan. Seamus is inconsolable—"

"So you're on good terms with him," Danny said.

Malcolm paused in the midst of picking a minute particle from his jacket. "Were we ever on bad terms?"

"The business about pub politics. You did accuse him of the graffiti on your windows. Plus, your issues with Brendan."

"By Christ, I'm not about to hold a man's lazy son against him at a time like this. Time to turn the cheek and offer support. I don't mind saying that I know how to relegate the past to the past. Start fresh with each day is what I say."

"Magnanimous of you, I'm sure," O'Neil said.

With a final particle flick, Malcolm announced that he might like tea, after all. Danny let him natter on about the annual fundraising auction that occurred each September during the festival. Malcolm rather thought his donation of several Aran wool scarves would fetch nice prices. Mrs. O'Brien, self-proclaimed village matriarch and auction organizer, had come to him personally to welcome him to her committee. For a woman with highly attuned organizational skills, Malcolm concluded, she was sadly in need of his guidance.

He sat down with a cup of tea for himself. "You'll see," he said, "the auction will fetch more money than ever this year. I haven't seen your wife at the meetings for weeks now, and I would hate to see her lose her standing in the community. I hope she's doing well?"

"As you might expect," Danny said.

"Back to Friday night," O'Neil said. "What time did you go to bed?"

Malcolm raised an eyebrow at Danny over a sip of tea. Danny raised his eyebrows right back. Malcolm set the teacup in his saucer and stirred in about three granules of sugar, taking his time. He nodded satisfaction after the second sip.

"Answer the question," Danny said.

"Friday night, that's easy enough to remember. I repaired Merrit Chase's necklace before bed," he said. "It needed a new clasp. So, let's say ten. Like I said, I didn't hear a peep."

Danny had been waiting for a chance to introduce his true topic of interest. He grabbed it while he could. "Merrit's necklace is a Firebird Design, correct?"

Malcolm nodded. "No surprise. It's my best line. I hope to expand it, you know. It deserves a wider audience. It always has, but sometimes the timing isn't right."

Danny asked Malcolm whether the name Toby Grealy rang any bells with him.

"Toby. Grealy." Malcolm shook his head, looking bemused. "Can't say that I've heard that name before."

"And John McIlvoy?"

"Of course. Whatever could he—"

"Did you know him when he was married to a Siobhan McNamara of Dublin?"

"Our current business relationship began when he moved back to Ireland. He'd been living on the Continent. As far as I'm concerned, anything about him from before then doesn't exist. I couldn't care less."

"Lucrative business relationship then," O'Neil said.

Malcolm sipped his tea.

"When did he move back?" Danny said.

"1996? Yes, around then."

"And how did you meet?"

Malcolm sighed and set his teacup aside. "What is this all about, good Danny?"

"We would like to speak to John McIlvoy. Routine questions. His name came up in conjunction with our investigation. Since you sell his work, you must have his contact information. We've been unable to find any records for him or even a phone number."

"That's because he's one of those off-grid types."

"Then an address will be fine."

Malcolm raised his shoulders and arms in an elaborate shrug. "Your guess is as good as mine."

"How's that possible?"

"The return address on his shipments lists a post office box, which is where I send his checks."

"I'd like his post office box address then."

"The problem with that," Malcolm said without a hint of apology, "is that of course I'll pass on your request to talk to him, and he'll react as you'd expect. He'll close the postal box."

"So don't let him know," O'Neil said.

Malcolm continued speaking to Danny as if O'Neil didn't exist. "I don't know why you need his address anyhow. You can contact him through his website."

"Not all the way off-grid, is he?" Danny said.

"Alas, even hermits need a website if they hope to sell their products." Malcolm fetched his laptop off a side table. "Here, let me show you. I helped him design it, if you must know. Simple but effective, I think."

169

The Firebird Designs site appeared on the screen. Close-up shots of his jewelry took up most of the page space. Malcolm clicked a button and the view changed to a contact page. "See? Maybe if you catch him on a good day, he'll agree to meet you somewhere."

He laughed, shaking his head as if he didn't believe this for a second.

"We'll email him. Meanwhile, we'd still like his post office address."

Malcolm made a production of navigating to a file and jotting down the address on a slip of paper.

"Don't alert McIlvoy that we have the address," Danny said.

Malcolm nodded as he buttoned his suit jacket. "If you'll excuse me, I'd best check on my new girl. How odd that I miss that little plonker Brendan. At least he knew how to handle the register."

Malcolm opened the door and bowed them out with a sweeping hand gesture. Danny let O'Neil exit ahead of him so that Malcolm wouldn't catch O'Neil's mocking eye roll.

"The man's so shiny everything bounces off him," O'Neil said as they walked the length of the Turkish rug.

"You're just peeved because he shined you on. Next time, try using your lady charms on him."

"If you don't mind my saying, Sir—sod off." He grinned as he said it and continued with, "Malcolm must know all about McIlvoy's past."

"And he doesn't seem to care."

"I'll wager you Malcolm's keeping a hefty portion of the sales in return for helping McIlvoy stay off-grid. Quid pro quo."

"Could be."

Danny stepped back into the shop with its colorful displays. From this vantage point, the Firebird Designs case appeared center stage, the darling of the store. Malcolm's golden goose. He always had a gleam in his eye, but upstairs just now the gleam had sharpened when Danny had brought up McIlvoy.

THIRTY-THREE

LIMESTONE TERRACES GAVE WAY to a gentler terrain as Merrit drove south toward Ennis, the County Clare seat. More houses, fewer cows, but the same ancient rock walls undulating along with them. After a year in Ireland, Merrit had gotten the hang of maneuvering on the narrow roads. It was fun, actually, and she never grew tired of the changing landscape, the way sun and cloud and rain and wind continually refreshed the scenery.

Beside her, Gemma was lost in her own world. She sniffed and dabbed at her nose with a tissue. Fresh black nail polish decorated her fingernails.

It occurred to Merrit that the graffiti had begun after Gemma and Dermot arrived in the village. But that had to be a coincidence. Not everything happened for a reason, and not everything was connected to everything else. Random chaos was part of life too. But then again, maybe it was *too* coincidental that they'd arrived right before the graffiti began.

Lost in thought, it took a second for Merrit to notice the slip of paper that Gemma held up at eye level near the steering wheel.

I can feel you wanting to talk to me, she'd written.

"That obvious, eh?"

Gemma nodded.

"Danny told me to stay out of your affairs because they're Garda business. I didn't think I was interfering with anything…"

She let the thought dangle and Gemma didn't disappoint.

He's referring to Lost Boy. Toby. My cousin.

"Oh my god, I'm so sorry. I had no clue." Once again, she petered off, but this time because she didn't have the words to console Gemma. After a minute, she admitted this out loud. "And here I am dragging you off to a paint store. We can turn around if you want."

No. I need the distraction. She hesitated, then jotted again. *Why are you helping me?*

Merrit opened her mouth and closed it again. She'd been about to say something altruistic—because it was the right thing to do— which was true. However, and this was a big *however*, there were also her selfish needs.

"Maybe I'm trying to prove myself to the locals. I'd like to be part of the community." She tapped her fingers against the steering wheel, unsatisfied with that answer. "I need to find a reason to stay in Ireland. My own reason apart from being Liam's daughter. It's just an accident of birth that I'm supposed to be the next matchmaker."

Gemma relaxed back into her car seat. *Thank you for telling me the truth. I understand.*

"I thought you might." A cemetery with hundreds of Celtic crosses slipped past their windows. So picturesque, so peaceful. Merrit loosened her grip on the steering wheel. "Besides, you could use the help, couldn't you? There's a lot going on what with the graffiti, your cousin,

Brendan too. Not to mention the whole thing with McIlvoy and your mom. But how is it all connected?"

I'm not leaving until I know. I don't care what Dermot says.

Gemma turned away from Merrit and grabbed a clean tissue from her pack.

"Thanks for letting me drag you along. I'd forgotten what it feels like to hang out with someone who doesn't know me, or think she knows me. I had a friend in the village—Marcus—but he's not around right now."

By the time they arrived in Ennis, Gemma had wiped her eyes and returned to blinking at nothing in particular. She was out of the car and walking toward TK Paint & Décor before Merrit had opened her car door, but her bravado faltered when she reached the entrance.

Catching up with her, Merrit quipped, "Okay, let me do the talking," and was gratified to see Gemma's lips soften into an almost-smile.

A pudgy man with the roundest face Merrit had ever seen stepped away from a display of color swatches. "'Allo, and what'll I be helping you with today?"

"Are you the in-house color consultant?" Merrit said.

"That would be me wife, the K in TK Paint & Décor. Kathleen!"

Kathleen stood a head taller than her husband and just as pudgy. She wiped orange-spattered hands on her smock as she approached. Gemma wandered toward the swatches.

As soon as Merrit mentioned the word *graffiti* Kathleen clapped her hands in delight and said how much she relished working with artists. "We have a fine line of spray paints that you can use on masonite board, plywood, canvas, you name it."

"Not graffiti as art, unfortunately. Here, let me show you."

Merrit led Kathleen outside. Ripping away the garbage bag that was still taped to the car door, she explained that she was new to

Lisfenora—a year but that was nothing by Irish standards—and was hoping for some clues about the paint. Maybe it would help her narrow down who had vandalized her car.

"Oh, love, that's a shame. Why, look at that. How interesting. Your vandal used a paintbrush, not a spray can. I can tell you right now that he's no artist."

"I could have told you that," Merrit said.

"Not for the reason you think—the shoddy penmanship, not an inch of creative flair to be seen. I'm after telling you no graffiti artist in his right mind would use a paintbrush or this type of paint. This is a semi-gloss for pity's sake. And an inferior brand if I'm not mistaken."

Kathleen scraped at the paint. "Just as I thought. Already flaking away. Well!"

By then, Gemma had caught up with them.

"What does it mean?" Merrit said.

"This is interior paint. Your average wall-painting paint. Won't stand up to the weather. And this particular hue—it's been out of fashion for a few years now. The good thing is that a car shop should be able to fix you right up, good as new."

Kathleen patted Merrit's shoulder. "Poor you—the village slapper, are you? And American too, by the sounds of it. Ah well, live and let live I always say."

Gemma didn't bother to hide her grin as they drove away. Merrit didn't mind that it came at her expense.

THIRTY-FOUR

ELLEN TOSSED ASIDE HER novel, dismissing its romanticism as pure bollocks. She couldn't concentrate. Earlier, Danny had bundled the children off to his car and reminded her that Gemma and Dermot needed to find a new place to stay. She still didn't understand what the fuss was about. He didn't live here anymore, and it wasn't like she had any connection to his investigation. But that was the least of her worries.

During confession the previous day—the first in months—Father Dooley had suggested that her recent behavior was her final wake-up call, that now was the time to reconcile with her daughter Beth's death and to mend her marriage. "What's next for you?" he'd asked.

"Yes, what's next for me?" she said under her breath.

She'd fixated on the word *behavior*. Her behavior. Bad behavior. She'd wanted Danny to catch her, and she'd longed for him to *hear* her. She'd done everything but scream in his face, hadn't she? She felt as mute as Gemma, signaling from the bottom of a pit.

She pulled her diary out of her robe pocket and tried to jot her agitation away with a diary entry, but it didn't work and a few minutes later she wandered toward the kitchen where Gemma had retreated after Merrit, of all people, had dropped her off. Merrit couldn't help herself, could she? She had to link herself to Danny, even if only through Ellen's houseguest.

Shaking her head in annoyance, Ellen peeked in at Gemma. Gemma waved and went back to washing dishes. No conversation to be had there, poor thing. Ellen continued through the living room and into her bedroom to hide her diary away, checking on the kittens while she was there. On her return trip to the living room, she peered into Beth's room. The room had a new smell to it now, a combination of the fungal odor that emanated from the sleeping bags and the minty chemicals from toothpaste and shaving cream.

She inhaled the scent of the living. This room did have life to it. It deserved life. Danny had been correct to urge her to yield the room back to the living, to their warm-hearted and rambunctious Mandy, who currently shared a bedroom with Petey.

Outside, a wall of fog hung in front of the windows. Shivering, she pulled the curtains closed, not wanting to look into darkness anymore.

Maybe it was time to crawl back up to the light. She opened a bureau drawer. She'd start with Beth's toddler jeans, brand-new and worthy of the donation box.

She'd made it through half a drawer when a bang from the front of the house startled her.

"Dermot, you returned?" she called as she headed toward the living room. "We need to chat about your staying here."

Tuesday

No one ever knew his own father.

Theodore Alois Buckley

THIRTY-FIVE

DANNY SAT ON HIS shabby couch with a plastic action hero digging into his thigh. Superintendent Clarkson stood over him, but Danny saw him as if through a backwards telescope: tiny, distant, blurred. Clarkson's mouth moved but his words didn't translate.

Just after midnight Danny had received the call from Dermot McNamara, who'd still had Danny's card in his pocket. The *chirrup-ing* mobile had jerked Danny out of an exhausted wasteland of a dream, a dream that featured white limbs stretching out of silage bundles and skeletonized sparrows picking at rotting flesh.

Now, a voice broke through Danny's daze. "Go, we have this," O'Neil said. "You see to Ellen in the hospital."

Somewhere in the background, amidst the industrious bustle of the scenes of crime officers, Dermot's voice rose with high-pitched agony. "Where's Gemma?"

Danny's knees wobbled as he stood. They felt as shaky as his thoughts, jumping from the mundane to the practical in confused leaps. The kittens needed a caretaker; Mandy and Petey would be heartbroken if their pets died. What about the kids? He'd have to hire a nanny, or Grandpap Marcus could move back in with them if he'd managed to maintain his sobriety. Of course, Danny would move back home now. How strange to think of himself back in the marital bed.

He stared at the jumble of purses and backpacks piled near the front door. Someone had ransacked them. Lipsticks, books, and wallets littered the floor.

"The intruder was looking for something," he managed to say before Clarkson's hand landed on his shoulder. With a little shove he ordered Danny to go with the ambulance. But Danny didn't want to go with the ambulance. He could wait hours at the buzzing and claustrophobic hospital in Ennis, hoping for word on his wife's injuries, or he could help track down Gemma while waiting for word on his wife's injuries. He could drink bad coffee in a forlorn waiting room or he could drink bad coffee while helping find the person who'd laid waste to what was left of his marriage.

The paramedics had immobilized Ellen's neck in a thick brace and attached an oxygen mask. On the gurney, she appeared impossibly young, her skin pale as an infant's. Danny concentrated on her eyelids, smooth and still, rather than her matted hair or the bloody rivulets dried to her neck and face. He blew on her eyelids, hoping to see them twitch. A twitch would be a hopeful sign, he thought.

"Off with you then," one of the technicians said.

Ellen had been conscious when he'd arrived. At the sight of him, she breathed "my fault" then slipped into unconsciousness. She'd been waiting for him, he knew this, and her strength of will so long buried under depression made him want to laugh and cry and feck all who knew what else.

He slapped the paramedic on the back and stepped out of the way. Danny kept slapping at nothing for a few beats before letting his arm drop to his side. Within a minute the ambulance was gone with siren blaring. Danny pivoted toward the master bedroom. The closet door stood open. He dropped to his knees. Almost weeping with relief, he picked up the kittens. Their little claws grabbed at the towel they slept on and dragged it with them. Carefully Danny unhooked them and snuggled them each into a pocket of his jacket. Safe. They were safe.

He tossed the towel aside. Ellen's diary stared up at him. He grabbed it up and shoved it into his waistband.

"What the bloody hell are you doing?" Clarkson said from behind him.

Danny shouldered him aside and strode outside, away from the metallic stink emanating from the kitchen and the shush of fingerprint powder brushes, away from the tossed drawers and emptied cabinets. Thank Christ the children weren't here. Thank Christ Merrit had run down the track from Liam's house to Fox Cottage to watch the children, unheeding of how she appeared in her bathrobe and Wellies.

But then, perhaps with a full house, Ellen's assailant wouldn't have dared enter. Not to mention, perhaps if he, Danny, still lived at home—

But then he couldn't go there. The guilt was already too much without going there.

Danny turned in a circle. He cursed the fog that had swallowed up the wailing ambulance. He cursed the house lights that lit the ground around him. Outside their circle of light and sound, the unnatural stillness of pre-dawn was a wall of silence.

"Ahern, you're out of here."

Danny turned full circle again, staring into the fog, expecting—hoping—that Grey Man would solidify out of the murk so he could beat it, him, whatever, to a bloody pulp. He'd predicted a Morrigan third, hadn't he? To go along with the three graffiti messages. And he'd been right. His sense that something more lurked out there had come true as if he'd willed it into being. He'd warned Merrit to be careful when he should have remembered the hovering sparrow. Lost Boy had tried to warn him to take care of his own.

"'Allo, Ahern!" Clarkson barked. "Get the hell out of here."

Danny snapped back to the hushed scene. He didn't like this, being on the other side of the violence. Powerless, flayed—a victim.

"Also, I don't need to tell you that you're too close," Clarkson said. "You're not to so much as burp near the evidence. You're off the current investigations. Hell, best to take it a step further: You're on compassionate leave as of right now."

Danny blinked, confused for a moment. His thoughts stuttered back to the larger picture and its various connections. Gemma had been staying with Ellen, and Gemma was missing. Gemma, Dermot, and Toby were siblings, and Brendan was part of the equation too. Of course this assault was connected to the deaths. It had to be. Didn't it?

O'Neil stepped off Danny's porch with a large brown evidence bag. The alabaster statue of entwined dancers appeared through the bag's clear plastic window. Aware of Danny's stare, he tucked the bag closer to his body and hurried it into the trunk of his car. *Too late,* Danny almost yelled. *Too fecking late!* He'd noticed the red-stained implement as soon as he'd entered the house. He'd almost pulled Ellen's blood-soaked hairs off it in a nonsensical fit of shame. Shame that this could happen in his house.

"We bought that statue in Italy," he said. "Our last great splurge before the children started coming. Lots of alabaster in Italy, the Leaning Tower of Pisa, you know. We bought that statue from an artisan out in the countryside somewhere. I can't remember where, one of those Tuscan hill towns. Ellen would know. She's good with names."

He broke off, detesting the sound of his vague and rambling comments. To think, earlier in the evening he'd laughed with his children as they'd eaten dinner at the Plough, where the crows and everyone else had fussed over them as usual. The children hadn't noticed anything amiss with Dermot and Seamus slaughtering themselves in a silent battle of the pints while Malcolm tried to rally everyone's spirits before declaring it useless and taking his leave.

Back at Fox Cottage, he'd had a devil of a time settling them down, and had just drifted off himself when he got the call from Dermot.

"Ahern!" Clarkson said. "Go."

A yowl of pain erupted out of the predawn fog. Dermot appeared, flailing from one guard to another with O'Neil in tow. "She left her mobile!" he bellowed. "She wouldn't have left her mobile. Why won't anyone listen to me! If no one's going to search for her, then I will."

In the midst of his panic, his gaze landed on Danny. He pushed past O'Neil and shoved a mobile into Danny's face. "What's this number here, in her contacts list? This is a Clare exchange, isn't it?"

The number loomed into Danny's sightline then disappeared when Clarkson swiped the phone from Dermot. "We need to get him out of here too," he said.

"I'll take him back to Fox Cottage," Danny said. "That's the easiest. Where's he going to find lodging at this time of night?"

"Ahern."

Danny ignored Clarkson's warning tone and Dermot's continued bellowing. "It's fine," Danny said. "No problem. He was Ellen's guest. Now he'll be mine."

"Go then, but I'm ordering you not to get involved with the investigation. None of your bullshit."

Fine. No bullshit from him. He was *on leave.*

Danny pulled Dermot to his car by the elbow. "Detour first. That was Alan's number on Gemma's mobile."

THIRTY-SIX

THE BANGING STARTED INSIDE Alan's dream of peeking into a window with his fists bloodying themselves against the glass, and then he was awake with someone banging on his front door and Bijou woofing in her deep-throated way, sounding like a guard dog despite her friendly intentions. He checked the clock. Jaysus, half four.

"Open the bloody door," Dermot called.

So Alan did. Dermot pushed past him and Bijou. Danny followed.

"Gemma!" Dermot called.

Sleep-fogged, Alan followed Dermot as he raced through the small house and pulled back the tangle of blankets on his bed. "I don't care if you've had at her, just tell me she's here."

"If Gemma were here," Alan said, "she wouldn't be hiding."

If Gemma were here. Alan backtracked from the thought. "What the bloody hell is he on about?" he said to Danny.

"Your phone number is in her mobile. Did Gemma text you tonight?"

"No. I gave her my number in case she ever needs a lift."

Danny's face was a series of craggy planes outlined by deep grooves that reminded Alan of the limestone terrain he hiked most days with Bijou: hardened by time, eroded by nature. It looked like it wouldn't take much to crack him apart. Meanwhile, Dermot searched through closets and behind and underneath furniture. He'd already cracked, that much was obvious.

"I knew it. That fecking McIlvoy ventured out of his lair and snatched Gemma. He's got her, I'm telling you, and we have to do something. Now."

"I don't understand," Alan said.

"The man who killed our mother!" Spittle flew out of Dermot's mouth. "He's here somewhere, and he took Gemma. He saw her, and he grabbed her."

"Why?"

Dermot pushed Alan against the wall. More spittle sprayed out of his mouth. "Because Gemma saw him kill our mom. Why the fecking hell do you think she's so paralyzed in life? She suppressed it all and went silent." He stumbled backwards, choking on his pain. "She could put that bastard away if she'd just get her memories back."

Without thinking, Alan crossed himself, that old habit from a bygone era in his life. The gesture didn't comfort him, but Bijou's weight leaning against his leg did.

Danny stirred, weight shifting from foot to foot. He spoke in a low tone. Alan knew that tone well. "You complete and utter gobshite."

Dermot didn't flinch, didn't seem to notice when Danny stood over him. Muscles twitched in his forearms. "You sleep in my house, put my family in danger, and now my wife's in the hospital because you couldn't be bothered to tell me that Gemma witnessed your mom's murder?"

Alan stepped between them. "I've got Dermot. You go to the hospital."

"Fine. Hold out your hands." Danny felt around in his pockets, handed two kittens to Alan, and strode to the front door. "I knew that bloody sparrow had something in store for me."

———————

Outside Alan's house, Danny paused before ducking into his car, trying to expel all emotion with loud breaths. He needed to think straight. Needed to set aside Dermot's utter shite for brains. *Think*.

He propped his mobile on the car roof and punched in O'Neil's number. "Here's what needs to happen."

THIRTY-SEVEN

DANNY GULPED DOWN A cup of bitter coffee while watching his men shuffle out of the incident room after a morning meeting he hadn't been invited to because he was "off duty until further notice." They lifted fingers in vague salutes as they passed. Most, he could tell, preferred to give him his space after what had happened to Ellen, but he still caught a few shoulder pats and murmured condolences.

After calling O'Neil outside Alan's house, Danny had spent what remained of the night in the hospital, and by dawn the surgeon had told him he'd better get some rest. The emergency surgery on Ellen's skull had gone well, but she would be unconscious for some time yet. The surgeon had bandied the terms "traumatic brain injury" and "skull fracture" around like confetti, and now Danny couldn't get the phrases out of his head. His teeth felt fuzzy. He needed a shower like a fish needed its gills. Sweat coated the mobile that he clenched in case the hospital called. He'd already contacted his cousin in Galway, who'd agreed to fetch the children for the next week. They'd been so overjoyed to miss school, they hadn't questioned him, and he hadn't had the stones to tell them what had happened to their mother.

Now here he sat, the ruse being that he'd arrived to give his statement. Garda or no Garda, as Ellen's husband he was automatically a person of interest. Fine. He didn't mind; it gave him an excuse to linger in the station. He wasn't a serious contender as suspect anyhow, because of the signs that the intruder had been looking for something inside the house.

He jotted a sentence or two of his statement while listening in on the conversations around him. Thus far, all he'd learned was that Clarkson had taken over the investigation, stating that Phoenix Park had no extra officers to spare. At the moment, he had O'Neil in his grips. The two of them spoke behind closed doors. Around Danny, a low murmur of expectation rose.

The incident room door swung open and bounced against the wall. "You, with me," Clarkson said to Danny. "O'Neil, sit and stay put until I get this sorted."

Danny followed Clarkson into the visitor's office. Clarkson leaned back in a swivel chair. He stretched his arms over his head and cracked his knuckles before motioning Danny to sit down.

"What are you after, Ahern? You think I don't know that pulling in Malcolm Lynch was your doing?"

"I'm here to give a statement about my wife, that's all," Danny said. "I'm glad to see O'Neil took the initiative on bringing in Malcolm. We need to find a man named John McIlvoy, and Malcolm is the man with the information. If Dermot McNamara is correct, then McIlvoy might have gone after Gemma and injured my wife in the process. Malcolm knows more about McIlvoy than he's letting on. If McIlvoy has anything to do with my wife's attack, I want him. So I'm hoping Malcolm will cooperate with you."

"And if he doesn't, what then?"

"I don't know."

While sitting alone in the hospital, Danny had emailed John Mc-Ilvoy, but he doubted he'd receive a response. Later, he'd met O'Neil and two other DOs at the bakery, where he'd coached them about how to invite Malcolm in for a few more questions. Of Malcolm's own volition, of course. As with most witnesses, all it had needed was a little ego flattery.

"Are we done?" Danny stood. "I need to finish my statement."

Out amongst the warren of desks, empty coffee mugs, and ringing telephones, the men quieted when Danny reappeared with Clarkson.

"O'Neil, with me," Clarkson said. "Time to talk to Malcolm Lynch."

Danny finished up his statement and handed it off to a barrel-chested officer with a chronically grim expression. A loaner officer from Ennis.

"Has anyone checked into John McIlvoy's post office box?" Danny said.

The officer glanced around before answering. He spoke in a low voice. "Ay, but he'd closed it down right enough. The permanent address he'd used to open the box led to a home in Shannon. Family there had never heard of him and knew nothing about a post office box."

So much for Malcolm not warning McIlvoy.

A door opened and Clarkson's voice rose over murmurs and paper shuffling. "Ahern, get over here!"

"Watch your balls," the officer said. "Last time he yelled like that a rookie had hurled on a body."

Clarkson, along with O'Neil, waited in one of the monitoring rooms. O'Neil avoided his eye.

Clarkson's face was red enough to glow in the dark. "Nothing new you want to tell me?"

"About what?"

Malcolm's image appeared center stage on the television monitor. He sat erect and relaxed in the neighboring room. He sipped coffee and grimaced. "Inexecrable," he said into the camera.

"Here, Ahern. Listen." Clarkson pointed to another television screen, pressed a button, and a second later Malcolm appeared. In the replay, Malcolm smiled his welcome at the men sitting off-screen. First to his right, then to his left. O'Neil had just introduced the session with the date and time when Malcolm interjected.

"I know, even if you don't, that much as I'd like to help you, I can't—no one can accuse me of being uncooperative, not even Danny. Is he here, by the way?" On the monitor, his smile turned petulant. *"I'd prefer to talk to him."*

"I'm conducting this interview," O'Neil said. *"For the record, this is Detective Officer—"*

"Like I told Danny, you can't compel me to reveal what I don't know about John McIlvoy's whereabouts. I have an alibi, quite the alibi, for the night of the boy's death besides."

"You're not here as a suspect," O'Neil said.

Malcolm waved a magisterial hand. *"Please. Danny asked about John, which is close enough. I didn't like his attitude while he was questioning me, by the way. I will be making a formal complaint—"*

"Posturing," Danny said. "No clue why, but he's definitely having us on."

"Never mind that," Clarkson said. "Listen up."

"—and though it pains me to air Danny's marital woes like this, I can't see that I can help myself. I have a business to run, after all, and Danny never bothered to investigate the nasty graffiti. I can tell you

that sales had been down since that day, and my shop is one of the most lucrative in Lisfenora—"

"You were saying about your alibi? For which death, by the way?"

"Oh, for that boy, Toby something."

"And?" O'Neil said.

"As I was saying," Malcolm said. *"I have an alibi, so if you think I'm the dead ringer for Grey Man, as the newspapers are calling our phantom boy killer—brilliant moniker, Grey Man, don't you think?— you might as well forget it now."*

"That's all fine, but we're after information about John McIlvoy," O'Neil said.

"You might want to talk to Ellen Ahern. She'll know all about my alibi that night. I trust I don't need to spell out what I mean by that."

THIRTY-EIGHT

ALAN PUSHED BIJOU'S RESISTING snout into a plastic bag that contained a pair of Gemma's dirty socks. Dermot cast a dubious glance at Bijou's underbite and squashed-in snout. Alan had his doubts also—she was more of a drooler than a sniffer—but he'd had to do something to get Dermot out of his house. The man just about tore down the walls in agitation, and Alan couldn't stand his stricken expression for a second longer. He'd been afraid it had mirrored his own.

"Looks to me like she wants to fetch them not sniff them," Dermot said.

"She got us this far. Good girl."

But this far was where, exactly? Two hours of tramping around the countryside had led to nothing. Now they stood catching their breaths on a hill that from afar had shimmered purple with turning heather. Around them, ancient drystone walls divided the landscape into nothing but boggy fields. Fog gathered along the coastline, ready to roll over them. Wind bent grass tussocks and rustled the heather.

"This is useless," Dermot said. "Your dog couldn't sniff her way out of a blanket. Gemma!" He bellowed into the wind, and the wind whipped the words back at them. "I'm heading back to Ellen's house to have at the guards. They should be out here also. Coming?"

"Soon. I'll meet you back there."

Dermot saluted and marched down the hill, stumbling and slipping as he went. His voice carried back to Alan in a plaintive call to his sister. Alan hunkered down on his haunches, feeling plaintive himself. The wind echoed in his ears, a hollowed-out noise that reminded him of too many other solitary moments. Since he'd left France, he'd collected these moments around himself like a security blanket, burrowing himself inside the safety of the known. He was comfortable with his life, and there was nothing wrong with that.

Yet, he couldn't deny that, like Bijou, maybe he was hard-pressed to sniff his way out of a blanket.

"Bijou, come."

Bijou sat at his side with nose lifted into the wind. It trembled and glistened. He could see that it worked; she was enjoying a world of scent he couldn't imagine. Perhaps without Dermot's distracting presence, she'd do better with the tracking. Alan lifted the plastic bag that contained wadded-up black knee socks. He sniffed but didn't catch anything except a faint leathery smell. Still, they had to be pungent from a dog's point of view. They'd been pressed up against Gemma's feet by her clomper boots. She probably had dainty feet underneath it all. Did she paint her toenails? Did she wear sandals in summer?

Scowling, Alan entrapped Bijou's nose once again. Bijou reared her head back with a whine and trotted off in the direction Dermot had taken. Alan could still see him, a greyish shape summiting the next hill.

According to Dermot, Gemma had left a bit of the human world behind when she lost her voice. He hoped that Gemma's uncanny touch with animals, her semi-feral ways, had led her to safety. "Gemma's a survivor. She'll have followed an animal path to a sheltered area. You'll see."

He hadn't been able to hide the desperation from his voice, though.

Alan turned around in a circle. Nothing impeded his view—not a rooftop, not a tree, not a standing stone or other megalithic monument. There didn't look to be shelter for miles.

Bijou looked back at him and whined.

"Okay then," he said, "painkillers for you and we'll try again later."

Alan let Bijou lead the way back toward Danny's house. When they crested the next hill, he caught sight of the abandoned famine cottage the next hill over. Twenty minutes later they arrived.

From the cottage that Ellen called her folly, he spied on the activity below him. Garda and unmarked vehicles crowded the lane in front of Danny's house. Several uniformed guards stood at the hedge line to warn spectators away. A flash went off: journalists. By now, the *Irish Times* had caught on to their local drama, as well as the newspapers from the neighboring counties. Alan didn't recognize the man who led a gesticulating Dermot away from the journalists. He seemed to be in charge, though, as he handed Dermot off to one of the guards for safekeeping. The house blazed with lights, well-lit in the perpetual twilight of this particular day. Inside, figures passed back and forth, all bustle and buzzing he was sure. He hoped for Danny's sake that the attacker had left a trace of himself.

Alan called Bijou to him before she caught wind of the dozens of new friends to be made below them. Stooping, he led her into the folly. Bijou settled herself near the door. Alan squinted into the corners and along windowsills littered with powdery animal droppings. Perhaps Gemma had run in here.

"Bijou, you ready?" he said and covered the dog's snout with the plastic bag again. This time around, she allowed it with a patient blink and then followed him to the scuffed dust where the McNamaras had bedded down their first few nights in Lisfenora. He angled her head downwards. "Sniff?"

Bijou complied with a few whiffs and wandered away. Once again, Alan covered her snout. Then he directed her head to the second disturbed area about the size of a sleeping bag. "Gemma here?" he coaxed.

To his surprise, Bijou kept her nose to the ground, snuffling. Her tail rocked back and forth, and, by Christ, his clown-faced girl might have finally gotten the point. After giving her a treat, Alan pushed her sniffer back into Gemma's dirty socks, then pointed her head to the ground. She circled a bit, then honed in on the second patch of disturbed ground again. This wasn't science, but it seemed to Alan that Bijou had caught Gemma's scent.

He led her toward the door, covered her nose again, then pointed to the ground. Bijou sniffed at the threshold, then up the doorframe. With a huff, she sat and started sniffing the wind again. She was clearly done for the day, and Alan didn't blame her.

Alan took one last look around before heading back to his car. Westward, the direction he and Dermot had hiked, held nothing. North led to the barren, rocky Burren, also unlikely for a woman who sought covered refuge. East led to the neighbors, cows, sheep, and the village.

The view south looked a lot like the view toward the Atlantic: rock walls undulating over the hills and heather purpling the hillsides. A hedgerow followed the lane past Danny's house on its southern route toward the next village. A blurred patch of green disappearing around one of the hillsides looked like a mirage.

Pressure gathered in Alan's chest. That same quickening that had accosted him when Camille had entered his orbit. It was an instinct that he'd often tested by seeking her out. He'd always found her too.

It seemed he couldn't resist his compulsive stalker tendencies even after all these years. At least they had a legitimate use now. If anyone could track Gemma down, it would be him.

THIRTY-NINE

CLARKSON REPLAYED MALCOLM'S MOMENT in the spotlight as he revealed his alibi and made a cuckold of Danny at the same time.

"*Shame that I'm compelled to spill secrets,*" Malcolm said. "*I don't kiss and tell. I'm a gentleman. I'd tried to break it off—in fact, I thought I had—but you know how women can be. At least that's what I've found. Women grow so attached, don't they?*"

Danny was too stunned to be angry. "He was playing with me."

Clarkson paused the video. "What's that now?"

"During our interview yesterday, he made a point of mentioning Ellen a couple of times. He asked about her. He couldn't resist dangling her to see if I knew about their—thing."

"You're telling me that pulling him in this morning wasn't some kind of vendetta?"

"No, Sir. It was about finding McIlvoy. And I didn't pull him in. O'Neil did."

"Give me some bloody credit, yeah?" Clarkson said. "You're supposed to be on leave, yet in you come to write a bloody statement without a prompting. And now this revelation. You were hoping for something."

"Like I said, about McIlvoy. But I'll tell you what, Malcolm is on my shit list now. He doesn't provide the information about McIlvoy, I'll see to the obstruction charges myself."

"Don't you go there," Clarkson said. "Now get out of my sight. You look like shite, you're not thinking straight, and you're so tainted we need a warning label on you." Clarkson ordered O'Neil next. "Get Lynch the hell out of here too. With our apologies."

At the door, Danny paused. "How's the hunt for Gemma McNamara going?"

"We're on it."

"I hope so because she's the key."

"To what?"

"To nailing McIlvoy."

Danny dragged a plastic chair until it bumped up against the hospital bed and sat down. Ellen laid quietly, eyelids smooth and twitch-free. An enormous bandage encased her head, which he'd expected, but not the wire that extended from somewhere within the bandages—no, from within her skull—into a monitoring device. More bloody phrases: "intracranial pressure" and "drainage."

He'd understood quickly enough and urged the nurse to be on her way. He was fine, he'd said, even though he wasn't. Weariness collapsed him onto folded arms with Ellen's hip warm against the top of his head. He closed his eyes against the shadows within his arms and felt for Ellen's hand. Her skin felt the same at least, pearly almost, that soft and lustrous fairness he'd always admired. Still admired, he reminded himself.

The scent of soap and citrus clung to her skin. The smell of steam rolling out of the bathroom. Ellen loved her long showers at the end of the day. He pictured her scrubbed and fragrant and bundled in her thick robe, enjoying a cuppa in her favorite chair, letting her hair air dry in long waves under the lamp. With a rare night off from the children, she'd been relaxing when—

No, stop thinking about it.

Exhaustion overwhelmed him. In addition to the nurse, the surgeon had also come and gone. In a tone somehow both businesslike and commiserating, he'd explained Ellen's condition with yet more words: "induced coma." In other words, someone—perhaps McIlvoy—had hit her so hard with the alabaster statue from Italy that he'd cracked her skull wide open. "Her brain needs time to heal. We need to run more tests and wait."

Beneath the exhaustion, a current of anger burbled on low ebb. Rising bubbles of pain and regret and rage grew and burst with sticky *pops* that hurt Danny deep in his soul. For now, it was manageable. For now, the current anchored him.

Danny sat up and pulled Ellen's diary out of his jacket pocket, wondering what it had been doing in the bedroom closet. Ellen could have dropped it, or set it down in a distracted moment with the kittens, or hidden it away from his prying eyes. Not that it mattered. Ellen had always been prone to mislaying her keys, her reading glasses, anything, really.

He opened the journal to a random page and caught Merrit's name. *I wouldn't have thought she was Danny's type, but can I blame him if he shagged her? Not hardly. But that doesn't mean I have to like the twit.*

"Jesus, Ellen, would you listen to yourself in here?" he said.

A few pages on, Ellen wrote: *It's nice to be wined and dined, and to be noticed as a woman. I know what M is doing—a seduction—but he's very good at it. I find that I'm rather drawn to him.*

Danny's stomach churned. That was disgusting. He let the book fall open to a page bookmarked by a pen. Ellen's last entry, last night, after the shower but before her attacker had arrived.

… I can't get Danny's look out of my head when he picked up the children tonight, like he didn't know me anymore, like I wasn't worth knowing anymore, and maybe I'm not.

Danny flipped the diary pages back to the previous week. And there, indeed, screamed Ellen's words confirming Malcolm's alibi for the night of Toby Grealy's murder. Danny still couldn't fathom why Malcolm had offered up the alibi unless it was to humiliate Danny. He hadn't prioritized finding the phantom graffiti artist, true, but surely Malcolm understood that vandalism didn't rate as high as murder.

No, the alibi had to be a good old-fashioned diversionary tactic. Most likely to distract Danny from prying into Malcolm's relationship with McIlvoy.

Whatever the reason, if that was the game they were playing now, then he, Danny, owed Malcolm the next jab. The thought comforted Danny, gave him something to think about as he continued reading the diary passage.

… he dared to pawn me off with a pair of earrings. I could care less about parting gifts. I wanted closure, an apology, an explanation, something, after the way he'd dumped my sorry arse after weeks of fawning over me. Malcolm's all about being the big man, but in private he's an insidious little whisperer, seeping into you like the bloody fog, and before you know it your clothes are off yet once again.

I'm still not sure what I did to deserve his contempt toward the end of the night. Dare to slap him so his bloody contact lens fell out? He didn't like that at all. Slapped a hand over his eye and refused to put on his specs. He's after being the vainest man I've ever met.

My poor ego. What fool was I.

Danny's mobile vibrated. He grabbed it out of his pocket, and glancing toward the corridor, whispered hello. He wasn't supposed to be using it on the ward.

O'Neil spoke fast and hushed without greeting him. "Something came back about our mysterious John McIlvoy, after all. Hold a sec."

Danny closed the diary and tucked it back into his pocket. He placed his hand on Ellen's and promised himself that he'd return with a novel to read aloud to her and her favorite lavender sheet spray.

O'Neil returned to the phone. "You there?"

"What about McIlvoy?" Danny said.

"Dead as last spring's lambs."

FORTY

AT 4:00 P.M., LIAM said goodbye to his last love-starved festival participant for the afternoon, and Merrit tried not to appear too relieved. A pall had fallen over the plaza, what with the seeping fog, the increased Garda presence, and the whispers of serial killer faeries.

Her lungs spasmed, that unsubtle warning that the anxiety she'd struggled with since childhood was building up.

"I could use a drink before dinner," she said.

"Agreed."

Merrit was too busy maneuvering Liam across the plaza to check his expression, but his voice sounded beat. The day had dragged, both of them preoccupied with Ellen and Gemma.

"I can't get the graffiti out of my head," she said. "The *slag* on my car doesn't seem to fit. If there's a pattern, shouldn't the graffiti have been on Ellen's car instead—or Dermot's car, for that matter?"

Liam paused before opening the door to Alan's pub. "In someone's mind you connect—to something."

There went her lungs again. She forced herself to inhale deep into her diaphragm.

Alan's pub echoed the grey pall outdoors. He'd lit a fire but most of the wall sconces remained dark. A few candles dotted the tables. Crazy shadows flickered over the walls and though a few customers had started to find their way inside, the room was nowhere as boisterous as usual. That said, Seamus and many of the crows sat in their usual spot near the taps while Alan stooped over Bijou spread-eagled on the floor in front of the fireplace. He stood and approached when he saw them.

"How's Bijou?" Liam said.

"Sore. She needs more rest before I take her out again." Alan rubbed his shoulder. "To search for Gemma."

"I'd like to help if I can," Merrit said.

"You just missed Danny. He picked up Dermot and left, no explanation. He'd come from the hospital."

"How is Ellen?" Liam said.

By way of answer, Alan shook his head. Several locals acknowledged Liam with waves. Merrit repeated her offer to help Alan.

"I'd rather you didn't come along. No offense intended."

Merrit nodded, but she felt the sting nevertheless. Alan led Liam to an empty barstool beside Malcolm. Malcolm held his brandy snifter as usual and beamed around the room before greeting her with a wave toward her necklace.

"It's a miracle how well expert craftsmanship holds up over the years, isn't it?" he said.

Out of the silence rose desperate laughter, cracked, hysterical. Seamus tottered toward them.

"Malcolm, you grand pretender. I hope you rot in hell with your precious jewelry and your precious shop."

He swayed and grabbed Nathan Tate's arm to steady himself. His distressed mirth couldn't have been more shocking than if he'd started tearing out his hair.

Malcolm swirled his brandy. "Ah well, we can forgive Seamus in the realm of his sorrow. I'm nothing if not sensitive to others' pain. In fact, I was thinking that in honor of my former employee, Brendan, I'd offer a sale, entice people in with a memorial sign."

Seamus stared at Malcolm. *Gobsmacked* was the slang word that popped into Merrit's head. Utterly gobsmacked. She dug her hand into her oversized shoulder bag and grasped her inhaler. The various tensions around the room closed in on her like one of her panic attacks.

"A tasteful sign," Malcolm continued. "I don't mind saying that I have sound design instincts. I could—"

A pint glass crashed against the floorboards at Malcolm's feet. Guinness splattered onto his linen trousers and he shut up properly then. Slow and considering, he blinked down at spots of beer.

"Best get home to clean yourself, you preening sack of shite," Seamus said.

This wasn't going well. Everyone on edge, the claustrophobic greyness of the past week pressing in on them. Merrit breathed against her clutching lungs and entwined her arm through Seamus's. "I'm so sorry for your loss. Maybe I can walk with you—"

"Get off me, you." He stepped away and jerked his arm up to loosen her grip. Being taller than she, and drunk, and none too coordinated, his elbow caught her square in the mouth.

She stumbled back, eyes watering with the sudden jab of pain in her lip.

"You don't belong here, you fool girl." Sweat trickled out of Seamus's hairline. "You're no better than Malcolm, swanning around the village like royalty. Do you think we don't know that Ellen's in the hospital because of you? You broke up their marriage—we all know it."

Merrit tasted blood. Her lower lip tingled, ready to swell. Liam pushed his way toward her, trying to get Seamus to shut up, but Seamus seemed determined to strike out at the closest target.

"If Danny had been at home where he was supposed to be," he said, "Ellen would be okay, so don't you be trying to placate me."

Merrit patted her chest against tension gathering around her lungs. "I wasn't—"

"Listen to me, girly, you aren't one of us, and you'll never be one of us."

All around Merrit, the other pub-goers stood transfixed. "That may be true," she said, "but you're mistaken if you think I care about that."

"Oh, you care, all right," Seamus said. "Your desperation practically drips off you."

Shaking, Merrit turned away from the staring Lisfenorans and tourists while Seamus's words continued to sting her like open-palmed slaps. She pulled the inhaler out of her purse and shot the mist into her lungs. She did care. Of course she did.

"You're like Malcolm here," Seamus said, "another grand pretender. You two belong together." He waved his arm. "Liam, you old scoundrel, give Merrit and Malcolm a try. They'd be perfect for each other."

"We'll accept your apology tomorrow," Liam said. "Someone get Seamus the hell out of here. Time for him to grieve at home."

Merrit's heart rate slowed and her breath eased. She wanted to slink away, but she held her ground against the pitying smiles. There was no way she'd let anyone chase her away from the pub, or Ireland, for that matter. If she left, it would be her own decision.

Alan strode around the bar and made a grab for Seamus, but he shifted away. "This isn't about my grief. This is about family—"

204

Malcolm placed a hand on Seamus's shoulder. "I must say, you do have a point about family. Family can be so difficult at times."

Merrit tilted her head to catch Malcolm's lowered voice. He spoke like a confidant, his voice as susurrating as wind through leaves.

"Yes, yes," Malcolm said to Seamus. "We don't like anyone upsetting the balance, I understand. You know I do. We know that things happen sometimes. You know this better than most." He paused. "But, Seamus, my dear man, lashing out at Merrit or me or anyone else for your troubles? It's grubby. Best to take responsibility and let go with what is done."

Malcolm angled Seamus toward one of the wingback chairs near the fireplace and gave him a little push. Seamus stumbled forward and lowered himself into the chair. A collective breath released and several people approached Merrit.

"I'm fine," she said. "Really. Just one of those things."

Malcolm twirled the brandy within his snifter. His voice rose. "There now, all's well. It's nothing other than what I do with customers. The art of persuasion I call it."

"And what did you just sell Seamus?" Nathan said.

"Perspective." Malcolm held up his snifter. "Alan, what about a round for the crows? On me."

Alan fetched the crows their drinks and announced that soon he'd be leaving them in the hands of his able junior barman.

"Where are you off to, abandoning us?" Elder Joe called.

"The forestry lands out there past Danny's house. It struck me that Gemma might make like a fox and find shelter there."

Merrit still stood beside Liam, her panic attack now nothing more than a blip to everyone but her and Liam. She pressed a napkin against her swelling lip and knew better than to offer her help to Alan again. There was only so much rejection she could take in one day.

"Maybe I can be of help?" Malcolm said to Alan instead. "I have excellent night vision."

"Oh, that's too brilliant." Seamus spoke loudly from his spot near the fireplace. "You'd like to be the center of attention, wouldn't you? Malcolm here's the big man! You'll put a sign up on the shop to let the world know what a hero you are."

"Grubby. Remember that, my friend," Malcolm said.

He handed his snifter off to Alan. With a hand-swipe down the front of his suit and a tug at the lapels, he was gone without paying for the last round. The picture of regal affront despite the mottled flush that showed clear through to the back of his neck.

Nathan wandered out of the pub too, saying, "Craic's over for tonight." He patted Merrit's shoulder as he passed, and with that commiserating gesture, Merrit decided it was pointless to stay any longer.

FORTY-ONE

DANNY PULLED INTO THE parking lot of the regional hospital in Galway City. Agitated, he tapped his fingers on the steering wheel and stared into the twilight lurking around the edges of the lot. Cigarette glow near the corner of the building caught his attention. As the orange light flared on an inhale from its smoker, he made out scraggly and grey-haired Benjy the Bagger, waiting as they'd planned. Benjy was nothing if not religious about his cigarette breaks.

Danny roused Dermot, who snapped awake with twitchy eyelids. "Where are we?"

"Galway. This is the closest morgue facility to Lisfenora."

Dermot went rigid. "No, that can't be. Gemma—"

"Jesus, no," Danny said. "The guards are still hunting for her."

"Why are we here then? When you said I could help you, I thought you meant with Gemma."

"This is related, believe me."

Benjy had caught sight of them as they exited the car. He ambled over in a cloud of smoke. Danny held out his fingers in a gimme

207

gesture. *McIlvoy dead* rang like a siren in his head. He'd heard the words from O'Neil but refused to believe them without Dermot's corroboration.

The cigarette dangled from Benjy's lips as he spoke. "You owe me for this one, Dan-o."

"You like me owing you."

"Fecking straight." Benjy dropped a folder onto the car's trunk. "Copies of the morgue photos, but you can't keep them. I'm glad someone's looking at these photos. Everyone needs a person to care."

He shoved the folder toward them and lapsed into a relaxed perch, staring off into space as he lifted and lowered his addiction. His index and middle fingers were stained yellow.

Danny passed a dozen photos to Dermot.

"Who the bloody hell am I looking at?" Dermot said.

"John McIlvoy. You don't recognize him?"

Dermot shoved the prints back at Danny. "No, no, no, that's utter bollocks and we both know it. It has to be." He jerked away from Danny, practically choking on his emotions. "McIlvoy has to be alive, or"—he swallowed—"or, I don't know what."

"He's quite mad with it, eh?" Benjy said. "Three, two, one … "

Dermot ran to the edge of the parking lot and bent over to heave up the contents of his stomach. By the time Danny caught up with him he was crouched against a low wall, head in hands. Dermot raised his head, desolation stripping his expression dry. "You can't know what this means. I might as well shoot myself now."

"Take a look at the photos," Danny said.

Back with Benjy, Dermot swallowed hard and studied the images. "I remember the ugly beard," he said. "Never understood how my mom could stand it."

John McIlvoy had worn his life roughly. Besides the beard, his lips were drawn back from a mouth full of decaying teeth. Wrinkles connected the corners of his eyes to his mouth, and oily wisps of hair dangled onto the silvered autopsy table that served as backdrop. A blue tint peeking through half-shut eyes looked like the beginnings of glaucoma veils.

"That McIlvoy?" Danny said.

Dermot browsed through the rest of the photos, which showed McIlvoy in profile. "But he's skinny."

"Malnourished more like," Benjy said.

Dermot shuffled through the images again, worrying their edges with his fingers. "McIlvoy had a belly on him and a double chin. His teeth were okay, as I remember. Nothing special. I don't remember the eyes. It's not like I looked too closely at him. I can't tell for sure. I mean, this could be him."

"Life on the streets changes a person," Benjy said.

Danny passed along more photos from the folder. These showed full body views. Dermot shuddered.

Smoke leaked out the sides of Benjy's mouth when he spoke. "Ay, he'd lived rough for years. That much was evident."

"Living on the streets," Dermot repeated. "Not that I care, you understand, but he'd always squeaked by with his jewelry making."

"Unless Malcolm Lynch, the man who sells McIlvoy's jewelry, was cheating him at every turn," Danny said.

"Or he spent all his money on alcohol and drugs. Doesn't take much to end up on the streets." Benjy angled a transcript page into the light cast by the hospital. "All this says is 'self-employed, artist,' which means nothing. Died three months ago, and the identification we found on him was years out of date, which wasn't surprising."

Dermot squinted at yet another photo, this time of an identification card that showed a younger, robust McIlvoy. "It's a crap picture but, yes, that's him. I don't understand. Toby told us he'd found McIlvoy."

"Someone lied," Danny said.

"No, no, that can't be." He held out his hand toward Benjy. "Be a gent, pass me that fecking fag."

Benjy handed over his cigarette and lit up another one for himself. Dermot huffed twice in fast succession. The action seemed to steady him.

Danny rocked back and forth, almost wishing for a cigarette himself. "You never told me how Toby found out that McIlvoy was his father. Is it related to the missing earrings he was wearing—the ones that were stolen off his ears?"

"Ay, indirectly like. It started out silly enough. He wanted a trinket to give to a lass—his first great love, to hear him tell it. He rifled through Aunt Tara's jewelry box for something she wouldn't miss. Aunt Tara's my mom's sister, and she raised Toby as her own. A conspiracy of silence that ended for Toby when he found the earrings in—what do you call it?—like a keepsake pouch? For mourning? Aunt Tara makes them whenever someone in the family dies."

"He found Siobhan's earrings—" Danny prompted.

"Yes, they matched a necklace that McIlvoy had given her when they got married. The earrings were inside the pouch along with a headshot of them from that day. One look at the wedding photo and Toby knew McIlvoy was his father and Siobhan his mother and that his life had been a lie."

Benjy stirred. His gaze sharpened. "How so?"

"What do you mean?" Dermot asked.

"How did the lad know they were his parents from a photo—resemblance to McIlvoy?"

"Ay, seemed obvious enough to Toby anyhow, and Aunt Tara admitted the truth when he confronted her. Then the next day, Toby made excuses about visiting friends and caught the train to Ennis before landing in Lisfenora."

"You wouldn't happen to have the wedding picture on you, would you?" Benjy asked Dermot.

"No. Toby brought it with him, so it's probably still with his personal belongings." He glanced at Danny. "Anyone found his things yet?"

"Not yet," Danny said.

Dermot returned to shuffling through McIlvoy's morgue photos. The cigarette dangled between two fingers, precariously close to the images. With a look of dismal triumph, he pushed one of the photos out at them. The image was overexposed, leaching the detail out of the silverwork and the color out of the stone, but there was no mistaking that they peered at a Firebird Designs necklace. It reminded Danny of the pendant that Merrit wore, which made a kind of sense. Gemma wouldn't have torn it off Merrit's neck otherwise.

"Found on the body, as I recall," Benjy said.

"That's my mom's necklace," Dermot said. "The one she was wearing when McIlvoy killed her. He kept it as a souvenir."

"Do you think seeing this necklace, the real necklace, would jar Gemma's memories loose?" Danny said.

"Maybe, but you lot have to find her first, don't you?" He jabbed at the picture. "I want my mother's necklace back. How do I get it?"

Benjy flicked his cigarette butt away. "Paperwork, laddie, good old bloody paperwork. Body's long gone, but if there was no next of kin to claim his belongings, the necklace should still be locked up somewhere. You'll need proof it was your ma's."

"Right." Dermot's expression crumpled. "Where are you, Gemma?"

Danny had no words for Dermot, and apparently Benjy didn't either. They watched as Dermot ducked back into the car. He leaned his head against the headrest and closed his eyes. His lips moved in silent pleas.

Benjy spoke between smoke puffs, the cigarette never leaving his mouth. "Now off with you. I've got dinner plans. Sweet divorcee with a randy soul."

Driving away, Danny pictured his hands reaching out, his fingers circling around Malcolm's neck, throttling the prattling barker for bedding his wife and for playing coy with McIlvoy's contact information when he'd known McIlvoy was dead. Danny wanted to rattle the smug bastard's cage.

He pulled over, fetched out his mobile, and navigated the Internet until he reached the Firebird Designs contact email form.

You might as well answer this message, Malcolm. I know you're playing at being the talented Mr. McIlvoy. Are you making the jewelry now too?

FORTY-TWO

GEMMA'S FULL BLADDER FORCED her out of a fitful sleep. It took her a second to remember where she was and how she'd ended up curled under a fallen tree trunk inside a den dug by some enterprising woodland creature. She blinked at mist-enshrouded conifers, a mix of pine, larch, and fir that a diligent forester had planted years ago and then let go to their natural state. Normally, the dank but beautifully green smell of vegetation, both fresh and rotting, soothed her nerves.

Listening to the increased fluttering and creep of animal life readying for the coming night, she tried to decipher sounds that hinted at danger. Beyond the trees, cows lowed and magpies chatted. Closer by, leaves rustled overhead. Unsure but desperate to relieve herself, Gemma eased herself out of her cramped position. After peeing behind the fallen tree, she made her way toward the edge of the forestry lands. A broad vista of farm fields stretched out before her. In the distance a farmer led a small herd of cows from one field to another. She hesitated, picturing watering troughs, then retreated back into the trees. Her thirst would have to go unquenched until nightfall.

She wasn't sure what to do. Her initial terror had waned to a low-grade jitter. She felt herself on the edge of either healing or madness, each attractive in its own way. Health was the ideal, but madness had kept her safe. It had insulated her from most of life's turbulence. It had comforted her. How to quit such an addictive habit?

She swiped away a tear—not for herself, no, because she was used to herself, but because of Ellen. She reviewed the previous evening and found herself wanting. Utterly useless. Why couldn't she have offered Ellen reassurance after her husband left with Mandy and Petey? Instead, she'd retreated to the kitchen, to sudsy water and sponge, and cleaned each plate until it squeaked. She'd just started on the first water glass when she heard a knock. Ellen had called out something that Gemma hadn't caught over the sound of running water. After that, footsteps and another voice, one that froze her as solid as the glass that fell from her floppy fingers and sank under the suds with a quiet *plonk*.

Her throat had worked against itself, traitorous as ever. She'd dropped to the kitchen floor in sheer terror and crawled toward the back door. Rational thought vanished. All that remained was, *Get out now*. After that, her memory turned hazy, as if the bottomless well had sucked it away from her. All she knew for sure was that she had not helped Ellen, that she'd hidden and then fled.

She wasn't sure she'd recognize the man's voice if she heard it again. She wasn't sure if it was his voice or something he'd said that had panicked her. This is how her memory went—a traitor. She'd even stared at the artist's statement picture of John McIlvoy when she visited the gift shop with Merrit, willing the image of him to jump-start her memories. She'd always hated the floppy leather hat he wore, but all she'd gotten for her efforts was nauseated.

She leaned against a pine tree and inhaled its sharp tang. The scent stirred something within her, cozy yet uneasy, and she willed herself to examine the sensation of it knocking against her faulty memory banks. Other scents intruded from memory: lavender and detergent overlaying an older mustiness. And an image of her mam hand-washing three generations' worth of antique lace, yellowing and fragile as spider webs. And another image of the cedar linen chest that sat in the kitchen beside the door to the den.

Her mother's annual cleaning-out of the linen chest, yes. Each lacy doily, baptismal blanket, and fusty table runner had had a story, a memory she associated with her lean but contented childhood. She'd set to hand-washing each scrap of the past, telling Gemma that the mementos were as good as a photo album for her—better even. Gemma now recalled their filigreed mosaic swaying on the breeze. She remembered how she'd dance beneath them while they dried on the line, watching clouds pass behind their lacy spaces.

Such a lovely memory. It didn't make sense that she'd forgotten it until now—did it?

A twig cracked. Gemma pressed herself against the pine's rough hide while, around her, twitters and rustlings paused and then sprang back to life. A squirrel chattered a warning and a scuffling animal made a trail of waving fern fronds. In the misty twilight, Gemma thought she made out a human shadow merging and parting from the tree shadows. She dropped to the ground and crawled toward her safe haven under the tree trunk.

FORTY-THREE

On the edge of the forestry land Alan caught Bijou's head and ducked it back into the sock bag.

"Come on, come on," he said.

He was tempted to call out for Gemma except that he knew that Bijou would take the sound of his raised voice as a sign for play. For all Alan knew, his voice or Bijou's clumsy thrashings through the undergrowth might scare Gemma off. He pictured her as a woodland animal, skittery and wary. No, worse. He imagined her as a traumatized woodland animal after trusting mankind once too often. He didn't like to think she'd fear him, but then he didn't know what last night's violence had reaped in her mind. In the end, he preferred to approach her in a gentling manner, if possible.

He completed a circle along the perimeter of the woods in hopes that Bijou would smell Gemma's entrance point. No such luck. To his right, dull grey twilight slanted over the countryside. To his left, misty outlines of trees fell into a wooded black hole. He stepped left into the forest.

He sensed her proximity like a homing beacon. Peculiar or not, he had a gift for stalking. In a low voice, he sang a French children's song, hoping this would entice her out. "*Dans la forêt lointaine on entend le coucou.*"

Singing about a cuckoo in a faraway forest, he felt a bit cuckoo himself. Nevertheless, he continued in the half-light while intermittently forcing Bijou's nose up against the socks. She liked what she smelled, if her wagging tail meant anything, but so far she hadn't shown extraordinary interest in anything but rolling in mushrooms and suspicious decaying matter. The painkillers were working wonders on her morale but not on her tracking abilities.

Rustlings and crackling up ahead caused Alan to freeze. "Quiet," he whispered to Bijou and she stood at alert, ears pricked. There was something up ahead. An alarmed *kuk-kuk-kuk* from a squirrel dittoed the sentiment.

Alan carried an electric lantern, but he hadn't turned it on yet. He could still make out the shadows of tree trunks against the gloaming. He eased forward with Bijou at heel. Pine needles brushed his cheek and the moist oily scent of resin wafted through on a cool breeze. Above him the trees whispered and everywhere he turned his ear brought new, undefined evidence of unseen life. Faint squeaks, ghostly chirps.

And something else. He stepped forward at the sound of agitated rustlings. At his side, Bijou gave a low woof and just about tore his shoulder out of joint in a sudden lunge that yanked the lead out of his grip. A few seconds later, her yelp ricocheted off the trees.

"Bijou!" Stooping, he groped around in the near dark until he felt her. She lay on her side, but she lifted her head to lick his hands. "What just happened, girl?"

A movement caught his eye, a distinctly human-shaped shadow melting into the murk. Alan had dropped the lantern somewhere among the ferns, so he aimed himself in the direction he'd seen the shadow. Up ahead, the foliage came alive with thrashings and footsteps. Two people—men, by the sounds of their grunts—flattened a stand of ferns as they writhed against each other. One of the men rose up with a furious roar. The man held a thick branch high over his head and began swinging it in a frenzy while his opponent shimmied backwards.

The attacker's grunts and growls turned into words. "You—" He swung and the branch hit a tree with a resounding *thwack*. "Son of a fecking whore."

Alan grabbed the man's leg, and the attacker crashed down against him. He straddled the man and spied the would-be victim already swiping dirt off his suit.

"Well," Malcolm said, "I always knew you were nothing but a grub."

A strange guttural sound, like someone being strangled, silenced Malcolm. The squirming man beneath Alan went still. All of them, including Alan, froze as a new shadow disengaged itself from the trees near Bijou. A moment later, the light from his own lantern seared Alan's retinas, forcing him to look down at Nathan Tate's face. Nathan's gaze had hooked on the person holding the lantern. "Is that—?"

Alan blinked toward the lantern, attempting to make out who had joined their unlikely threesome. Trees and other foliage leaned toward them and away as the lantern swayed.

Gemma. Her hand shook, and as the light swung toward her, Alan caught sight of dirt streaking her face and mats weighing down her usually bouncy hair. Terror worked itself around Gemma's face in muscle spasms. Her mouth worked, her eyes bulged, and Alan cringed at the warped and tortured noises that found their way out of her.

"What, Gemma, what are you trying to say?" Alan said.

Gemma's scratchy voice tried and failed to claw its way out of its long-held silence.

"Nothing but a grub," Malcolm said.

Nathan shoved Alan off him and lunged toward Malcolm. Leaving those two to fight their own battle, Alan made his own lunge, trying and failing to catch Gemma as she collapsed.

FORTY-FOUR

DANNY FOLLOWED THE TREE line along its western edge. His torch barely penetrated the blackness of the deep country night.

"There," Dermot said from behind him.

Light mingled with the foggy ground cover and created a hazy glow through the trees. "Alan?" he called.

"Hurry up then," Alan called back. "Took you long enough."

Dermot ran ahead toward the lantern light, almost braining himself against a low-hanging branch in the process. Danny grabbed tree trunks for purchase as he followed. He stepped around a tangle of branches and made out the outline of the lantern. A few steps on, he stopped. He'd expected Gemma. That much was the point of this outdoor adventure. What he hadn't expected was Malcolm and Nathan Tate fighting like a couple of hooligans.

At the sight of Malcolm, Danny had to swallow back the urge to pull him aside for a wee chat. Nathan stood over him, brandishing a branch as thick as a man's arm. Further on, Gemma and Bijou lay atop a mass of flattened ferns, back to back, both breathing in shallow pants. Alan knelt beside Bijou, while Dermot brushed back Gemma's hair and whispered in her ear.

Danny approached and shone his torch at Malcolm and Nathan. They appeared wilted. A nasty bump rose out of Malcolm's temple.

"This is outrageous," Malcolm said. "I came out to help search for Gemma. I did say I have excellent night vision."

"The hero, you are," Nathan said.

"Quiet, both of you." Danny studied their ripped clothing and oozing scratches. Malcolm straightened his jacket while Nathan shifted from foot to foot.

"He attacked me," Malcolm said. "I want to press charges."

Dermot stumbled to his feet. Before Danny had a chance to stop him, Dermot had yanked the branch out of Nathan's grasp and raised it like a bat. "Which one of you did this to Gemma? Tell me now or, on my mother's grave, I'll kill the both of you."

"No one touched her," Nathan said.

Danny pulled the branch out of Dermot's grasp. He didn't look like he had the energy to use it, but it wouldn't hurt to lessen the chances.

"Malcolm, Nathan, I need you to sit down while we wait for the guards. And don't move."

Malcolm buttoned his suit jacket. "I'd prefer a bath. I can meet you at the station."

"Sit. Down." With more force than necessary, Danny grabbed Malcolm's shoulder and pushed. "Now."

Malcolm smiled. "Ah, Danny, you've heard about my alibi, I see. No matter." He pulled a handkerchief out of his pocket and dabbed at the bloody lump rising out of his big, bald head. "I assume you will be getting me an ambulance as soon as possible."

Danny retreated while Dermot hovered near the two men, not letting them out of his sight. Danny called the station while staring down at Gemma's curled form. Her back rose and fell but otherwise she didn't move. With a whimper, Bijou struggled against Alan's restraining hands. "Son of a bitch hit Bijou."

"Which son of a bitch?" Danny said.

"Nathan was the branch-wielding madman I saw."

"I told you, that was Malcolm," Nathan said. "I got the branch away from him."

Malcolm sighed. "Believe me, I was aiming at Nathan. I had to defend myself."

"Was there anyone else out here?" Danny said.

"Could have been, but he'd be long gone by now. It was utter chaos with those two brawling like a couple of eejits," Alan said. "Gemma appeared out of nowhere, and she was on the verge of speaking, I swear it. Then something must have spooked her because she deflated. Now look at her. I haven't been able to get a response out of her."

Dermot tossed the branch aside. "What am I doing? I've got to get Gemma out of here." He knelt next to his sister. With care, he eased his arms beneath her body and gathered her up. She was limp as a towel, her gaze wide and staring into nowhere. "We need a ride and somewhere to stay. Danny, your place?"

"We'll get an ambulance out here—"

"No!" He lowered his voice. "No. That won't help, believe me, I know. We need a quiet place away from here."

"As I was saying previously," Malcolm said, "I'll take the ambulance, and I'll take an officer so I can make my statement against Nathan."

"And what about my statement against you?" Nathan said.

"I was defending myself, also as I said."

"Not that, you shiny knob." Nathan addressed Danny directly. "I'd like to press charges against Malcolm for murder."

FORTY-FIVE

Two hours after coming upon the chaotic scene in the forest, Danny arrived at the Garda station with O'Neil driving and Malcolm in the backseat. Danny had lent Dermot his car so that he could transport unresponsive Gemma away from the scene. "No more hospitals for her," Dermot had said. "I'll not have her trussed up like my auntie's Christmas roast. I'll see to her."

By that time, O'Neil had arrived with a crew of guards. "We need to question you."

"What bloody questions?" Dermot had shouted, his eyes rolling. "My sister is almost comatose once again." He pointed at Malcolm and Nathan. "They're to blame. Now get the hell out of my way."

Dermot's departure left Danny to hitch a ride back into Lisfenora with O'Neil. Danny kept his gaze glued on the drystone walls that disappeared ahead of the headlights, counting in his head while Malcolm droned on about *preposterous* and *troubled* Nathan Tate, whom he, Malcolm Lynch, had tried to befriend, and wasn't that the way when it came to his generosity, his so-called mates taking advantage of his kind nature, libeling him, and who knew what else?

Danny reached number 1,753 as they pulled into the station's parking lot just behind the Garda vehicle transporting Nathan.

O'Neil herded Malcolm ahead of him into an interview room, but not before Malcolm twisted back and whispered to Danny, "Hadn't you better get back to the hospital?"

Danny went weightless with rage, imagining Malcolm using the same intimate tone to persuade Ellen into his bed. He inhaled the scent of burned coffee and dust from the heating vents—1,754, 1,755—and exhaled as O'Neil retreated with Malcolm. Danny would've liked to see Malcolm pinned down like a bug in a display, see him squirm, for anything. Clarkson was right to want Danny nowhere near the investigation.

Clarkson approached. "I'm sure you'll come up with something good and correct about your presence at a scene you shouldn't have been within a prick's one-eyed view of."

"Alan Bressard called me. And as any friend would, I went out to lend him a hand."

"And you just happened to have Dermot McNamara with you?"

"Yes." Clarkson didn't need to know they'd been driving back from the morgue when Alan called.

"Right. And where's the missing girl? I thought you were bringing her in."

"Looks like it will be a while before she's fit to communicate. She's had some kind of relapse."

Clarkson stood in the middle of the jumbled desks with hands on his hips. His eyebrows formed a consternated line. "And your good friend, Alan Bressard, who found her?"

"At the vet. His dog got caught in the middle of it."

"Oh, for the love of—" He rolled his shoulders and cracked his neck. "Okay, let's get on with what we have here, shall we, gents? I'll be with Malcolm Lynch in room two. O'Neil will remain with Nathan Tate. Whatever else those two have to say, we know Tate whacked Lynch a good one."

With that, he was gone, leaving Danny at loose ends while around him uniformed guards on the end of their shifts gathered their belongings and saluted him on their way to the pubs or their cozy homes. With a pang of guilt, Danny remembered the novel and lavender spray he'd promised himself he'd bring Ellen.

Had she sprayed her sheets for Malcolm?

He shook the unwelcome images away and launched himself toward interview room one. Inside the monitoring room, the barrel-chested officer from Ennis glanced up and away again. "Eh?"

"Ignore me. I'm just here to see what Nathan Tate has to say."

Nathan was in the midst of explaining why he had followed Malcolm into the forestry lands. Under the fluorescent lights, his skin was the color of a fish belly and the bags under his eyes stood out like purple flotation devices. The cool-cat *artiste* of few words wasn't in evidence at the moment.

"I already told you that I followed Malcolm because tonight was the night I meant to have it out with him. He killed my father."

O'Neil remained silent while Nathan rubbed his side as if in pain. His voice, when he spoke again, was low, completely done in. "I meant to catch up with Malcolm outside the pub and invite him to have a chat with me in the plaza, there to tell him what I know."

"Know or suspect?" O'Neil said.

"Either way, close enough for me."

"Go on."

"Malcolm had left the pub in a huff because Seamus spilled beer on him. It was earlier than usual for him and for once he wasn't chatting his way out the door with one of the other crows. Seemed a good time for a word, so I followed him. Only, he didn't go to his flat as usual. Off in his car." He shrugged. "So I followed him some more."

"You've lived here for some weeks now so what was the hurry?"

"No hurry. Just seemed a good time, like I said, because he was already out of sorts. I thought I might catch him off guard and get a chance to say my piece. It's like pissing in the wind with that man most of the time." He straightened up, twisting in his chair to stretch out his back. "In the forestry, he came after me with the branch first, not the other way around."

"That'll have to be your word against his. Right now I'm more interested in the story of your father's death. Malcolm must have had something against your father."

"No. That's just it. He didn't. My father fit a type, that's all." Nathan lapsed into silence, staring at his feet.

Danny itched with impotence and with the urge to call O'Neil out of the interview room and deposit himself with Nathan instead. Come on, O'Neil, do me well, Danny thought. Ask the right questions. Get Nathan talking again.

"And what type was that?" O'Neil said.

Pretty good, pretty good. Danny pulled up a chair and sat forward on his elbows. There had to be something here he could use against Malcolm.

Nathan disappeared out of camera range, reappearing with a glass of water. He gulped it down and set the empty glass on the ground beside his chair. "John McIlvoy's type, of course."

O'Neil's tone sharpened. "John McIlvoy?"

"Ay, that's the whole bloody point. My dad fit the approximate height and appearance of McIlvoy, well enough anyhow. I don't know how they met, but I'm sure Malcolm had been keeping an eye out. My dad had the misfortune to catch his attention."

"You're accusing Malcolm Lynch of planting McIlvoy's identification on your father after killing him. You're saying that McIlvoy is actually alive."

"Exactly," Nathan said. "Except, McIlvoy could have been the one to kill him. Either way, those two were in it together. Malcolm, the seducer; McIlvoy, the throttler."

Danny rocked back on the chair. What the hell? This case was more muddled than a herd of sheep in a garden maze. Quickly, he checked his email. And there, a message from the Firebird Designs email address awaited him.

At least you're right about one thing: I am a man of many talents. —The Talented Mr. McIlvoy

Cute. But at least Danny had received a reply. It was a start.

"Now I know why they killed my father," Nathan was saying. "McIlvoy is still wanted for murder. So my poor father was misidentified and his body sent to the incinerator without a proper investigation. Just another waste of space living on the streets. What did he matter?"

"If it was murder," O'Neil said, "there was an investigation."

"Yes, murder, but if there was an investigation it didn't last long. I was told no one came forward to claim the body."

"You skipped an important bit," O'Neil said. "How did you discover that Malcolm Lynch—or McIlvoy—allegedly killed your father?"

The words seeped out of Nathan, slow and steady. "My father used to visit me in my studio if his voices weren't too bad. He was a paranoid schizophrenic, to put the label on it, but what was I going to do? He was my dad, so I listened to him as he ranted about the

CIA, the IRA, Al Qaeda, even the Queen of England. One day, he talked about how he'd finally got an 'in.' He'd cracked the code of silence, so help him, with the help of a new friend."

Nathan paused for a moment as if to replenish the verbal well. "His description of his friend sounded like another one of his delusions. A fella with no hair—at all—and a great big smile, but it was the only fact I had. When my dad first went missing I gave the guards hassle, trying to light a fire under their arses to find him. Weeks later the guards fetched me. A homeless man had died—neck broken—but his identification said John McIlvoy. They showed me photos, and I'm all but shouting from the rooftops, 'No, you bloody eejits, that's my father, Sean Tate.'"

Nathan sat back, breathing hard. So did Danny. With or without Malcolm, McIlvoy had left devastation in his wake. Many years ago with Gemma's family and three months ago with Nathan's. And in the present with his own, if Danny's gut was correct on the matter. And now here they all were, the results of the devastation flung together with perfectly timed, one might even say sublime, chaos. Father Dooley would probably have something to say about this—fate or destiny or God's will. Danny liked to think in terms of karmic retribution.

"I wanted to identify my dad," Nathan continued, "but it was too late. He'd already been cremated. The guards didn't pursue the case in what I would call an in-depth manner. So here I am, having to do the confronting myself."

"But how did you connect your dad's death to Malcolm Lynch?" O'Neil asked.

Good lad. Keep Nathan focused.

"They had the decency to give me his effects, including a necklace. A nice thing. It took me a while, but I found a jeweler in Limerick who recognized the designer. Guess who? John McIlvoy of

Firebird Designs. Easy enough to find the website even though McIlvoy was supposed to be dead."

Indeed. But then, anyone could keep a website up and running.

"The website lists Malcolm Lynch as an agent of sorts. So I came to Lisfenora to meet him and—what do you know?—he was the spitting image of my father's description. That's when I decided to move here for a while. I move around a lot anyhow, so it was no problem."

"Have you met John McIlvoy?" O'Neil said. "We'd like to find him ourselves."

"Wish I could say that I have. But I did talk to him. His accent was pure Dublin."

"What did he say?"

"The website listed a phone number. Unfortunately, I went at it all wrong. Couldn't keep my temper. I didn't give him my particulars—I'm not that stupid—but I threatened him. A few days later the telephone number was out of order and not listed on the website anymore. That's why I was so intent on getting Malcolm to talk. He was my only connection to the man."

Danny had heard enough. He slipped out of the room and into the loo to slap cold water on his face. The story was so bizarre it had to be true. Or perhaps Danny wanted it to be true. Either way, he'd go with it. Coarse paper towels caught on his stubble, and he smiled at his sorry self in the mirror. Malcolm had some explaining to do. At minimum, regarding aiding and abetting the main suspect in Siobhan McNamara's murder. And from there, Malcolm would lead Danny to McIlvoy.

Buoyed by the thought, Danny combed wet fingers through his hair and settled it off his forehead.

The door opened and Clarkson entered. Danny tried to ignore the sound of Clarkson's piss hitting porcelain. "What's Malcolm saying?"

"You need to stay out of it. Are we square?"

229

"As a bathroom tile."

Back in the desk warren, Danny unclenched his hand from around a wadded paper towel. He tossed it onto O'Neil's desk, and then thought better of that and reached for it over a mess of paperwork. He caught sight of a crime scene photo of Blackie's Pasture with assorted houses and shops lining the far side. Danny squinted.

Jesus. How could he have forgotten? Danny grabbed up his jacket and jotted a quick note to O'Neil.

Tell Nathan Tate to call me as soon as possible.

FORTY-SIX

DANNY HADN'T BEEN TO O'Leary's Pub in a few years. Smaller and darker than the Plough, the O'Leary clan favored a nautical motif. A giant Captain's wheel hung over the bar and prints of galleons on stormy seas covered the walls. The effect wasn't cheery, so all the better that Theresa O'Leary graced the bar with her presence most evenings. Codgers and young fellas already filled the stools, all vying for attention from the girl. Her regulars appeared to be a well-behaved lot compared to Alan's.

Rumors that she had all the lads quivering appeared to be true. She laughed at something a business type said and fobbed him off with a, "You've got all the finesse of a kick to the balls, haven't you then?"

She was just feisty enough, and she sported a red bra beneath her mannish button-up blouse so she was also just sexy enough. In other words, she knew what she was about even though she was all of twenty years old. Her alert gaze swept over her customers, and she mixed drinks with a sure hand. Surely such expertise came from growing up in the pub.

Danny waited at the end of the counter. A few patrons raised their pints in homage to Ellen. Theresa plunked a pint of the black stuff down in front of him. She had kind eyes, grey-rimmed with dark blue and perceptiveness.

"On the house. How are you getting on?"

"As you'd expect. If you have a few minutes, I'd like to ask you about a lad you may know."

She beckoned him to an empty table with a "keep your peace" lobbed back at the codgers and fellas. "You're here about the lad in the paper? Disgusting, what happened."

Danny swallowed his surprise along with a mouthful of Guinness. "His name was Toby Grealy."

"I know. Brendan Nagel introduced us." She smirked and rolled her eyes, the first time she'd shown her young years, only to catch herself up with a grimace. "Sorry, that was tacky. I shouldn't smile, but Bren was a right lovable goof, but a goof all the same. He fancied me something terrible."

"If I were his age, I would too."

She raised a shoulder in a gesture somewhere between dismissive and flattered. "His friend, though, Toby, now he was more my type."

"Friend?"

"By the end of the night you'd have thought they'd known each other since the nappies."

"Tell me about it."

Theresa settled herself in the chair across from Danny. She had a languid way about her, with one crossed leg swinging and a hand drooping off the edge of the table. "Bren had been coming in more often, seeing as how he fancied me, poor sod. He tried to be charming, but you couldn't get him to shut his trap about Malcolm Lynch. Crap boss, sounded like."

Danny's couldn't help himself when he asked whether she'd ever seen Malcolm in her pub with dates.

"Oh no, not the likes of us. According to Bren, Malcolm considered this side of Blackie's Pasture the wrong side of Lisfenora, which is another reason Bren liked to come here. Malcolm sounds like a right tosser. Lisfenora isn't big enough to have a side."

"True." Much as Danny wanted to gather as much vicarious dirt on Malcolm as he could, he kept to the point. "So Brendan came in one night—"

"Week before last, yeah? The usual. Moping around the bar and trying to catch my eye. This other bloke, Toby, comes in and sits down next to Bren. Didn't have a choice, seeing as it was the last open spot. He smelled ripe, but he'd tried to clean himself up in the bathroom. I could tell because he'd wet down his hair." Theresa pointed toward the end of the bar. "They sat over there where I make drinks, so I overheard them. I hear a lot anyhow. Comes with the territory."

"Alan over at the Plough says the same."

"He's a good one. I like him even if my father's got it against the French." She sipped on a Coke she'd brought over with her. "That night Toby looked to be pretty grim. He probably would have kept to himself if Bren hadn't noticed his earrings. It's not like you could miss them. I would have commented myself but Bren got to it ahead of me. 'Hold on now,' he said, 'where'd you get those sorry things?'"

Danny was transfixed. This girl was bloody perfection. If only all witnesses were this observant and coherent.

"Then Bren couldn't help himself. He went on to make the saints weep about some blighter named John and how something was fishier than a selkie's twat—his words, not mine. As soon as he mentioned the name—"

"John McIlvoy?"

233

"Ay, that's it. As soon as he mentioned the name, Toby jerks up like a puppet on a string. 'You know John McIlvoy?' he says. I lost the conversation there, but when I returned they were still at it, whispering like a couple of girls. I'm just that curious so I pulled my special smile." She pulled it, a hint of teeth, lips just this side of pouty. "Daft really, but it works."

She laughed, and Danny joined in. She was an antidepressant, this girl; he'd have to come back for a fix now and then. He thought Ellen would like Theresa, which comforted him past the jolt of guilt. He shouldn't be enjoying her company even for these few minutes.

"I tell them there's no secrets at my bar," she continued, "and Bren's off the rafters about how he's going to help Toby find this John character."

"How was he going to manage that?"

"Not sure. Just that he knew a man who knew McIlvoy."

Malcolm.

"Did you see Toby after that?"

"That was the last I saw of them, that night." She gazed unseeingly at the bar, where one of her patrons signaled her with an empty pint glass. "Can't believe I'm saying this, but I miss the sorry blighter. Bren would have grown up to be a proper fine boyfriend for some lass." She rose. "Cheers then. I hope it helps."

Danny finished his pint and left before anyone had a chance to commiserate about Ellen. Across the lane from O'Leary's, Blackie's Pasture lay quiet and dark. A faint scent of wet grass tinged the air. Danny could just make out a footpath that skirted the silage bundles and disappeared into the dark. The fog would have hidden the struggle and murder. The bundles stood near the center of the pasture, beyond the light cast by the dimmed shop lights. After the pubs closed, there would have been no one to see and no way to see anyhow, with or without the fog.

The door opened behind him. "I'm glad I caught you," Theresa said. "I forgot something."

And conscientious too. Perhaps he did fancy her a bit.

"Bren was that polluted he insisted Toby come along to meet his dad, that his dad would love to hear his story about John McIlvoy. They left together."

———————

For the first time since Danny had known him, Alan joined him at the bar, arse planted on the stool, pint in hand. The crowd buffeted them from behind, an elbow here, a shoulder there. Danny couldn't hear himself think over the laughter and low roar of conversation. Only one week left of September, which meant one more week until the pub became a locals' haven once again.

"Bijou's sleeping in my office," Alan said.

"She's okay?"

"Ay, she'll be alright." He gulped at his Guinness. "Word on Gemma?"

"Nothing yet, but you'd better believe I'm going to visit her in the morning."

"Oh?"

"This investigation needs Gemma."

"Alan!" came the exasperated voice of the junior barman.

Swearing under his breath, Alan rose. Danny rose along with him, Alan to go about his work and Danny to his.

Seamus sat at his usual spot at the other end of the bar along with a few crows. His head bobbed on sagging neck. His face was puffy yet slack, the skin under his jaw so loose that it gave the impression that his jaw might clatter to the floor. His mouth moved with a strange, gummy clacking sound. Danny shooed Elder Joe and Mickey away, and sat down next to Seamus.

Seamus blinked at him. His voice slurred past the consonants and rolled over the vowels. "What of it then?"

Footsteps stopped behind them. Danny turned around to wave off their visitor. Mackey held out a carry bag from the Spar.

"Pardon a second, Dan-o. Got something here for Seamus." Mackey patted Seamus's shoulder and went on as if he'd received a response. "Bought a few things today, and you take them home and you eat, you sorry old sack. And then tomorrow morning you eat something else before you return to drink yourself to death."

Mackey shoved the bag between them onto the bar top and stomped away. Seamus peeked over the rim. He fumbled out a jar of peanut butter and proceeded to twist at the lid with fingers curled like gripless anemone tentacles. For the first time, Danny noticed his inflamed knuckles. They reminded him of his rheumatoid granny.

"Got the word on Gemma," Seamus said. "She is found, and good for Alan. The hero, though you'd never know it." He loosened his grip, shook out his hand, and tried the lid again.

Danny said, "Let me," and unscrewed the top. Alan plopped bread and a knife down in front of them on the bar counter.

The homey smell of peanut butter reminded Danny of his children, of Ellen slathering it on crusty brown bread along with homemade strawberry jam, back when she made jam. His stomach howled, and he took over the job of spreading the mashed peanuts on bread, first for Seamus, then for himself. Its comforting texture saddened him. He shoved himself past the feeling, thinking about how to break through Seamus's grief long enough to get some information out of him. The direct approach seemed the best bet.

236

"You lied to me," Danny said, "and I want to know why."

"Wha—?" Seamus gagged on his wad of peanut butter and bread.

"Theresa O'Leary says your boy met Toby at her pub. Why hide a fact like that?"

"Why indeed? Except that at the time, my son, he were alive, and I knew he had nothing to do with that boy's death. No way in hell. Call it a father's protectiveness." He broke into a shaky laugh that echoed around the room like an entrapped bird. "Knew you'd get serious with me sooner or later." Seamus blinked furiously and tried to twist the lid back on the peanut butter jar.

Danny helped him and dropped it into the grocery sack. "Best mates by the end of the evening, so she said."

"You're slaying me with this, you surely are. Only I don't feel like laughing."

"He brought Toby around to meet you. Why?"

Seamus rocked himself into a standing position. He clutched the grocery bag to his chest, teetering. "Slaying me," he repeated and shuffled out of the pub.

Wednesday

My father, now in heaven, is a keeper
of the birds. And his eye is on his sparrow.

Don Williams, Jr.

FORTY-SEVEN

MERRIT'S SWOLLEN LIP FELT like a slug hanging on her face. She tested its tenderness with a fingertip, wincing, and then forced her hand away from her face. She knocked on the door of Fox Cottage and entered when she heard the muffled sound of Dermot's voice.

Heat almost blasted her out of her shoes as she closed the door behind her. With fireplace tongs in hand, Dermot turned a bleary and flushed face toward her. His hair clung to his head in sweaty streaks. He must have kept the peat fire burning through the night because it had infused the room with its earthy, tar-like odor. He reminded Merrit of a horror movie she'd once seen, something about cabin fever, in which the young and nubile characters went mad with stir craziness. Bulging eyes, twitchy lips, jerky movements.

"I hope you don't mind the intrusion," Merrit said. "You know that Liam and I live down the track, right? Liam owns this cottage."

"Danny mentioned as much. Thanks for letting us stay here."

Merrit waved away the gratitude. She wasn't much of a help to any-one these days, whether out on the plaza with Liam or at Alan's pub yesterday, but here she was anyhow, hoping to be let in. She held out a box of corn flakes and a container of milk. "Thought you might need breakfast food. I'm not sure what Danny has stocked in the kitchen."

"Just about nothing." Dermot squinted at her, his leg jiggling. "What happened to you?"

"I stepped in where I didn't belong."

Merrit edged along the back of the couch. Gemma appeared placid under a mound of blankets, the way she stared up at the crossbeams and blinked slow as an owl. Flushed as Dermot, yet she shivered in spasms that belied her calm appearance. Dermot shoveled more peat pellets into the grate.

"Is she—?"

"Catatonic. You can say it." Dermot grabbed the cereal from her, opened it, and started eating the corn flakes dry. He spoke through hasty handfuls. "Just like after our mom died. Trauma-induced. Though, I take that back. She's not as bad this time." His eyelid twitched. "No need for feeding tubes, at least."

"What happened? Last night in the forest, I mean."

"Bloody hell if I know. Alan was looking for her, and Malcolm was helping until he ended up brawling with Nathan. All I know is that something frightened Gemma back into her shell. It could have been anything." He stuttered to a stop, then continued as if compelled to say what he was thinking out loud. "Even something as small as the sound of flesh hitting flesh."

Dermot hoisted Gemma into a sitting position and settled her back on a pile of pillows. He placed a corn flake on Gemma's lower lip, murmuring for her to *chew and swallow, just chew and swallow, please.* Gemma continued blinking without expression. Dermot pushed the cereal flake, no longer an inconsequential one of many, but a crunchy harbinger of Gemma's fate, so that it tipped into Gemma's mouth.

Merrit could feel Dermot's desperation—*just chew and swallow, just chew and swallow*—and then his relief when her jaw moved and the muscles shifted beneath the thin skin on her neck.

Dermot breathed. "You see? No hospital needed. I can take care of her until she comes out of it, which she will. You'll see." He placed another flake just inside her mouth. "That's my Gems, you've got it. A little nourishment, a rest, buckets of fluids, and you'll be right as rain, won't you?"

Gemma continued blinking, Dermot continued pleading with her, and Merrit left the room to wipe away her tears in the privacy of the kitchen.

"Can you bring out bowls and spoons?" Dermot called.

So she did, glad for the task. "Why don't you show me how to feed Gemma so you can take a break? You look like you're about to lose your mind."

"You could be right. I'll pack our stuff at Ellen's house." He paused. "If the guards will let me in. And run by the pub to thank Alan—I owe that man my firstborn child—and buy some adult nappies, just in case." His grunt sounded more like a soul in despair trying to fly free of its body. "Jesus, I don't think I can bear it. Not again."

"Take your time," Merrit said. "I'll look after her until you return."

"All you do is feed her as if she were a baby. And maybe you can walk her to the toilet now and again. Somewhere in there she knows what to do." He kissed Gemma's cheek. "Back straightaway, Gems."

Dermot tapped the front door closed behind himself. He'd forgotten a jacket but Merrit supposed he wouldn't notice the cold outside. She lifted a spoonful of cereal and milk to Gemma's lips. She remembered her babysitting days, shifting plastic spoons in pastel colors into the tiny mouths of her charges. She'd done so with indifference to whether the infants ate or dribbled, almost with a cavalier attitude, thinking of it more as playtime than caregiving. Now, with Gemma, she focused on landing every atom of nutrition into her mouth.

Gemma didn't dribble. At the slightest pressure of spoon on her lip, she opened her mouth. She chewed and swallowed, all the while staring into a middle distance. It was like feeding a giant doll. This opening, chewing, swallowing, and opening, chewing, swallowing was devoid of Gemma's essence, that intensity and odd grace that characterized all her movements.

But she was eating. This had to be good.

"Ah, Gemma," Merrit said, "if you were awake, what would I say? Something about Alan, because I've seen the way he looks at you. At least it's obvious to me that you like each other. I'm supposed to be a matchmaker. Somehow I'm supposed to be charmed for it the way Liam is. Runs in the blood, so he says, over generations. Gemma?"

No response. She nudged another corn flake into Gemma's mouth.

"I'm not sure I'm cut out for living in such a close-knit community. I don't know what I'm trying to achieve. Sometimes I don't know why I'm still here." She stared into Gemma's fathomless eyes. "Are you less lonely in there, Gemma? Does the catatonia lessen the pain of your isolation?"

Sometimes loneliness was worse when you were surrounded by people. Maybe Gemma had learned this lesson long ago.

"Gemma, can you hear me?" The nothingness of her. "They say that coma patients register on some level and you're more awake than that."

Merrit pictured Ellen Ahern under a crisp sheet, laid out like an Egyptian mummy. Danny—what he must be feeling. She'd have liked to visit the hospital to show support, but that would probably just be her desperation leading the way again.

From far away a voice filtered into Gemma's dark and safe corner where nothing affected her. Sensory inputs washed over her and away before she could make sense of them. Some things, like the cool press of metal against her lip, set off a bigger signal—food, eat—that also slid away, leaving her floating again without knowing whether her mouth had responded or not.

Memories beckoned, but had no effect. She floated, aware but not aware, preferring her imprisonment with its peace and its simplicity. In this nothing place she could relax her vigilance. Rest her weary brain, hear voices through cotton, recognize her five senses signaling from afar, trying to rouse her from her safe place.

For now, she knew without awareness of having produced the thought, that she preferred floating in her dark and safe corner.

FORTY-EIGHT

DANNY WATCHED A NURSE help settle Ellen into her private room on the women's acute ward. Wires, tubes, and monitors still surrounded her but somehow Danny felt more breathing room outside of the ICU. The shushed atmosphere upstairs had sucked the oxygen out of the rooms. Here, nurses chatted as they passed in the corridor and laughter floated from the bedsides of recovering patients. Perhaps the noise would be good for Ellen.

"Right then. Now we wait." The nurse held out her hand. "I'll get an orderly to bring the flowers she's received."

After she left, he pulled Ellen's lavender sheet spray out of the small suitcase he'd brought from home. His hands ached and a deep abrasion left a smear of blood on the spray bottle. He hadn't been able to sleep last night, alone in his family home for the first time in a year and with Ellen's blood soaked into the kitchen floor. The scenes of crime officers had released the house to him, but it had still felt like a crime scene. At 2:00 a.m. he'd heaved himself out of bed and torn out the stained linoleum until his fingertips were raw. And once started, he hadn't stopped until his kitchen floor was laid bare, tarry linoleum glue stuck to what were once lovely pine floorboards.

He'd have those floorboards sanded and varnished like new by the time Ellen returned from the hospital. For now, he'd make do with spritzing her hospital sheets and pillows with the lavender spray. A flap of the sheets scattered the scent in the direction of her nose. Next, he shuffled through various nightgowns he'd stuffed into the suitcase and pulled out Ellen's sterling silver hairbrush and mirror set, inherited from her very Victorian granny. Danny thought she might like to see some of her favorite belongings when she woke up. He set the antiques on the bedside table beside a handmade wooden box that contained the children's first baby teeth, their infant bracelets, their locks of baby hair.

Next came a romance novel called *Broken Promises*. Feeling ridiculous, he nevertheless opened it at the bookmark and read aloud from the top of the page: " ... *and Anna pressed her face against his chest, smelling his musk that aroused her yet further. She flicked her tongue in ever-tightening circles around*—Jesus, Ellen, this is utter shite. I can't read this to you. I'm sorry, but I can't. How about I bring in one of your old favorites? I could stand reading *Rebecca*."

He imagined a twitch of humor around her eyes. She'd foisted *Rebecca* on him years ago, insisting that he give it a try because of its literary merit. He'd tried, but given it up for her to read aloud to him. Every night for a month, he'd drifted off to sleep after half a page. Her voice had been his lullaby.

"I'll bring it next time," he said over a sudden clamor of voices from down the hall.

Laughter filtered into the room. Danny tensed. He stood as Malcolm's voice grew louder. The man couldn't help himself; he had to announce himself all over the ward.

"Of course, you must visit my shop. I'll give you a ten percent discount on your first purchase. How's that for incentive?"

More laughter, and then Malcolm appeared in the doorway with the nurse. They each carried several floral arrangements that friends and family had sent to Ellen.

"Such colorful bouquets," Malcolm said, "and so many more still upstairs, aren't there, Maggie? This one is from me. Of course, I couldn't arrive without a token."

He settled his dozen lilies center-most on a narrow shelf that ran the length of one wall. "I picked these out one by one, never mind the florist, I can always spot the best blooms. It comes with working with beautiful objects my whole life."

To Danny's disgust, the nurse looked like a woman in love. Her cheeks rosy, her smile glued in place, a finger twirling her ponytail. "I'm off on my rounds. I'll get that orderly to bring around the rest of the flowers."

Malcolm's gaze followed her angular form as she left. Funny. Danny had never noticed how reptilian he looked with his eyelash-less blinks.

"Nurses are grand, aren't they? They pride themselves on pleasing others."

Malcolm settled a guest chair closer to the window, unbuttoned his suit jacket, and pressed his hands down the length of his body to settle the expensive cloth just so. He hadn't looked at Ellen once.

Danny's fingernails bit into his palms and with a force of will he said in a neutral tone, "What are you doing here?"

Malcolm patted the bandage on his head. "Came to get my head checked, just to be sure." His teeth flashed in the hazy sunlight that managed to sneak through the cloud cover. "Thought I'd check on Ellen while I was here. I'm glad to see her so peaceful. And, has she lost weight?"

No, Malcolm didn't just say that. He didn't just imply his working knowledge of her body.

"Now then," Malcolm continued, "what news have you about the graffiti on my windows?"

"We have other priorities, wouldn't you say?"

Malcolm cocked his head, looking puzzled. "We can't let a vandal go about terrorizing the village. For all we know, it's that Nathan Tate. He has something against me, some notion in his head about his father's death. And now I have a slight concussion on top of everything else."

"You're the victim right enough," Danny said.

Malcolm either hadn't heard or had chosen to ignore Danny's snide tone. Danny thought the former, which was odd. He'd never noticed Malcolm's social obtuseness before. Danny slid onto the mattress next to his wife. He leaned back against the headboard. Now Malcolm was forced to at least see his wife while he spoke to Danny.

"It doesn't worry you that Nathan accuses you of killing his father on McIlvoy's behalf?"

"Of course not. What nonsense."

"What about the Firebird necklace and John McIlvoy's identification found on the body? You know you're in a world of hurt if you're helping McIlvoy hide, him being a suspect in a murder and all."

As I'm sure you know, he didn't say.

"Danny, Danny, even off duty, you're a Garda officer at heart." He settled back in his chair, expansive, as if the two of them were sitting before a roaring hearth with Scotch in hand. "I'd consider letting go of the assault charges against Nathan if the man would leave the village. Return to wherever. I don't mind telling you that I didn't sleep last night, I was that distressed over the whole business."

247

Danny brushed back Ellen's hair. Malcolm reignited his smile, turning it on like a reflective coating, bouncing everything back out at the world. He still hadn't looked at Ellen.

"This is all a bit much. I might have to consider a vacation. Perhaps to St. Tropez, though I have to take care with my skin. Wouldn't do to sunburn."

"I would advise against leaving the country."

"Now you're just being petty."

"Why were you in the woods last night?"

"Oh, that. Alan needed help, and I'm nothing if not civic-minded." Malcolm stood and rebuttoned his jacket. "I must be off then. I have a dinner date in Ennis. The French restaurant? You must know it. *Le Bouchon?*"

Oh yes, Danny knew the restaurant, and Malcolm knew well enough that Danny couldn't afford it on his salary.

Malcolm twitched at the lilies he'd brought, rearranging them with his back facing Danny and Ellen. "There, quite nice." Turning, he asked, "How is the girl, Gemma, by the way? Last night she seemed quite, well, stupid, shall we say?"

Nice of him to ask about Gemma but not Ellen. Most genial of him, to be sure. Keeping his tone even, Danny said, "She's not well. Back to a catatonic withdrawal is my best understanding, the same as before, when your dear friend, John McIlvoy, murdered her mother."

"Oh, now you're just trying to get a rise out of me, aren't you? Police tactics, brilliant, but I'm too perceptive for that. I'll be off. Cheers then," Malcolm called with a backwards wave, only to backtrack from the hallway a second later.

"I can't believe I forgot to warn you." Malcolm leaned against the door frame, at ease and loving himself for it, Danny was sure. "Ellen's doctor is meant to be on his rounds and should be arriving to talk to you sometime this morning. He has been trying to contact you—"

Danny's heart banged against his sternum. Contact him? He hadn't received any messages. He yanked his mobile out of his pocket—dead.

"That Maggie, such a kind nurse," Malcolm continued. "It never takes me long to draw people out, and I did ask about Ellen, obviously. Maggie was only too empathetic and as a family friend she didn't see the harm in telling me what she'd heard."

"Did you just say 'family friend'?" Danny leapt off the bed, ready to head butt the smarmy bastard into next century. In the nick of time, the doctor in question came abreast of Malcolm.

"Mr. Ahern, I'm glad I've caught you. We need to talk."

FORTY-NINE

A KNOCK STARTLED MERRIT. Milk spilled down Gemma's chin. But, like a doll, Gemma was impervious to the inconvenience and mess. The knock sounded again, louder. Merrit waited, hoping for a reaction out of Gemma, but when none came at the third knock, she rose. She opened the front door to find Danny in his black trench with cockeyed collar. He looked like a drowned man, face puffy and pale and blurry.

She blinked in surprise. He blinked in surprise. A thousand questions flitted through her brain, but he preempted her. "Why aren't you on the plaza with Liam?"

"Liam is fine for today. I needed a breather from the festival." She opened the door wide to let him pass. If he noticed her swollen lip, he didn't let on. Merrit returned to feeding Gemma. "I sent Dermot out for a break. He might be at your house packing up his and Gemma's stuff, if you want to talk to him."

Danny paced around the couch a few times before throwing off his coat. He crowded in next to Merrit on the couch. She stiffened at the unaccustomed proximity of him, his smell like lavender and antiseptic, the press of warmth.

"I need Gemma to wake up," he said. "I need her to remember John McIlvoy."

Merrit slipped a spoon with one milk-soaked corn flake on it into Gemma's mouth. A hair curl swung forward and blocked her mouth. Danny moved it out of the spoon's way.

"With McIlvoy out there, Gemma is still in danger." It may have been Merrit's imagination, but she thought she saw a spasm of fear deep within the blank depths of Gemma's eyes. "How come no one's talking to Malcolm? He knows the man."

Danny snorted. The puff of air tickled Merrit's ear. "Oh, I'm doing my best when it comes to that, but Superintendent Clarkson has his own ideas. Nathan Tate's the one looking at a charge for assault while Malcolm"—Merrit glanced up when Danny spat out his name—"is in his good graces."

Danny leaned around Merrit to catch hold of Gemma's chin. A gentle nudge turned her head. Danny stared into her near-black eyes. "What will bring you out of there, Gemma McNamara?"

He let go of Gemma's chin at the sound of a car braking to a halt outside the door. "That will be Nathan. I told him to meet me here."

"The guards let him go?"

"For now. He's all right. He dislikes Malcolm even more than I do." Danny hooked her gaze, studying her. "You must know what I'm talking about."

She did. Malcolm's affair with Ellen. Liam heard everything through the Lisfenora grapevine.

Merrit opened the door to see Nathan's fist about to knock on her forehead. Despite the chill, he only wore a baggy sweater with the sleeves pushed up to his elbows, displaying powerful forearms.

Nathan faltered when he caught sight of Danny. "No disrespect intended but you look like skewered shite."

"Nice of you." Danny rolled to standing. "Did you bring it?" Nathan shifted his head toward Merrit.

"Hardly matters, does it?" Danny said. "We're all of us outcasts at the moment. And Merrit doesn't have anyone around the village to confide in anyhow, except Liam, and he's okay."

"Gee, thanks." It was the truth but he didn't need to be so matter-of-fact about it. Merrit settled a blanket over Gemma's shoulders. "You mind telling me what's going on?"

"This." Nathan pulled a chain out of his jeans pocket, at the end of which dangled a shimmering blue stone.

"Where did that come from?" she said.

"This is the necklace that was found on my dad's body. It came back to me as next of kin."

He rehashed the story in a few quick sentences. Nathan held a Firebird Designs necklace found on dead John McIlvoy, who wasn't John McIlvoy but Sean Tate, and, logically—if any logic existed—the necklace shouldn't have come within miles of a down-and-out Limerick man.

"Dermot identified the necklace as his mother's," Danny said, "stolen off her corpse by John McIlvoy."

"If he wants it back, it's his," Nathan said. "It's nothing to me."

"Now we need to find the matching earrings, the ones that disappeared off Toby Grealy."

"Oh." Merrit stirred uneasily. "Gemma told me about the matching set. You're sure this is her mother's necklace?"

"Yes," Danny said.

Merrit plucked the necklace from Nathan's fingers, still unnerved, but now certain about one thing, a thing that Danny might have noticed if he wasn't a typically clueless male when it came to jewelry.

But she needed to be sure before she said anything, because what she was thinking wasn't good. Not good at all.

FIFTY

DANNY LEANED AGAINST THE wall, fatigue and the ever-present bur-
ble of anger making him limp. A skimpy patch of light lit the necklace that Merrit held up in front of her. She made a noise, a pensive
click of the tongue, and turned away to burrow into a pile of clothes
draped over the rocking chair that stood in the corner of the room.
The floorboards creaked when the chair swung into motion, sounding eerily female and sad. Ellen flashed through his head.

"Could you stop that thing rocking?" he said.

Merrit nodded and unfurled a quilted, waterproof jacket. "Gemma's," she said. She rifled its pockets until she found what she was
looking for and showed it to him. The black box with the earrings
that Danny wished he'd never seen.

Merrit retreated into the kitchen, saying the light was better
there. Danny followed with Nathan fast on his heels. By the time he
entered, Merrit had the black box opened and sitting on the kitchen
table beside the necklace. The pendant sparkled with the same luminous blue hue as the earrings.

Merrit picked up one of the earrings and squinted at its backing. The stone was set into what Danny would describe as a backless silver frame that allowed light to play through the stone.

"There it is, but we knew that already," she said.

"You need a microscope to see," Nathan said.

"The jeweler stamped in his signature beside where he soldered on the post. Something that looks like an *F*. For Firebird." Merrit turned over the necklace Nathan had brought. "Same here."

Merrit held an earring up to the light, then the pendant. She squinted at the pendant's silver backing, then back at the earring. "These are a set, made to be worn together. We don't need Dermot to confirm that both these pieces were his mother's. Which means—"

"Show me your proof," Danny said.

She handed him the opal jewelry and directed his gaze to where she pointed on the back of the pendant and also on the back of one of the earrings.

Merrit had good eyes. It took Danny several seconds of blinking to bring three lines into focus. The same three lines in the same configuration on each piece. He wouldn't have noticed them, and if he had, he would have taken them for a scraggly backwards *N*, some kind of artistic signature. But now he deciphered a *1/1*.

"One-slash-one. So?"

"So, according to what Malcolm taught me when I brought my necklace in for repair, this means that this design was a one-off. The only one of its kind. These earrings and this necklace are a matching pair. They were designed together."

The ramifications hit Danny like an ax buried into his brain. "This whole bloody time these earrings were staring me in the face? In my house? Pointing the way?"

Danny banged open a cupboard, pulled down the Glenfiddich, and swallowed a mouthful straight from the bottle. The whiskey burned right back to his optic fibers, sending fireworks through his vision. Whatever scant objectivity he'd maintained had just evaporated. McIlvoy. He'd entered Danny's life, dared to make jewelry that insinuated itself into his family, jewelry that Malcolm had given Ellen.

He wasn't sure whom he wanted to nail more, Malcolm or McIlvoy.

Merrit was explaining to Nathan that if the necklace used to belong to Siobhan McNamara—which it had, according to Dermot—then the earrings had also. And since the earrings were Siobhan's, then these were also the earrings that Toby Grealy was wearing when he died, and if these were the earrings he was wearing, which they were, then somehow Malcolm had gotten his hands on them, given them to Ellen, who'd given them to Gemma, bringing them full circle back into the McNamara family.

"That's twisted," Nathan said. "So that must mean Malcolm offed Toby Grealy because how else—"

"He has an alibi," Danny said.

"So then McIlvoy."

"Perhaps so. The talented Mr. McIlvoy." Danny swigged again and let the dizziness ride through him, welcoming it. Sublime chaos, that was what it was, full stop. He banished the image of Toby's infected earlobes. Those tender bits of skin carrying all the boy's hope by way of a pair of opal earrings.

"Hold on there," Nathan said. "Why didn't Gemma recognize her own mother's earrings?"

"Somewhere inside her, she did," Merrit said. "She recognized something about my necklace also, so I expect it was the generalities of the look rather than the specifics, you know what I mean?"

"Near enough," Nathan said.

Danny set the whiskey aside. "Near enough isn't good enough. Never is. Ellen is near enough to life to be called alive, yet we won't be getting any insights from her about Malcolm and the timing of their rendezvous the night Toby died. She's not near enough to consciousness for that. In fact, she may never be again. Ellen may never wake up. Ever."

FIFTY-ONE

DANNY STOOD IN THE dark breathing through his mouth. A part of him observed himself from afar with something between shame and surprise. He hadn't known that he cared about his marriage to this extent, much less that he could be moved by rage and jealousy. He'd held back on his emotions for too long—especially when it came to Ellen—and now here he stood in Malcolm's flat with lock picks and a metaphorical ax of loathing to grind.

And he felt grand. Like a maverick cowboy from a classic John Wayne film. He'd hear about this break-in from Clarkson, but Danny was on compassionate leave. A civilian—kind of. A civilian who had gone around the bend.

So be it.

He'd vetoed his own idea to interrupt Malcolm's fancy date at the fancy French restaurant. He'd pictured the lilies that Malcolm had brought Ellen, the way he'd avoided looking at her. No, not avoided. Avoidance implied some kind of emotional reaction. Malcolm had simply not cared enough to see her.

Danny felt along the wall through the kitchen area. The endless fog had retracted its tendrils and moonlight glanced off the spit-shined countertops. A faint glow from streetlights saved him from knocking over the scalloped Waterford vase located pride of place in the center of a sideboard. Malcolm owned plenty of expensive bits and pieces, no doubt bought at his wholesale discount.

A set of bookshelves displayed classics bound in creamy leather. Gold-embossed lettering announced Beckett, Faulkner, Dickens, and the rest of the usual literary canon. Danny pulled out Shake-speare and opened it at random. The book spine creaked. A new-book smell of glue and paper and tooled leather wafted up at him.

Cervantes, Rilke, and Tolstoy proved to be in the same immacu-lately unused condition. Danny stepped away from the books, ad-miring how well they appeared next to the reading chair and lamp with a tulip-shaped shade.

Continuing on, he reached the bathroom. He closed the door and turned on the light. A contact lens case, along with an electric toothbrush, sat on the counter. Malcolm was proud of his teeth, wasn't he? He liked to flash them around.

Inside the medicine cabinet Danny found colognes, deodorant, aspirin, dental floss. The usual, but Danny was expecting more for some reason. He backed out of the bathroom, turning out the light, and let his fingers trail over the wall until he came to the closet. A quick look confirmed that Malcolm loved his fancy suits to go with his fancy dates at fancy French restaurants.

Danny hovered near the bed, gazing out at stars and church spires, trying to absorb the essence of the man who lived here. Elu-sive, but he was here, somewhere.

From the bed, Danny retraced his steps to the kitchen area.

One of the cabinets held a bottle of Calvados brandy. Malcolm was true to his word when he said he wasn't one to drink alone. To maintain a trim figure, he said. The man was obsessed with his trim figure and dapper appearance.

Once again, Danny's mind ricocheted back to Ellen, pale and limp in her hospital bed, the massive bandage encasing her head, the feeding tube chafing her nostrils, the catheter bag dangling beside the bed. Malcolm had fooled her with his charm.

But then, she'd been ripe for the fooling. Danny had left her to wander her own sad orbit alone.

Continuing where he'd left off with the Glenfiddich at Fox Cottage, Danny chugged a mouthful of Calvados, sputtering at its burn. He peered at a bulletin board hung beside the refrigerator. Snapshots showed Malcolm in the midst of his Lisfenoran life, smiling on the threshold of his shop, smiling on a plaza bench with newspaper folded over his knee, smiling at what looked to be a committee meeting for some local event, smiling in Alan's pub.

The images centered on Malcolm and only Malcolm amidst random arms and legs. The star of his own Malcolm Show.

Danny tipped back a long, lingering sip of Calvados, now savoring its initial harshness and noting the earthy apple and cinnamon aftertaste. He decided that Ellen would like it.

He emailed John McIlvoy from his mobile. *Come out of hiding and meet me at Malcolm's flat. I dare you.*

Within five minutes he had his answer: *Tempting, but I'm more for disappearing.* —The Talented Mr. McIlvoy

Danny tried the door to Malcolm's workroom—double-locked—and settled himself on a rolling chair to gaze at the play of streetlight through the Waterford vase. The Calvados glided down this throat, stinging less than the nagging sense that he was missing a crucial connection.

FIFTY-TWO

MERRIT ROUSED HERSELF WITH a jerk and stumbled out to the living room where Gemma slept on the couch next to the fireplace. She surveyed the lamp she'd left on as a nightlight, the banked peat fire, and Gemma curled under three blankets. All as it should be.

She checked her mobile. Dermot had texted. He'd decided to drive to Dublin in the middle of the night to fetch his Aunt Tara back to Lisfenora. Arrival sometime in the morning.

"Shoot."

Returning to the bedroom, she sank onto the bed and tossed around for a while. But it was no use. There was no way she was falling back asleep now. She turned on the bedside lamp. A framed photo of the Ahern family in happier times stood next to the lamp. Laughing Mandy and Petey with a hugely pregnant Ellen. Merrit angled the picture toward the lamplight for a closer look.

Ah, jeez. She closed her eyes, pressing the picture against her chest. How much could a man like Danny take?

He had crashed out of the house hours earlier. She'd felt a peculiarly male steam coming off him, a mix of impotence and recklessness and determination. If he was thinking clearly, he hadn't shown it.

And here she was, in his bed, precisely where the villagers had thought she'd been cavorting all along. How perfectly ironic.

A faint creak settling into the sound of the wind rattling the casement windows drew her out of bed again. Merrit peeked out the curtains but saw nothing but darkness. The inactivity, the waiting, the expectation of an answer gnawed at her. Gemma lay in the living room like a totemic cipher, inviting the rest of them to circle around her in prayerful desire for her to bequeath her secrets unto them.

In the living room, Merrit poked at the peat pellets until they glowed orange. There had to be food in the house besides the cereal she'd brought. A draft slithered around her ankles as she entered the kitchen. She froze at the sight of the back door creaking on its hinges. A long line of night stared back at her. Grey Man, she thought. Could be it was about to ooze inside and flip her off her feet and drag her away into the murk.

"Oh, stop it."

She pushed the door to slam it good and shut, but the wood pushed back. Hard. Her face exploded in pain. She bent over and cupped her nose as footsteps shambled past her, none too steady, stealthy, or fast.

Catching her breath, she ran into the living room. She gasped at the sight of a man with hands encircling Gemma's throat.

"What are you doing?" she yelled. "Seamus, stop!"

She grabbed Seamus around the shoulders and used her body weight to pull him away from Gemma. He fell on top of her in a fug of unwashed grief and struggled like a stuck beetle before rolling off her. Merrit scrambled to her feet, but as quickly as the violence had occurred, it died.

Seamus approached Gemma again. He raised his hands, but this time his shaking fingers grabbed at air before landing on Gemma's shoulders. Gemma opened her eyes and stared into space.

Merrit despaired of her. If Seamus's hands around her neck weren't enough to wake her up, then what would?

Merrit grabbed Seamus by the arm. He almost went down again, but she managed to prop him up and push him toward the bedroom, picking up a wrought iron fire poker on the way. She let go of Seamus and pointed the poker at him.

Seamus buried his face in his hands. His Hail Marys and Holy Fathers lacked conviction, as if he knew it was too late for him.

"Have you gone insane?" Merrit said.

Seamus was too caught up in misery to heed her, now muttering that he didn't know where it had all gone wrong.

"Seamus!" She nudged him in the arm with the poker. "You had to know someone would be here with her. What were you thinking?"

He raised a bloodshot gaze toward her. His face crumpled. "My son."

He curled into a ball on the bed, mumbling something about not caring anymore.

Merrit grabbed her mobile off the dresser. "I need to call the guards now."

"I know what you're thinking, lassie, and you don't know the half of it. You don't know anything." He curled tighter into himself and buried his hands between clenched thighs. "All I wanted was to ensure Brendan's future."

Seamus's attempt at a smile was nothing but a ghastly effigy. "In for a step, in for a mile to hell."

FIFTY-THREE

BY THE TIME MALCOLM arrived home after his fancy date, Danny had finished the Calvados and let his senses relax into a mellow swirl of impressions and half thoughts. It helped that the alcohol had diluted his anger. Without the excess emotion, he thought things might make sense. But they didn't. He'd have to go with his instinct when it came to talking to Malcolm.

Malcolm appeared with welcome smile prepared. He wore a slim blue suit and a mauve tie with a faint sheen of silver threads sewn into the weave. His woo-the-lassies tie, no doubt. A little bold but sensitive at the same time. He was like a standard poodle, showy and sociable.

"McIlvoy warned you I was here," Danny said. "Nice of him."

Malcolm checked his watch and glanced around the place. His gaze landed on the empty Calvados bottle. "Danny, Danny, Danny, is this perverse payback for my *liaison* with Ellen? I might have to get you fired. You know that, don't you?"

"I admit to a *perverse* pleasure in breaking into your place, so let's call it even for shagging my wife. I do have some bad news, though."

Humming a little, Malcolm slid the jacket from his shoulders. "Honestly, Ellen and I had a fine friendship through the auction fundraising committee. I didn't realize I was leading her on. But then she began showing up at my place." He held the jacket up, gave it a shake, and laid it carefully on the kitchen countertop. "I swear, sometimes I think I ought to check my charm at the door. Gets me in trouble I'm sad to say."

Danny counted to three and exhaled. "Women can be tricky. I feel for you."

With gentle tugs Malcolm loosened his tie and drew it from around his neck. He held it up so the two ends dangled at exactly the same length, gave it a shake as he had the jacket, and folded it in half before laying it on top of his jacket. "Versace. Silk. Available in Dublin, but then you don't get there often, do you?"

"Too true," Danny said. "But then I don't have a good income from a jewelry business, do I?"

Malcolm wagged a playful finger in Danny's face. "Now, now. I'll fix us tea. A nice green tea sent over from Harrods of London."

Danny transferred himself to a bistro-style table that sat opposite the sink. Despite himself, the more he observed of Malcolm, the more fascinated he became. It was a special breed of fascination tinged with loathing.

"There now." Malcolm set a tea tray on the table and slid into place across from Danny. He poured hot water into loose-leaf tea strainers that perched on their teacups. "Milk, sugar, lemon?"

"I'm fine without," Danny said. "You're not the least bit curious about the bad tidings I bring?"

Malcolm stirred milk into his tea. "You'd be a likeable fella if you weren't so tedious."

"Related to Firebird Designs, I'm afraid."

Danny made a show of rifling through his pockets. He placed the opal necklace that he'd borrowed from Nathan alongside the matching earrings that Merrit had retrieved from Gemma's jacket pocket. "As you can imagine, I didn't notice the workmanship on the earrings when I found them in my wife's jewelry box. So kind of you to give them to her, I'm sure. But I wonder at anyone breaking up a set like this."

The teacup tinged against its plate as Malcolm set it down. His hand crept toward the necklace. Danny slapped it away. "Now, now, I may be an unimaginative member of the Gardaí, but even I know a good story when I hear one. And there's no use telling me these aren't a set, a special set made for Siobhan McNamara, because we've got corroboration and all that boring Garda shite."

"Of course these are Firebird. That goes without saying," Malcolm said. "I'd vouch for them myself, but as to anything else—"

"McIlvoy must have panicked after he killed Siobhan because he didn't take the time to grab her earrings as well as the necklace. That was quite the sorry mistake on his part, wasn't it? Imagine, years later, they appear on a boy named Toby Grealy—McIlvoy's own son. And no mistaking it this time. They were stolen off him well and good."

"I wouldn't say John was the panicky type," Malcolm said, "and, anyhow, you're farting in the wind with your conjectures. But entertaining, I must say."

"Oh, I'm sure. The bad news for Firebird Designs is that now we have to investigate the business. In depth, you see. Who knows what we'll find?"

"This is preposterous."

"Indeed. Preposterous that our lost boy's mother's earrings went from his earlobes to my wife's jewelry box. You gave these tainted things to Ellen, so that gets me wondering how the devil you got them." He raised his hand. "I know it. You were with my wife the night Toby Grealy died, and I'll be the first to admit that my imagination hasn't plumbed that oddity yet."

"Because there's no oddity about it."

"Then there's this necklace, found on the itinerant Sean Tate, Nathan's father."

Malcolm sniffed and sipped. "Nathan. He's not one of us."

And you are? Danny didn't say.

"Planting the necklace on Sean Tate was a handy way to unload a piece of incriminating evidence in the Siobhan McNamara murder case."

Malcolm reacted by cocking his head like an inquisitive—what?—cocker spaniel? Danny wondered what it would take to bring out his inner pit bull.

"Altruistic of you to befriend Sean Tate on behalf of McIlvoy. Whether you or McIlvoy, we know—"

"Please don't talk about us as if we're interchangeable." Malcolm shuddered. "You can't imagine how that irks me."

Danny paused. "I imagine so, because you're the real brains behind the operation, aren't you?" He was feeling his way in, trying to get at the heart of Malcolm. "What you'd love most of all is your picture on the artist's statement in your shop."

"And why not?" Malcolm said. "I'm the face of the brand, after all."

"You like to deflate others and inflate yourself, don't you? That's not a healthy recipe for seeing reality clearly."

Malcolm's lips thinned, sharp as ice chips. "You talk to me about reality, when you're sitting here telling ridiculous stories to take your mind off your almost-dead wife. But if it helps you cope, who's to say what's healthy and what's not healthy?"

Danny steadied himself by squeezing his knees. "We have a theory about why you faked McIlvoy's death. We call it the Golden Goose Theory."

Malcolm merely raised his eyebrows and checked the water level in the teapot.

"You help protect McIlvoy in return for a greater share in the business. I imagine your share has grown over the years. You're a persuasive fellow when you want to be."

"That's the closest you've come to an astute thought since I arrived." Malcolm gazed down at his fingernails and gave them a quick buff against his trousers. "But still, there you sit looking like you know what's what. But how could you? You don't know how I've languished under his name. I'm the proper figurehead, but you can't just go changing a brand, not one as well-respected as Firebird. I'm after maintaining its brand integrity, and that's meant living with McIlvoy—"

"I didn't realize Firebird maintained *brand integrity*."

"You doubt me?"

"Seems to me Firebird is Firebird. That's the brand. Not McIlvoy, not you." Danny set his teacup aside. "Who gives a fat cow's arse about you?"

Malcolm swung out of his chair and shoved his empty teacup into the sink. He flushed. "I'm the brand. Me, Malcolm Lynch, and my designs, yes, *my* designs, will see their way to the best shops in Dublin, and from there—"

Here we go, Danny thought. "Like I said, rather full of yourself then."

Malcolm picked up the teacup again. He smoothed his index finger around its rim. "There now. No harm done. I wager you don't know the difference between bone china and fine china. This set is antique bone china from Royal Ascot. Hand painted. And look what you almost made me do, break one of my pieces. You don't know how to handle fine collectibles, do you?"

Now it was Danny's turn to cock his head. This episode of the Malcolm Show had just turned bizarre.

"Even though I'm the true soul of Firebird Designs," Malcolm continued, "I've had to live under McIlvoy's endless presence. It's all me, it's always been me. My initiative. My business acumen. Even my design ideas. Some of us have a greater purpose. But how could you possibly understand that?"

In a moment of clarity, Danny understood the crux of the man. This wasn't his overactive imagination creating stories out of sparrows either. Malcolm loathed McIlvoy. How it must chafe not being able to preen and fawn with the credit of Firebird Designs.

And then Nathan Tate's father happened along, who looked similar to a picture on an identification card.

"How long had you been on the prowl for some poor bastard to die as John McIlvoy? I imagine that could take years. You needed to find someone the same height and coloring. Someone no one would miss. The Golden Goose Theory isn't quite correct, is it? It's not so much about protecting McIlvoy as about getting rid of him permanently." Danny leaned back, thinking it through. "A fake death to camouflage a real death later?"

Rather than an inquisitive spaniel, Danny thought he glimpsed something more fierce going on alert as Malcolm stood.

"Would you like some ladyfingers?" Malcolm excused himself and stepped the two steps to the refrigerator to fetch a pink bakery box. "Lovely, these. I discovered this bakery in Ennis not two months ago and have been talking it up. In fact, I helped triple their business. The *Clare Challenger* reviewed them last week—a smashing review, I might add. I don't eat many sweets as you might have guessed, but my palate never lies."

A *brriing* caused Malcolm to jump toward his mobile sitting on the counter. He grimaced when he realized that the sound wasn't coming from his phone, but from Danny's pocket instead.

"Sir," O'Neil said when Danny answered, "a couple of officers are picking up Seamus at Fox Cottage. He attacked Gemma, but Merrit got him under control. Merrit's coming to the station too. No one seems to be hurt."

Danny kept his voice casual. "She's an anxious one, is our Mandy."

O'Neil picked up on Danny's subterfuge, saying, "You're not after doing something stupid, are you?"

"Perhaps so. You settle a hot water bottle against her stomach and she'll fall back asleep right as rain."

O'Neil got the hint and rang off.

"No hassle," Danny said into empty air. "You didn't wake me. Right. Cheers."

Danny clicked off. He stared into the pink bakery box where a dozen perfect confections coated with powdered sugar beckoned him to indulge. Bloody hell. Seamus? Something loosened itself from deep inside his brain, but he didn't have time to think it through. He'd have to wing it to get under Malcolm's slippery suit of skin. Somehow. Talking about John McIlvoy wouldn't do it.

"Excuse me," he said. "I'd better wash my hands before I eat."

Malcolm nodded his agreement and waved Danny toward the bathroom. "The guest soap is to the right."

A bloody guest soap. God, how he wanted to see the bastard squirm.

Inside the bathroom, Danny ran the water and texted O'Neil. Without waiting for a response, Danny wetted the guest soap, mussed the hand towel, and returned to Malcolm.

Sitting down, he picked up a ladyfinger and pointed it up at Malcolm. "Did you know that Ellen kept a journal?"

FIFTY-FOUR

ALAN ALWAYS FELT MOST restless during this quietest time of the day, beyond the height of night but well before light peeked over the eastern horizon. He stood in Fox Cottage watching through the window as Merrit drove toward the Garda station. The guards had already left with Seamus. Merrit had chosen to follow them and had called him to watch Gemma. She liked to be involved, that one. Maybe she would make a good matchmaker in the end.

He dropped his hand to Bijou's head. "Good girl."

She wagged her tail in response to his voice. She was dopey from the painkillers but otherwise her usual self.

He raised a window sash to inhale quietude. Gemma's presence was loud behind him with her abundant curls tangled in all directions and spine erect against the sofa back. She wore an ancient U2 concert t-shirt, child's size by the looks of it, and a pair of Dermot's boxers, making her look more childlike than ever.

If she'd been aware and reactive, moving her hands in that graceful way of hers, he'd have found the whole tangled, half-naked mess of her arousing. While she was still catatonic, thinking that felt like a taboo, so he banished it from his mind.

Telling Bijou to stay, he approached Gemma. He wasn't sure what to do with himself. He was still a stalker, watching her while she was unaware of him. One would think he'd feel comfortable with that, but he twitched with embarrassment. For her, for him.

"Gemma?" he said. "Do you know I'm here?"

Her gaze remained fixed in space and her expression vacant.

He fetched orange juice with a straw and stooped in front of her. She sucked when he touched the straw to her lips, went lax when it dropped away. It was eerie, like a machine, obedient yet unresponsive at the same time.

Behind him, Bijou inched toward the sofa. The big gulumph thought she was being stealthy, but her heavy breathing gave her away.

"Bijou, stay." Bijou poked the back of his neck with her wet nose. "Bijou," he warned in a louder voice.

Gemma rocked forward the tiniest bit. Toward Bijou. At least, Alan could have sworn she did.

"That's right, Gemma, Bijou is here too."

He placed a hand under hers and signaled to Bijou. *Good dog, come. Good dog, come.* It didn't matter that Bijou couldn't see the movements. What mattered was that somewhere in her brain Gemma register that her canine friend was nearby.

Bijou sidled up beside Alan and plopped her head on Gemma's lap. Her tail thumped harder than ever and she drooled with excitement. Her head canted to the side with ears perked as she gazed at Gemma like she was a doggy savior.

Alan knew his dog's body language. She was now waiting on a game. So much stillness from one of her humans meant that next there'd be wild movement and tumbling playtime. She woofed in response to the suspense of the wait.

Alan hesitated, unsure whether eighty pounds of keyed-up dog colliding into 110 pounds of immobilized woman was a good idea. On the other hand, given that Gemma preferred animals to people— one of her best qualities, in fact—there might be nothing better than mounds of fur and slobbery tongue to awaken her.

"This might be a go," he said to Bijou, who whined in response.

Alan maneuvered himself so that he sat next to Gemma.

"Time to try," Alan said. "Bijou, go!"

Two seconds later, the force of Bijou's joy toppled Gemma sideways against Alan. The dog head-butted her, licking her legs, pawing her arms. When she didn't receive a response, her tail sagged. She aimed a whine at Alan.

"It's okay, girl," Alan said. "Go on, play."

Alan watched, amazed as Bijou nestled against Gemma's supine form so that she was half on top of her. With a whine that Alan swore sounded distraught, she started licking Gemma. Her arm, her chest, her neck, her face. That great tongue of hers lolled over Gemma's chin, mouth, cheeks, nose, even her eyes, which Gemma shut automatically.

Gemma's nostrils flared.

"Careful," Alan murmured. "I don't think she can breathe."

Bijou placed one paw over Gemma's shoulder and covered her face with even more slobber.

Gemma's chest hitched up, trying to gain purchase against Bijou's weight.

Alan grabbed Bijou's collar, but he hesitated. He was witness to a small, extraordinary event, here, now, that defied logic but that somehow made all the sense in the world: his dog knew what she was doing. Alan believed this without question.

Bijou continued licking. Gemma's mouth popped open on an inhalation. Bijou's tongue lapped over her nostrils, her lips, drowning Gemma in saliva.

Alan's hand hovered, primed to pull Bijou away. Gemma's struggles increased as her body sought more oxygen. Alan's pulse accelerated, fearful, hopeful, undone. His chest ached with tension.

Gemma's face turned red with exertion. Alan positioned both hands around Bijou's collar and just as he was about to give up the delusion about his wise dog, he saw consciousness like a torch beam rising out of Gemma's soul. In three rapid blinks, she was gasping and squirming beneath Bijou. Bijou backed off with chest heaving as much as Gemma's.

"Holy mother," Alan breathed.

His beast couldn't track worth a damn, but licking, ay, licking enough to suffocate, she could manage. He couldn't think of what to say other than doggy words, but then, if there was anyone who'd understand, it was Gemma.

"Good dog, Bijou. Good, good dog. Best dog ever."

Gemma's gaze traveled over the ceiling. After a long moment, her eyes widened. Her mouth opened in a big O. Before Alan had a chance to react, she'd scrabbled over the back of the couch and run to the closest door, opened it to see a closet, slammed it, and run on until she reached the front door. She shot out of the house, heedless of her bare feet.

"Gemma!"

Alan had no trouble catching up with her, but once he did she squiggled and slid around in his embrace. His grip slipped. It was like trying to hoist an eel.

Sounds rasped against unused vocal cords, piercing and incoherent. Alan cringed against Gemma's high-pitched shrill. She had to be ripping out her vocal cords she was trying so hard.

Her chest heaved on a long inhale. After a pause, a lifetime of a pause it seemed to Alan, her scream shattered the night quiet.

FIFTY-FIVE

Danny bit into the ladyfinger he held. "For the last few months Ellen has been writing in her journal more than usual."

Malcolm used a spoon to transfer another one of the sponge biscuits from the box to a small plate. "I've cultivated a skill. Transformation I call it, and I can't help admitting that I could write a book. I'd call it *Transform Your Thoughts, Transform Your Life.*" He settled back in his chair with a dreamy smile. "It's about moving on. And you, good Danny, need to move on."

Danny squeezed his knees again. Remain calm. Just for a little longer. Don't think about moving on, about the real truth—that he'd moved on a little too fast, that in the past year he'd been happy in his own quiet space away from Ellen's turmoil, happy to play daddy every night and weekend.

"Transformation," Danny said. "That's quite a word right there. It makes me wonder how you'd transform yourself into a good lover. I have it straight from the source, dated some time last month, that Ellen was less than enthusiastic about your—shall we say—abilities."

Malcolm's ever-pleased smile remained, but Danny heard the beginning of a crack when he said, "Nonsense. She was mad for it even on that last night."

"I can understand your embarrassment. I've had to face the fact that I couldn't satisfy her, and I'll admit I'm relieved that I'm not the only man—"

"I told you—"

"And then Siobhan McNamara's earrings—the ones Toby was wearing—your parting gift, I take it? Frankly, I don't know how you could be such an utter bollocks. Alibi or not, you're pointing right at yourself for Toby Grealy's murder. Because how else could you get your hands on them unless you'd ripped them off him yourself?"

Malcolm cut a piece of ladyfinger and forked it into this mouth. "Poor Ellen. That was my last night with her, the final breakup after the breakup. Sometimes it takes women a few rejections to realize the truth."

"How did you get the earrings?"

"If you must know the truth—and I do hate to say this because he's my friend—Seamus gave them to me."

Danny swallowed hard against a wad of ladyfinger. Seamus again.

"Does this mean he killed that poor boy?" Malcolm continued. "That's not for me to say. I don't judge. All I know is that Seamus thought I might like them, which of course I did. He was forever trying to—what's that saying?—'grease the wheels' with me for Brendan's sake."

"Oh, really?"

"Well, yes, how else could I get the earrings since I was meeting Ellen that night? I can't be in two places at once. I did not kill Toby Grealy."

"So Seamus—who you're *not* accusing of killing Toby—somehow gets his hands on the earrings and gives them to you, then later that evening you turn around and give them to Ellen."

"Quite right. As you said, a parting gift. A nice one, I might add."

As interesting as this thread was, Malcolm's "transformation" shite had distracted Danny. He'd felt his phone vibrate with O'Neil's reply text message, so now it was time to cut through Malcolm's greasy distraction tactics. The man was oddly convincing.

"The reason I bring up the earrings is that Ellen couldn't pawn them off on Gemma fast enough. In her journal, she had quite a lot to say about your vanity in addition to your lack of prowess in the sack."

Malcolm's smile dipped toward tepid and the telltale flush started its creep. Danny was rather fond of Malcolm's colorful skin. It was a convenient barometer.

Danny bit and let crumbs fly out of his mouth as he spoke.

"But wait, that's not the best part. The best part is when she wrote that she was relieved that she didn't have to pretend to like your hairless hide anymore, said it gave her the willies." He paused as Malcolm's skin darkened to almost purple. "She always thought that no hair around the little laddie would cause it to appear bigger. I guess not, if she's to be believed."

One of Malcolm's eyelids twitched. He shot out an arm toward the pastry box and shoved a ladyfinger in his mouth. Powdered sugar drifted onto Malcolm's five-million-count, Christ-only-knew-what-kind-of-imported-cotton dress shirt. While chewing, he glanced at his heavy gold watch.

"You wouldn't be waiting for a phone call, would you?"

"I don't know how many times I've seen it in my life," Malcolm said. "Unreliable people. And Seamus most of all. I don't mind telling you that sometimes the weight is high indeed, especially when you have a so-called friend foisting his idiot son on you. Fecking waste, like father, like son." He shoved another ladyfinger into his mouth and chewed. "Tit for tat, one less grub."

"What tit for what tat?"

"Haven't you been listening?" Spittle flew out of Malcolm's mouth. "This wasn't supposed to happen, not to me. It's jealousy and ineptitude—a lethal pair, when it comes to a man like me— with people out to ruin my livelihood and my good name. And what do you do about it? Nothing. I still haven't heard anything back about the graffiti or assault charges against that Nathan Tate."

"Who's out to ruin your livelihood and good name?"

"Everyone!" Malcolm swiped the pink bakery box off the table.

"As far as I can tell, you, Malcolm Lynch, don't have a good name. All you've got is an oily smile and expensive suits. You're nothing."

With a sudden lunge, Malcolm's inner pit bull came to life. He launched himself over the little bistro table, knocking over the table and spilling Danny backward off his chair. The back of Danny's head bounced off the floor, but he managed to right himself enough to kick out with both his feet. His feet landed squarely on Malcolm's oh-so-flat stomach. Malcolm doubled over on a noisy exhalation just as the door to the stairwell opened.

O'Neil hopped into the room on nimble feet. Like a fecking caeli dancer, Danny thought.

"In the nick, that you are," he said.

"Waiting for the perfect timing," O'Neil said with his grin in place.

Danny rubbed at a scratch Malcolm had managed to leave on his cheek. "There's a consolation."

"Malcolm Lynch, you dapper son-of-a-something," O'Neil said, "seems like you assaulted an officer. That's all we need to keep you for a while."

O'Neil pushed Malcolm toward the door, but the man insisted on retreating for his tie and jacket. By the time he was suited up again, his coloring was back to normal and his smile back in place.

"I'll be home soon enough. I'm sure your superiors would like to know that Danny broke into my flat."

Despite his smug tone, he couldn't hide muscle spasms that played tag along his jawline.

Thursday

When the sparrow sings its final
refrain, the hush is felt nowhere more
deeply than in the heart of man.

Don Williams, Jr.

FIFTY-SIX

DAWN ARRIVED UNDER A grey cloud cover that matched Danny's mood. He hadn't slept between helping O'Neil escort Malcolm to the Garda station and returning to Blackie's Pasture once again. Mist lurked around the edges of the field. If not for the faint sheen of village lights, he could have been standing deep in the countryside.

But he wasn't. He was back where he'd started. Toby's death still hovered over him, trying to tell him something. But bloody hell if he knew what.

"You there, Ahern," Clarkson said. "Off to the side with you."

"I'm no longer on compassionate leave. I hereby reinstate myself."

"You're getting on my last nerve, you know that? You need to step away, step down, desist—phrase it how you bloody well like. You've already caused enough problems. You're in a world of bad when all this dies down."

He meant Malcolm, who'd arrived at the station talking about sanctions against Danny and how he was nothing but civic-minded, but he'd been stretched beyond his limits, and if they all wouldn't

280

mind he'd keep his mouth shut until his solicitor arrived to escort him home, because, of course, he'd done nothing wrong.

It had taken Malcolm a while to close his yammering maw, and by then they'd gotten the call from Milo of Milo's Silos that had led them back to Blackie's Pasture.

Meanwhile, Seamus was also waiting for them back at the station. The sublime chaos continued, and Danny wanted to be a part of it.

"I'll observe while I'm here," he said, "but I want a chance to interview Seamus later. The investigation is so off it's spoiled."

"And you think talking to Seamus will help?" Clarkson said.

"I have some thoughts, yes."

"We'll see. Get on with your so-called observing then."

Clarkson retreated to a tractor and flat bed that sat near the silage bundles. One of the three bundles sat on the flat bed and a swarm of scenes of crime officers buzzed around the other two.

O'Neil was already talking to Milo and the taciturn field owner. Danny arrived at O'Neil's side in time to hear the owner grunt in response to something Milo had said.

"It's not my fault a killer is on the loose on your land," Milo said.

The owner's voice turned out to be smooth as silk. "If you'd hauled them to my other property when I requested it, we wouldn't be standing here at all."

Milo turned to Danny. "Is it my fault the dead boy had no other place to doss down? There was enough space right enough, but who would expect that?"

"So you loaded the first bundle, and then—?" O'Neil prompted.

"I couldn't help but see the sleeping bag, now could I? And my first thought was that boy I'd found, so I had a closer look to satisfy my wits that I had found a clue."

The field owner mumbled something that sounded like, "Witless more like."

Danny excused himself and headed toward the crime scene activity. The two remaining mounds of fodder stood next to each other but with a space between them. The third had sat in front of them to form a loose three-leaf clover. Danny could see how there would have been a cavelike space in the center of the clover for Toby to shelter for the night.

Plastic flags marked various items lying within the perimeter of the shelter. A large pack that a hiker might use. A blanket. The boy had come prepared to rough it.

"What now, Ahern?" Clarkson called.

"That." Danny pointed beyond the hiker's pack. "I need a closer look."

"You better not be winding me up." Clarkson escorted him around the techs. "Well?"

They stood beside a marble Celtic cross mounted on a pedestal, common to many a tourist shop. It lay on its side—dropped, it looked to Danny. One of its arms was half buried in the dirt, the other pointing at the sky. It could be that the faint smudge on one corner of the arm was blood. Could be. Probably was. In other words, the probable murder weapon.

"I think it's time for me to talk to Seamus." Danny pulled out his mobile and snapped a picture. "Do I have your permission, Sir?"

"Oh, now with the respect, is it. Mind how you go. I want two of my team monitoring the interview. And I'd best not hear that you came within a fart's whiff of Malcolm." He raised his voice as Danny turned away. "Is that clear, Ahern?"

"Yes, Sir."

Fine. For now Malcolm was off the hook.

A whoosh of feathers passed overhead. Danny stopped to track the bird. He caught sight of a sparrow with a droopy wing hopping on one of the silage bundles, the one that announced *come home*.

"I see you," Danny said.

Across the field, an officer called, "You, get back!"

One look, and Danny changed directions, aware of the ever-present hovering at his back. None other than Merrit Chase had ventured into the pasture. She wore flannel pajamas under a rain-coat with slip-on gardening clogs, and her hair gathered up into a crazy sleep knot. She didn't seem to care, though, her impeccable posture as impeccable as ever.

She launched in without a greeting. "I walked over from the station when I heard that you—the guards—were back here again. Can you escort me in for a closer look at the 'come home' graffiti?" She met Danny's gaze, squinted at him, and looked away. "I want to compare it to what's on my car. Malcolm washed off his message before I could see it for myself."

"It's the same person. We've no doubts about that."

"Still. There's something that doesn't make sense to me."

"And what is that?"

She started ahead of him along the footpath that locals had pressed into the ground. They headed away from the plaza and toward O'Leary's Pub on the other side, with the bundles on their left. She paused to take in the police activity. "That's where they died—that's so sad."

She continued until she was abreast of the bundles and then slightly past them. From this vantage point, they could see *come home* scrawled across the bundle that stood closer to the O'Leary's side of the pasture.

Merrit sounded deflated as she said, "Oh."

"No great revelations?"

"I was hoping for a reprieve, I guess. The words on Malcolm's shop and these words both appeared the night Brendan was killed, right?" She looked around as if imagining how it might have been that night. "It was super foggy, if I recall."

She opened her mouth to say more, but closed it again. With head down, she turned around for the return walk to the Garda station. Danny gazed at the graffiti, trying and failing to grasp what Merrit had noticed. She'd latched on to something, though, because she wasn't one to walk with eyes aimed at the ground.

The hopping sparrow *tsip-tsip-tsip*-ed as it flew away.

FIFTY-SEVEN

GEMMA SHIVERED AND CURLED closer to Bijou's warmth and doggy smell. Dogs knew things, and they never lied. Bijou's relaxed behavior told Gemma that she was as comfortable here as if they were in Alan's pub. So that was good. Bijou felt safe, so Gemma could feel safe too, even though she lay on a couch in a room she didn't recognize.

She'd woken up to reality without realizing that she'd been gone, and then the memories had flash flooded her. Every ghastly moment that had lurked inside her bottomless well had threatened to pull her under. She'd had to run. The notion of being stuck in this house, like she'd been stuck in the linen chest with its knothole when she was a child, had terrified her.

She remembered it all now. How, after McIlvoy came to live with them, she'd spent huge swaths of time inside the linen chest. The way the towel that her mam laid over the old lace scratched her skin. The scent of cedar. The smell of a roasted chicken that her mam had taken out of the oven for dinner. The way Gemma's heart skittered around in her chest when McIlvoy's voice rose, enraged, because her mam dared to stand up to him. "The shop must stay in my name," she'd said. "It's the kids' inheritance."

And then. What came after. Her mam's gurgles as McIlvoy bashed her head against the counter before crashing out of the house. Gemma had managed to call 999. She'd known even then that she was closing down, that if she didn't whisper out a few words of help for the baby still inside her mam, she never would. She had managed this and held her mam's hand, willing her to stay alive but knowing that she was dying. Somehow she'd known that her baby brother could be saved. When the EMTs banged into the house, Gemma fled back to the linen chest.

And then. Toby's violent birth—more violent than McIlvoy's attack, it had seemed to Gemma, who had witnessed the second assault on her mam's body through a knothole in the chest. An emergency Caesarean that had looked like a massacre. A bloodbath.

And then. The squirming and squalling live thing that had come out of her precious mam's stomach. Nothing but a monster whose first loud wail had drowned out the world.

And then. Gemma had disappeared for a while, a long while, until she'd woken up one day in a care facility, awake but not whole.

And now? She wasn't sure she could live in the world with these memories. But then, this is what she'd wished for, hadn't she? She'd insisted on begging a lift to Lisfenora when Dermot had left. She had pushed herself toward this outcome. And now that she had the outcome, she wanted nothing to do with it.

She'd never be whole. She understood that now. She would always be the quiet girl who didn't handle people well. This was who she was. Her dreams of a miraculous recovery were nothing but a grand fiction.

"You've got some nasty cuts on your feet," Alan said. "But no stitches required."

Alan's voice startled her from her reverie. She'd have to watch that, the way she lost track of the outside world. Her hand snaked up, gesticulating in its automatic fashion. Oh, that too. She had so much retraining ahead of her.

Gemma opened her eyes. She'd sunk so deep into Gemma World that she hadn't realized they were closed. Alan sat next to her feet with a bowl of warm water on his lap. He submerged a wash rag and squeezed out the excess water. Rather than rubbing, he pressed the cloth up against the bottom of her left foot, then her right. He squinted and pressed harder near the ball of her foot. She twitched away from the pain.

He raised his hands, glancing at her, then away, then back at her and holding. "Oh. You're here then."

She nodded. Boy, was she.

"I wasn't sure if you'd—"

Fallen back into herself again. Yes, she knew what he meant. That would forever be the fear for anyone who knew her. And for herself too, she supposed. The proclivity would always be there. She understood this now also.

Alan excused himself and stepped out of the room. Rummaging sounds issued from somewhere behind her. A cabinet clicked shut, and then he was back with plasters and antibiotic ointment. "Right then."

His fingertips tickled when he tapped her skin with ointment. She'd never been as fragile as Dermot had treated her, and now here sat Alan also treating her like she'd break in half. But now she could talk, and with spoken words, maybe people wouldn't treat her like a porcelain doll. She opened her mouth.

Alan froze when the first scratchy sound came out. The skin on her face warmed—oh god, that reaction, the hard *tap-tap* of her heart—but she tried again. It was like her mam said to her all those years ago. *Say your words. It's okay to say what you need, baby.*

Gemma's eyes watered and the pressure increased in her chest. She hadn't realized she'd lost her mam's voice too. Her voice urging Gemma toward becoming her best possible self.

"I—I—"

Horrible croaky sounds. Gemma caught her breath, and then the next thing out was a gasp. The pressure in her chest so tight, she almost couldn't catch her breath. She struggled against every lost moment with her mam, the years spent in silence and despair.

"I—I—"

Alan held her hand. "You're grand, you are."

She almost choked on her need to speak the words, almost choked on backed-up tears. The words dribbled out of her. "I'm not that fragile."

"What?"

Her voice. It wasn't what she wanted. She'd always imagined something low, mellifluous, a cross between an actress and a blues singer. Instead, she sounded, well, girly. Not an ounce of feminine authority or wisdom to it. She sounded like the nine-year-old she was when her lips first glued themselves shut and her vocal cords froze.

"You can rub the ointment in harder," she said, louder this time.

There. She'd said them. Her first words in seventeen years. It didn't matter what the words were, just that they be.

"Right then," Alan said. "I'll press a little harder."

Alan continued where he'd left off. The sting was okay. She could handle it.

"See?" she said. "Not so fragile."

He smiled down at her feet. "You're a funny odd creature, you are."

Yes. She'd always been. She'd have to accept this about herself too.

"Where am I?"

"This is where Danny lives right now. Dermot brought you here after the attack and finding you in the forestry lands."

Ellen, where is she? Is she okay? Gemma struggled to her feet. *I can't believe I didn't remember that. We have to go.*

"You're signing," Alan said.

She crawled around the room looking for her shoes. "Ellen," she said.

The silence behind her was so loud she turned around. Alan folded a plaster over on itself. "Not good. She's still unconscious."

Gemma hung her head. It had been a repeat performance of her mam's death. A woman—Ellen—enraging McIlvoy so much that he lashed out. Just like before. This had been the refrain in her head—*just like before, just like before*—when she'd bolted from Ellen's house, her terror so vast—vast as the universe—that this time around she hadn't even had the brains to call 999.

"Dermot?" She scrabbled back toward Alan and plucked a new plaster from the box. She slapped it and two more on her feet and returned to the ground. "My shoes?"

She didn't care how her voice sounded now, or that she couldn't speak above a whisper. Along with every other emotion that had erupted out of her today, she felt a searing resolve most of all. She had to finish this once and for all.

"Over here." Alan led her to the corner of the room where someone had flung their knapsacks and sleeping bags. "Dermot is fine. He drove to Dublin to fetch your aunt. Aunt Tara?"

She nodded. Aunt Tara didn't travel well on her own, so that made sense.

Gemma grabbed the first knapsack, looking for clean clothes and socks. This one was Dermot's, but it didn't matter. She found a jumper and pulled it on. Amongst the dirty clothes, a photo caught her eye.

Her mam, her dear mam. Looking so happy. She remembered this wedding portrait sitting on the fireplace mantel, the hopes Mam had had for a happy family when she married McIlvoy. The image showed just their faces, cheek-to-cheek and grinning. McIlvoy hadn't seemed so bad. At first.

She pushed the photo at Alan, not wanting to touch it anymore. "Him. He did it. That's him."

Alan frowned. "I don't recognize him."

She found socks and trainers. She pulled them all on, including a scarf, and her hoodie, and stood without tying her trainers.

"I can talk now," she said.

The statement was a revelation, a small source of power.

"You mean to the guards?" Alan said.

She swallowed. "To Danny, please. Not to everybody at once."

FIFTY-EIGHT

SEAMUS SWAYED IN A gentle rhythm back and forth. "Now it can end. I'll gladly rest me head in the gaol to have it all end."

"Listen to me," Danny said. "Can you do that?"

Seamus continued swaying, lost in his own world, mumbling to himself. The hours of wait inside the Garda station had withered Seamus. His shoulders slumped forward and his head almost bounced against the tabletop. The room stank of him, alcohol mixed with despair. He'd refused coffee and a solicitor.

"Let's start with Gemma. Why did you attack her?"

Seamus swayed faster.

"The good thing is that you didn't hurt her. The DPP might not bring charges against you at all. But I'm still wondering about your guilt. It can't be about Brendan—"

"My son." Seamus covered his face with his hands. His shoulders shook.

Danny scooted his chair so he sat closer to Seamus. "—because you couldn't have killed your own son."

Seamus mumbled something. Danny pulled his hands away from his face. "You need to speak up." He felt bad but it needed to be done, so he continued with, "Brendan in a field, his neck broken. That wasn't you—was it?"

"You've got it all wrong."

Sometimes the trick was to get witnesses talking. Seamus was a far cry from Malcolm, who now sat in a room enjoying a chat with his solicitor while he waited for the team to return from Blackie's Pasture. Meanwhile, Seamus was so mired in his own agony that he didn't know what was good for him. Danny felt like a right bastard, but this was what he needed to exploit—Seamus's helplessness and despair.

"I have it wrong?" Danny said. "What do I have wrong—John?"

Seamus froze. Then a second later he was up and pacing around the room, half leaning against the wall to support himself. "I wish I'd never heard that name. I wish I didn't know anything about him."

"Are you John McIlvoy?" Danny said.

Seamus knocked his head against the wall. "No, no, no."

Danny grabbed him, turned him around, and helped him slide down the wall. "Okay, no 'John.' Okay?"

"It's all my fault. All of it. I might as well have killed Brendan with me own hands." Seamus grabbed Danny's leg, and for the first time since Danny entered the room, held Danny's gaze. "I let the Grey Man into our lives."

Danny slipped down the wall so he was seated next to Seamus on the ground. He'd felt the same thing: that he'd somehow let Grey Man into his life too. Slithering in with the fog and still hovering—but cloaked. Danny was blind, somehow, to the truth of things. But he wasn't sure which truth he was looking for anymore either. Too many truths had glommed together. Toby. Brendan. Gemma. Ellen. Malcolm. McIlvoy. Seamus. Nathan too.

And himself.

He'd missed the sign the sparrows had tried to convey to him.

"Malcolm said that you gave him Siobhan McNamara's earrings—the ones that Toby Grealy was wearing when he died. Someone had stolen them off his body. You can see how it looks between that and attacking Gemma."

Seamus stared at the blue wall across the room.

"You knew Toby Grealy. You can't deny that. Brendan brought him home to meet you."

Seamus closed his eyes and leaned his head back against the wall. "He was trying to be helpful, is all. He knew I had an interest in anything to do with John McIlvoy. Because of Nathan Tate. Nathan was the one to first get me thinking, see, about how I might ensure my son's future. I had befriended the man when he first arrived. And a most interesting story he had too. One mention of a hairless wanker who surely had a hand in his father's death, and I knew he meant Malcolm."

He spit out Malcolm's name as if he couldn't get the sound of it out of his mouth fast enough. Danny sat back, relaxed now. He had Seamus in the sweet spot; all he needed was a little prompting to keep talking. So, Danny prompted.

"So you pointed Nathan toward Malcolm—"

"Ay, and then I invited Nathan to be one of us crows at the Plough. Malcolm fancies he's one of us too, that he does."

"And Brendan?"

"Malcolm is always on about Firebird, how he's going to expand its brand. So I let him know that I'd gotten wind that McIlvoy was found dead—not giving Nathan away, you see—and that I had to wonder what Malcolm had been up to. But, I could stop wondering if he'd give my lad a job, teach him about business, get him going on a stable future."

293

"As a shop boy? That's no future, is it?"

"Of course not, but it were a foot in, and I hoped to see Brendan take over the shop in the future. Malcolm can't hold on to it forever. I wanted Brendan as safe as possible. That was always the goal."

"And how was that going to happen?"

Seamus grimaced with his eyes still closed. "Oh, I hear you. You think I'm an egg short of a full dozen, but I were thinking more and more that Malcolm hid something big, and I planned to find out what that something was, and when I did, Malcolm would have to let Brendan in on the business. We'd enter into a deal."

Danny thought about Brendan in all this: a son who'd almost died as a child; a son trying to please his dad; a son who wrote adventure stories that took him far away from reality. "What did Brendan think of your plans for him?"

Seamus opened his eyes. They were liquid with emotion. "If only he'd been the rebellious type. The type to tell me to feck off and let him be. The type to run away to make his own way in the world. But he weren't, and I thought myself lucky for it. Now look at me." Tears dribbled out the sides of his eyes, but he didn't notice or didn't care. "Like I said before, I might as well have killed Brendan meself."

"And Toby?"

"Oh ay, my boy brought him around like a gift to me. And so it went, as soon as that poor lad laid out the earring maker's blame for his birth mother's death, well then, I thought myself content indeed. John McIlvoy, that Toby said, he'd be the jewelry maker, he'd be the murderer. And it seemed like Malcolm had his hermit jewelry maker right where he wanted him, didn't he?" He bounced his head against the wall. "How could I know any better?"

He cracked his head once more against the wall, harder this time.

"Go on," Danny said. "You're doing great."

"We told Toby that Malcolm knew all about McIlvoy. The lad was practically pissing himself he was so eager. He went around to the shop the next day. And, of course, I had a wee chat with Malcolm myself."

Danny remembered Malcolm's description of the visit—the would-be thief with grubby fingernails. "Your plan in all this was to discover something to hold over Malcolm's head the way he was holding Siobhan McNamara over McIlvoy's."

Seamus continued bouncing his head against the wall too hard for Danny's liking. He laughed but not quite a laugh, more like a demented cackle. "Ah, Danny, you've got it wrong at the same time you've got it right. But the outcome was inevitable anyhow. Toby had to die."

"Why?"

"Because Malcolm deemed it so if I wanted assurance of Brendan's future. Simple as that. But I didn't think through the ramifications. Had no clue how Malcolm's mind worked. He's good, that one. Bent me over like a bare-arsed poof, and I had to take it. Even when it came to that wee Gemma who witnessed her mom's murder. I knew he had me. If I didn't off her, McIlvoy would eventually go down, and if he went, Malcolm said that he'd make sure I did too."

A smear of blood stained the wall behind Seamus's head, but he continued pounding.

"Seamus, stop," Danny said.

"I can't. Why should I? What difference does it all make now? Yes, I knew that Toby was dossing down in Blackie's Pasture. I couldn't let him stay with us. Yes, I went there to kill him—"

Seamus's head came to a stop.

"—but Malcolm had gotten there ahead of me. Toby was already dead, see, but now I've got the blame. Like I said, Malcolm's good."

He shifted sideways so he was facing Danny. His bleary gaze wandered over the ground and up Danny's body. "I've decided prison isn't any better, after all."

"Better than what?"

"Than a Devil's Pact. Malcolm was right about that, anyhow."

Seamus's hand shot out and in the moment Danny blinked in surprise, he grabbed a pen out of Danny's shirt pocket and jabbed it into his own neck.

FIFTY-NINE

"Don't pull the pen out of his neck!" Danny yelled as he ran out of the interview room. While someone called the EMTs, Danny found a scarf in the lost-and-found cubby under the reception desk and ran back to Seamus, cursing himself for not seeing it coming. Seamus had been hitting his head against the wall hard enough to draw blood.

He landed on his knees beside Seamus and wrapped the scarf around his neck to hold the pen in place. Beckoning an officer to hold the scarf, he ran back out of the room. The on-duty officers stood in clusters, talking louder than usual. Clarkson, O'Neil, and several others were still at Blackie's Pasture.

"Where is Malcolm Lynch parked?" Danny called across the noise.

Someone pointed down a short corridor to a small conference room reserved for suspects and their solicitors. Danny strode across the room.

"Danny."

Merrit stood near one of the desks, the one composed person in the room. She still wore the flannel pajamas and raincoat he'd seen her in at Blackie's Pasture. Her stillness could be unnerving, but

Danny saw it for what it was—a barrier. A barrier that sometimes allowed her to see things with scary astuteness.

"You've been waiting for me this entire time?" he said.

She nodded. "Two things, and then I'll go. Alan texted me. Gemma is awake. She can talk, and she remembers her mom's death. Alan's bringing her in."

Danny's fingers tingled with a spurt of adrenaline. This changed everything. "Brilliant."

Merrit held his arm as he turned away. "She only wants to talk to you. For now. She's still … you know."

Danny nodded, his brain in high gear, and continued to the conference room.

"Wait, Danny, that wasn't the second thing," she called.

But he was already entering without knocking first. Malcolm sat with legs crossed and tie loosened oh so artfully. The man at ease, with no worries. As reptilian as ever.

"Back for more conversation?" He nodded toward the man sitting beside him. "This is Ian Finn, my solicitor. I'll be in need of coffee soon if this waiting is going to go on much longer—"

"Shut your bloody mouth," Danny said.

"You need to leave, Detective Sergeant," Finn said. "You interrupted a private conversation with my client."

Finn stood, but Malcolm waved him down. "Danny and I, we're friends now, aren't we?"

Danny closed the door and grabbed a chair. He angled it right up next to Malcolm and sat so that their knees brushed.

Malcolm grinned, looking down at their legs, and didn't shift away. "Come now. Really?"

"Seamus rammed a pen into his own neck," Danny said.

"I'm not surprised. He wouldn't last five minutes in prison, a man like him. He knows that."

"You did something to him." Danny leaned closer, elbows on knees. The solicitor might as well have not been there. "Put a nasty little bug in his ear."

"Don't say anything," Finn said.

Malcolm mimed turning a key to lock up his mouth. "Apologies, good Danny. I must heed his advice."

"Oh, that's quite all right. I relish the chance to get a word in without your endless self-serving blather. I've come to various conclusions, you see. You believe that Firebird Designs means something, that anyone would care one way or another about a line of necklaces and earrings. It's all yours and only yours, to your mind at least, and along comes Seamus and Nathan Tate, ready to out you for killing Nathan's father."

For once, Malcolm kept his mouth shut.

"What else could you do but accept Brendan as an employee, let Seamus think he was going to get his way, and then bide your time." Danny needed to speak fast before Clarkson returned. He lowered his voice. "Because that's what you're good at, isn't it, Malcolm? Biding your time. You've been doing that all these years with Firebird and with finding a good candidate for McIlvoy's supposed death. So what's a few more months when it comes to getting Seamus and Brendan out of your life, eh? Because you don't share, and besides, the Nagels are beneath you."

"Of course they are," Malcolm said.

"Mouth shut," Finn said. "Is this an interview, Detective Sergeant? Because if it is, you must record it."

Malcolm was bursting to speak. His skin was starting to mottle with the effort to keep his mouth shut.

"Then a boy named Toby arrived, a boy who also wanted to pry into your tidy little life with Firebird Designs. Worse yet, he wanted to out McIlvoy as a murderer, and Seamus knew who he was too—McIlvoy's son—which meant you were even more entwined with the Nagels than before."

"You're only about half wrong there."

"Malcolm," his solicitor warned.

"I suppose you used your persuasive tactics—quite the skill you have there—" Danny said.

"Thank you. I come by it naturally—"

"—to have Seamus believing it was in his best interest for Brendan's future to get Toby out of the way. Poor Seamus. You used him to keep you immaculate hands clean. But then, if Seamus wanted in so badly with you, then he had to deal with McIlvoy's baggage too, right?"

"There's a cost to doing business, I always say," Malcolm said.

Finn looked about ready to pop a vessel. Malcolm waved down his protests before he spoke them.

"Yes, hapless Seamus," Danny continued, "who found himself doing your bidding to kill Toby."

"Ah, so you do understand that I didn't kill the poor boy. Perhaps you are smarter than you look, good Danny."

"Not so fast." Danny paused. "No one, least of all me, denies your alibi. Yet, Seamus insists that Toby was already dead when he arrived, and that you did the killing. I lean toward believing him rather than you. How did you manage it, Malcolm?"

"Note this, Finn. He's bending the facts to suit his needs."

By now Finn was stooped over a pad of paper, taking copious notes.

"There's no question," Danny said, "that the cross that struck Toby's head came from your shop. I've seen them there myself. Solid Connemara marble, am I right?"

"Bah. Point against Seamus again. Brendan gave him one as a gift not long ago. How it landed at the crime scene, I don't know. I can't imagine why a godless child like Toby Grealy would want such a thing." He sniffed. "And Brendan. Worse than useless."

"Yes, Brendan. He had to die too. Without Brendan around, Seamus would no longer have reason to pry into your shop affairs, and he wouldn't accuse you to the guards because as he put it, you'd find a way to take him down too."

"Malcolm," Finn warned. "Don't say a word."

"A son for a son," Danny said. "Is that what Seamus meant by a Devil's Pact? And somehow, you still persuaded him that it was in his best interests to kill Gemma for what she might remember about McIlvoy the murderer. Too bad for you he didn't have the heart for it." He tapped his fingers on the table. "Or perhaps it didn't matter whether he succeeded or not. Now he's arrested and will be on suicide watch. You'd like him to kill himself, wouldn't you?"

"Danny, Danny, Danny."

"And we can't forget Ellen," Danny said.

Finn stood. "Time to leave. I will be reporting this harassment to your superiors."

"I agree," Malcolm said. "You are quite obsessed with me, aren't you?" He smiled, looking pleased with the idea.

"Fine." Danny stood. "By the way, Gemma is awake and talking and remembering and arriving at the station any time now."

Malcolm blinked slow as a lizard with stone cold gaze.

SIXTY

GEMMA PAUSED IN FRONT of the Garda station to gather up her will. She had all kinds of coping mechanisms that her counselor had taught her. Unfortunately, they'd fled except for a breathing exercise. So she breathed. She could do this. She could walk into the station and she could talk. She had something to say. Many things to say.

Up ahead Alan said, "Ay, she's here. Gemma, you still back there? Come see Merrit."

Merrit appeared out of the fog and grabbed her in a hug. She smelled like stoked peat fires and facial cream. Gemma leaned into her, liking her more than ever.

Merrit pulled away but with her arms still around Gemma's shoulders. Her gaze penetrated Gemma, and Gemma's body responded with the breakable feeling like it always did. "You're fine, I can see that, but—are you ready to, you know, engage?"

No. But I have to now. It's time. She caught herself and dropped her hand. "Sorry."

"It's fine. I get it." Merrit thought a second. "Your signing is like my inhaler. A crutch. I still fall back on it sometimes for my anxiety. Do you need me to go in with you?"

"No, thank you. I have Alan."

Merrit's cheeks balled up when she grinned. A squirmy sensation, uncomfortable and thrilling at the same time, filled Gemma. Merrit let her go, glancing back in the direction of the station's front doors. A troubled frown dampened her smile. "I should go. Danny's expecting you."

With one fortifying breath, Gemma waved bye to Merrit and stepped through the door that Alan held open for her. After the insulation of the fog, the bright, noisy interior of the station almost sent Gemma fleeing after Merrit again. Her skin prickled with the beginnings of the sweats. But her bones weren't glass and her skin wasn't parchment. She wasn't going to fall apart. She never had before. Even so, the trembles were so bad she thought she was going to throw up.

She waved a hand in front of her face, trying to catch her breath. "I can't do this."

Care wrinkles deepened the lines around Alan's eyes. "I'll be beside you. If you want that."

An inner door opened and Danny greeted them. His hair stood in all directions and blood spattered his shirtsleeves. Tension radiated from him, and Gemma, ever sensitive to male energy, shied back behind Alan.

"You remember now?" Danny said.

"Go easy," Alan said. "Give her a chance."

Gemma handed over the wedding photo of McIlvoy with her mam. A niggling something caught at her and eased away before she could capture the thought. Her nerves were so tight she didn't think

303

she could hold on to anything right now, anyhow. Thank goodness she hadn't eaten in a while.

Danny stared at the photo. A crease ran down the center of it where it had been folded. "Where did this come from?"

"Dermot brought it," Alan said. "Gemma found it in his knapsack. He's off fetching their Aunt Tara from Dublin. That's why he's not here."

"I hope he returns soon," Gemma said.

Danny started at the sound of her voice. No doubt because of its unused scratchiness, its humiliating girlishness. But he surprised her.

"You are the best thing I've heard all day," he said.

He held out his hand for her. Her body quaked so hard she felt like it was going to crack open wide as a seismic fissure. She waved her hand in front of her face, trying to catch her breath as she placed her other hand on top of Danny's and let him escort her into a loud room full of men. She froze with hand still in front of her face.

"Let's get her to the loo," Alan said. "Give her a few minutes."

Danny led the way between desks. The men's curious glances might as well have been laser beams penetrating Gemma's skin. She pulled up her hoodie to create blinders. Alan placed a gentle hand on her back. Just for a moment, but it helped.

"This suffices for our public loo. Unisex. Take as long as you need."

Gemma rushed forward, turning and pushing the doorknob, and pushing harder until the resistance gave way and she almost fell on top of the uniformed officer who was exiting.

"Excuse me, Miss," he said. "We're through here."

A second man standing at the sink turned around. But he didn't need to turn around for her to know who he was. She remembered everything now.

Gemma grabbed the wall in response to what felt like every bone in her body shattering at once. Behind her, Alan and Danny entered the room behind the uniformed officer.

"I've got him," the officer said. "Back we go then, Mr. Lynch."

With every ounce of her being, Gemma tried to talk, tried to say two words. Only two. But just as in the forestry lands, she couldn't. She opened her mouth and nothing but pathetic croaks emerged.

Malcolm shrugged as if to say, *What do you expect?* His squint slit razor sharp against her skin, penetrating deep into her heart, cutting it open. *Use your words,* her mam had said.

But she couldn't manage both words and emotions. It was too much. The edges of her vision blurred. Malcolm's smug chuckle rasped into her, reminding her, doubling itself inside her head until she thought she would scream.

"The little grub seems quite incompetent to me," Malcolm said. "Now if you please?"

Something snapped. *Grub.* His favorite word for her back then, in Dublin. He'd said it in the forestry too.

One second Gemma was stumbling away from him and the next she was on him in one leap, wrapping her legs around his waist, forcing him backwards against the sink. She clawed at his smooth skin, skin he cared for, yes, of course. He would.

"Get her off me!" Malcolm yelled.

Gemma tightened her grip. She swiped at his right eye, then clawed, until Malcolm's eye teared up. His grunt of pain buoyed her, kept her going despite hands that sought to pull her off him. She focused all her attention on steadying her hand while she pinched.

Malcolm roared, a sound she remembered well from her childhood, and in one ferocious movement flung her away from him, propelling both her and Alan backwards into the wall. Malcolm swung toward her, his hands already raised, but Danny grabbed him around the neck in a chokehold.

Gemma struggled to catch her breath, dimly aware of Alan propping her up and Malcolm tussling with Danny. Several other men entered too, but Gemma didn't care anymore. She'd gotten what she wanted. Her proof even if nobody else had noticed anything amiss yet.

Malcolm hurled curses at her, his face mottling red. Yes, that too she remembered.

He held a hand over one eye. "Where's Finn?" he yelled. "That little hoor almost took out an eye. I need a hospital."

"Give us a look then," one of the men said.

Malcolm's voice had turned into a snarl. "Get your paws off me. I need a doctor."

Gemma raised her hand and uncurled her fingers.

"Danny," Alan said. "You need to see this."

One look at the brown contact lens on Gemma's palm and Danny was out of the room calling for a cell in which to lock Malcolm.

Gemma let her arm drop. Exhaustion settled over her. Alan sat down next to her. She leaned against him and closed her eyes.

"He's John McIlvoy?" he said.

She nodded because for now it wasn't that she couldn't talk. She didn't want to.

Friday

I watch, and am as a sparrow
alone upon the house top.

Psalm 102:7

SIXTY-ONE

DANNY SAT IN THE hospital with a copy of *Rebecca* cracked open on his lap. Ellen lay as before, insensate and peaceful. The machinery still monitored her brain, still drained her urine, still fed and hydrated her body.

In his pocket, he fingered his wedding band. He'd thought to string it around her neck so that when—not if—she woke up, she'd feel it and know—what? He wasn't sure.

He cleared his throat. "You'll be glad to know that we arrested Malcolm—or rather the Talented Mr. McIlvoy. One and the same man. No wonder McIlvoy seemed more figment than reality." He touched her hand, still so warm. "I saw Malcolm's contact lens case, but no specs. Too bad I didn't clock that like I should have. Point of fact, he doesn't need specs. He wears brown lenses to hide his eye color. Blue eyes, but one of them with a stripe of brown through the iris. Odd-looking. You can't miss it. Rare it may be, but Malcolm passed his strange eye color to his son, Toby."

After hours spent with Malcolm, who refused to respond as John, they now knew that his hair loss had occurred after he'd fled Ireland for Europe. *Alopecia universalis* it was called, and it could happen fast. From normal to reptilian in less than a year. Malcolm being Malcolm, he'd fallen in love with himself all over again and made himself into a sleeker, more urbane version of himself. The Malcolm of today with his impeccable wardrobe, thin frame, and pristine hairlessness bore no resemblance to McIlvoy of old. He was a regular Elijah Doolittle.

No, not Elijah Doolittle. Grey Man. Sucking hapless people like Ellen and Seamus and Sean Tate and even he, Danny, into his fogs.

"And then there's Nathan. Malcolm killed Sean Tate, his father. We know that too. That, at least, was like I thought. Malcolm wanted Firebird Designs for himself. He wanted to retire John McIlvoy out of existence. That's how much he detests his prior self, as if John is a separate person, even down to the P.O. box he used to send himself checks. It all made sense to him. The man's completely around the bend." He squeezed her hand. "I'm sure that doesn't surprise you."

A knock interrupted him. Merrit stepped into the room.

"What are you doing here?" His tone was too sharp. "Sorry."

"I visited Seamus. Seems to be mending well. His body, at least." Merrit walked around the edges of the room farthest from Danny's chair. "May I sit for a bit?"

She pulled up a chair so that she faced Danny across the bed.

Danny pulled his wedding band out of his pocket. It still gleamed despite his tarnished marriage. "Ellen used to like it when I told her about my cases. In the old days, I would have told her about Toby Grealy, the way he looked when he died, as if he saw angels in the sparrows above our heads. She would have wanted to know everything after that. Like how, with the help of Seamus and Brendan, he'd known that Malcolm was his lead to finding McIlvoy. And that he was the walking dead as soon as Malcolm got a good look at him."

"Ellen would have helped you cope."

"Hah."

But it wasn't funny; it was true. He didn't have the energy to roll his eyes at Merrit's hocus-pocus observations.

With a thoughtful crease between her eyebrows, she gazed at his hand clenching the wedding band, then at Ellen. "You can talk. I'll be your listener."

Just like that, thought fled. Instead he asked about Seamus.

"I told him that Malcolm had been arrested for Siobhan McNamara's murder, and he seemed relieved." She adjusted the edge of the blanket that covered Ellen. "Do you think you'll arrest Seamus for attacking Gemma?"

"Doubtful. Gemma doesn't want to press charges anyhow. And Nathan Tate will be fine too. Malcolm has been on such a roll that the DPP will have plenty of newsworthy cases to pursue."

"For Siobhan," Merrit said. "And for Brendan too?"

"Looks like it. He knew Brendan's dog walking schedule for Alan and watched out for him from his flat."

"Poor Seamus. To be the lucky one."

Danny looked up. He'd been fidgeting with Ellen's fingers, curling them up, straightening them out. "The man's unluckier than a bull at snipping time."

"Malcolm would have killed him eventually, don't you think? Because Seamus knew about his true identity. Seamus told me that Malcolm had told him the truth after Seamus confronted him with Toby's story."

"Ah, no wonder Seamus was so terrified of Malcolm. He hadn't known he was trying to manipulate a murderer. Then it was too late to wiggle his way out again."

And that's when the Devil's Pact truly began, whether Seamus knew it at the time or not. Malcolm's whispering Grey Man voice always in Seamus's ear. And in the end, both their sons dead.

"And Malcolm will be charged for Ellen's attack too?" Merrit said.

"He'd better be."

"About Ellen—"

"He never cared for her. She was useful for some egotistical reason and then she wasn't. Then he used her to give himself an alibi for the night of Toby's death. I found a passage in her journal. She didn't just show up at his place unannounced. He called her over. Ellen expected reconciliation but got the damned earrings instead."

Merrit fiddled with the zipper on her purse. "I'm the one who brought Gemma into the shop. He was right there, all over her—taunting her." She set the purse aside. "Of course he knew who she was because Dermot and she had been in the pub. He was practically daring her to recognize him."

"Of course. He would."

"That's how Malcolm saw the earrings." She shifted, looking pained. "That's how he knew Gemma had them, not Ellen after all, and he'd have heard through the pub that she and Dermot were staying at your house. It wasn't a secret. If he hadn't seen Gemma with the earrings—"

"Stop."

Danny closed his eyes for a moment. Merrit's meddling probably had worsened the situation. But now wasn't the time for recriminations, not here in front of Ellen.

"We'll never know," he said. "I had just been around asking Malcolm for McIlvoy's address. So maybe that put him over the edge to violence. Either way, he was compelled to get rid of the earrings and Gemma. Ellen was in his way."

Merrit didn't look convinced, but she went along with his train of thought. "He is still McIlvoy at his core. Full of rage when things don't go his way. He must have been fuming when Gemma got away."

"He went along to the forestry the next day in hopes of getting to her again."

"And what about Toby?" Merrit said.

The last loose end of the case. Seamus pointed at Malcolm, and Malcolm pointed right back at Seamus, and Danny still felt like he was missing something.

"I'm still pondering that one," he said. "Pointless, all of it. All for a bloody shop."

"Mmm." Merrit shifted the purse on her lap. "More than that. For posterity. Malcolm through his designs and reputation, and Seamus through his son's bright future as a local businessman. He was so hopeful."

"Only to get caught up in a false promise. Can you imagine Malcolm teaching Brendan the art of business ownership or leaving him the shop? It never would have happened. Malcolm was playing Seamus and playing with him like a cat with a mouse."

The novel that still sat on Danny's lap fell to the ground. As he bent to retrieve it, the wedding band dropped out of his hand. He'd been clenching it so hard it had warmed to the same temperature as his skin, so that he couldn't feel it anymore. He glanced at Ellen, at peace, her skin so smooth that Danny saw the woman he'd married. Perhaps over time they'd reached the same tepid temperature, so that they hadn't felt each other anymore.

He smoothed out the IV cord attached to Ellen's hand, then held out the ring. "I forgot string."

"String? That won't do." Merrit flashed a small smile. "Men."

Her fingers traveled to the moonstone pendant dangling within the dip between her clavicles. She unclasped the chain and slipped the pendant loose. Holding it up to the light, she said, "How could he be so talented and also so—"

"I know. It boggles the mind."

She held the chain out and Danny uncoiled it from her palm. His wedding band slid onto the chain and looked at home. The improvised necklace slid around Ellen's neck and also looked at home.

"Seamus was no match for Malcolm," he said. "He knew Malcolm had killed Brendan. Malcolm made sure that Brendan died in Blackie's Pasture. What better way to make his point to Seamus? Threat, revenge, and sadistic cruelty all in one go."

"Revenge?"

"For interfering with Malcolm's past. For using the past to force Brendan on him. For mucking about with the precious reputation of Firebird Designs. In the end, for threatening Malcolm's fragile ego, risking his perfectly curated identity."

He thought back to Malcolm's flat. No essence to be had there because it was nothing but set design.

Merrit still sat in her composed manner, watching Ellen sleep. "I'm sad for Dermot and Gemma. Toby was still alive when they arrived. They were so close to finding him in time."

Danny stared at Merrit, absorbing what she'd just said. His fingertips tingled.

She met his gaze. "What's wrong?"

He'd been a proper eejit, that's what. Bloody Seamus and the peanut butter. Bloody Dermot and the creased wedding photo.

Danny stood, pulled out his mobile, and was already dialing by the time he got to the door.

"Wait, Danny," Merrit said. "I never did tell you—"

"I can't now." He placed a hand over the end of the phone. "Thank you for the chain. I'll buy a new one and return yours soon."

SIXTY-TWO

MERRIT STOOD IN THE doorway. She'd risen as soon as Danny had left the room. He waved "sorry" at a nurse and hurried down the corridor with mobile stuck to his ear. He didn't notice how many of the nurses looked after him. What did they see? Tall, determined, strong, careworn. Perhaps. She saw a man with a cockeyed jacket collar and worn-down heels, a man who would now need to drop by Liam's house to return her chain.

And, a man who maybe didn't need to know the whole story, after all.

She returned to Ellen, this time perching beside her on the bed.

"I tried," she said.

A monitor beeped; the feeding tube dripped. A small wooden crucifix hung high on the wall, unobtrusive but still there. The crucifix seemed strange to Merrit, like so much of her life in Ireland. Her relationship with Liam, her status as outsider, her doubts about her abilities to follow Liam as matchmaker, her need for community and connection.

Which was why she'd latched on to Gemma. Maybe Gemma could become a friend if she stayed here. Maybe Merrit could foster a private matchmaking session between Alan and Gemma.

She smiled. Silly. Gemma already knew what was what. So did Alan, for that matter.

She picked up a silver brush from the side table and ran her fingers over the soft bristles. People were mysterious, yet they gave themselves away if you knew how to look. Danny, for example, the way he'd talked to Ellen while Merrit had observed from the doorway. His near constant contact with her body while he talked. This hairbrush for a woman with a shaved head beneath her bandages. He was in the process of realizing that he still loved her.

"Danny holds on to his feelings, doesn't he? Even if he thinks he's let go." The brush was lovely, a heavy silver antique that felt good in her hand. "I wish I'd gotten up the nerve to tell you that I hoped that Danny would become a friend, that's all. There was nothing else. If you were awake, you'd be happy to know that he tolerates me at best. I'm not a slag."

She set aside the brush. "The thing of it is that I want to bring him back into the fold. For Liam's sake. Danny hasn't let go of his feelings for Liam either. You and I both know Liam was, still is, like a father to Danny. So I need to continue working on that. And village gossip be damned."

Merrit rooted through the giant purse she always carried around with her. Below a half-completed scarf, yarn, knitting needles, a water bottle, and her camera, she found it—the Ahern family picture from Fox Cottage. An exuberant Ellen waved a paintbrush toward the camera with little Mandy and Petey hugging her legs. Her giant belly pushed out a smock so that it was almost a tent over the children.

"You were lucky that Malcolm didn't see you that night." Merrit shivered. "You probably just missed him in the pasture with poor Brendan."

Come home, Ellen had painted on the silage bundle. A message meant for Danny that anyone crossing the pasture would have seen. Danny would have learned about it soon enough even without Brendan's death.

Merrit set the photograph in its cheap plastic frame next to the antique brush, right where Danny would see it. When his head cleared, maybe he'd notice what Merrit had seen right away. Granted, Merrit made the connection because she'd talked to the color consultant at the paint shop. But still. You couldn't miss the splash of color across the front of Ellen's smock and the painted wall trim in background.

It must be a sweet baby's room with its magenta trim.

"Maybe you'll remain the final mystery." She smiled. "Men. They're obtuse sometimes, aren't they?"

She continued looking at the photo for a while. Home. Merrit had a chance to make a home for herself in Ireland. In fact, Ireland itself was home even if navigating local life felt like rough seas. The pull of the land grounded her, filled her up. She'd been home all these months and hadn't realized it.

SIXTY-THREE

ALAN GATHERED UP HIS jacket and called Bijou. The dog jumped off the couch. Gemma shifted under her mound of blankets. She hadn't moved from the couch except to go to the loo since she'd returned from the station after attacking Malcolm. They should have been celebrating now that she'd vanquished the John McIlvoy spectre from her past and now that Dermot had returned with Aunt Tara.

Gemma's listlessness worried Alan, but he couldn't do anything about it for the moment. He didn't need to be here, anyhow. Aunt Tara would return from her walk to continue her desperate hustling and bustling, cooking food no one ate, making endless calls about funerals and body transport, making something she called a "mourning pouch" in memory of Toby. She would take care of Gemma.

"I need to get back to the pub," he said.

He kept his voice down because Dermot was sleeping in the next room. He'd been subdued also. Malcolm's arrest hadn't seemed to mean anything to Gemma and Dermot in the end. Maybe they didn't trust their good fortune yet.

Gemma pulled the covers down. Those brown, fathomless eyes of hers gazed beyond him. She pointed to the front door and yanked the blankets back over her head.

Alan checked the window. Several Garda vehicles approached. He could hardly miss them with their neon yellow stripes and GARDA emblazoned in all capital letters. Danny and O'Neil approached and knocked on the door. The rest of the guards stood back but on alert. They'd pretty much surrounded the house.

"You'll need to stay out of our way," Danny said. "We're coming in now."

The door wasn't locked and in they came. "Where's Dermot?"

The bedroom door opened. Dermot squinted against the light. A lifetime's worth of grief coated him in a second skin.

O'Neil stepped forward with handcuffs. "Dermot McNamara, you're not obliged to say anything unless you wish to do so, but anything that you do say will be taken down in writing and may be given in evidence."

Dermot bowed his head, tears streaming down his face.

"Explain," Alan said.

"I remembered that Seamus can't open a bloody jar of peanut butter. No hand strength," Danny said.

"What?"

"Malcolm has an alibi for Toby's death, yet there was no way Seamus with this arthritic grip could have wielded the marble cross. You have to be strong to pick it up, much less wield it as a weapon."

"No," Dermot said with clogged voice. "It wasn't like that."

"You should keep quiet," O'Neil said.

"No!" Dermot struggled forward with O'Neil maintaining his grip on his arms. He dropped to his knees beside the bundle of blankets on the couch. "Gemma, please, listen."

The blankets shifted. Gemma peered at her brother.

"I didn't swing the cross like a weapon. I'd never do that. Do you believe me?"

"I'm not sure."

"You have to believe me. We fought, yes, because I wanted to bring him back to Dublin and talk about what to do next. Talk about your welfare most of all. Him larking off like that. It wasn't the way to do it. We had to think of you. We couldn't spring it all on you like that."

She sat up. "You have to stop with that."

Dermot placed his head on Gemma's lap, and she ran her fingers through his hair. Her look of despair just about shattered Alan's heart. He stood there, stymied beyond the help of insightful chalk-board quotes.

"Toby finally called me back," Dermot said. "There must have been a hundred messages on his mobile by then, between Aunt Tara and me. So I met him in the pasture. His life had been a lie and he meant to bring it out in the open. He was hurt, angry—betrayed. He thought he'd be the family savior all on his own. I couldn't get him to talk to me or to listen to me, so I ordered him to help me carry his things to my car. We were leaving. I picked up the cross. He tried to yank it away from me, so I raised it above my head, backing away, ordering him to grab his backpack."

Dermot shifted and looked up at Danny. "Toby yanked on my arms one too many times and the cross, it came down like a tree, cracked into his head. But I swear he was back up again straightaway, insisting he was fine. I don't understand it. How could he have died?"

"You left him there," Gemma said.

Dermot bowed his head. "That was my fault, leaving him. I should have known better. I said, 'Fine, you stay here, break Aunt Tara's heart.' Something petty, in any case."

"You took the wedding photo with your mother and McIlvoy in

it away with you, though," Danny said. "That makes it seem not quite as accidental as you describe."

"It had fallen out of his pocket, that's all. I grabbed it up as I was leaving. I told him I was going to burn it once and for all."

"We'd better go," Danny said.

"You'll be fine now?" Dermot's tone beseeched Gemma. "Please say yes."

"Yes."

In less than ten minutes they'd come and gone, and now all Alan could hear were Bijou's pants. Without finesse, he whipped the blankets off Gemma. She said she was not so fragile, so let her be not so fragile.

"Talk," he said. "Did you know?"

Gemma pushed curls out of her face. Alan relented as soon as she started shivering. He sat down next to her and wrapped the blankets around them both.

"Did you know?"

"I suspected," she whispered, flinching as she spoke. She'd told him she detested the sound of her voice. "The picture we found in Dermot's knapsack. Aunt Tara would recognize it. Toby took it from my mom's mourning pouch when he took the earrings."

And so what?

Alan caught on a second later. Dermot could only have retrieved the photo from Blackie's Pasture.

"It still doesn't make sense," he said.

Gemma's determined expression wilted. "It does make sense. Toby died because of me." She clutched the covers and jerked them over herself. "Please leave me alone now."

Alan hesitated. She was fragile, but not that fragile. Most of all, she was her own person, who knew her own mind. "I'll be at the pub if you need me."

"No, stay. Leave me alone and stay at the same time."

SIXTY-FOUR

GEMMA'S MEMORIES WERE ON overdrive now. She recalled too well the night her mom died. McIlvoy had lost his mind when her mom told him that she'd never said she'd share ownership of the family gift shop with him, she was sorry if he'd misunderstood but the business was held in trust for the children, there was no use talking about it, and why did it matter anyhow because her income was his, and his jewelry was selling well, and—that's where McIlvoy had silenced her words.

She wasn't sure how much time had passed since Dermot's arrest, but enough that Aunt Tara had returned from her walk, gone into hysterics, and called a taxi to drive her to the station. Gemma heard it all from the safety of her woolen cave. Her need to retreat was almost a physical pain, like she had an addiction.

Perhaps she did. To silence and darkness and quietude away from reality.

But now she had to face that reality. Ultimately, she was to blame for what happened to Toby. Dermot had spent years watching out for Gemma. He longed for a family of his own. He longed for her to get better. He feared that with any sudden shock she'd relapse into catatonia and he'd be back to the beginning. He feared what Toby's revelations might do to her.

His fear had caused him to confront Toby, to bully him.

Gemma pressed fingertips against her eyes to keep from crying. But she could have handled the truth. She *was* handling it. Right now. She was.

"Gemma?"

She unwrapped the blankets from around her head. Alan's face loomed, green eyes and a scar on his cheekbone and the barest dimple on his chin. Alan.

Concern crinkled up his face. "What's the matter?"

She shook her head. She needed to be strong for Dermot now, the way he'd always been strong for her. Hopefully, Alan would understand.

Gemma swallowed and ground out between rusty vocal cords, "Can I not talk for now?"

In response, with halting precision, he signed the letters *G, E, M, M, A*, and retreated fast. Heart fluttering, Gemma scrambled off the sofa to follow him.

He spoke as he headed toward the kitchen. "There's no denying it's twisted the way the fates played Malcolm's hand back at him. The way he tried to get at your mom's shop, and then later Seamus tried to get at his. And all because of his grand plans to take over the world of jewelry with Firebird Designs. It's beyond comprehension. A special brand of lunacy."

Gemma pointed to Alan's arm tattoo with its swirling temptations that could ruin a man.

"And I have my own brand of lunacy too. As do you, I might add." He got industrious with sponge and a dirty glass. "Nothing we can't work out."

Gemma's skin grew hot as she tried to process his words.

Alan finished washing the glass and pulled something out of his back pocket. A sheet of paper. "Merrit found this when she fetched your mom's earrings out of your jacket. She didn't mean to pry." He held out the sheet. "Here."

She'd forgotten. The flyer she'd pulled off the cork board at the fancy vet clinic. A local animal aid organization sought volunteers.

"Bijou's local vet could use an assistant," Alan said. "Could be a thought."

Gemma pulled back the kitchen curtain to reveal crimson and orange light spreading the day's last soft shadows across the pastures. Alan closed in behind her, but without touching her.

"Are you ready?" Alan said.

She nodded.

"For anything?

She nodded.

"For everything?"

She nodded. But, she told herself, she'd use her voice on her own terms.

SIXTY-FIVE

ONCE AGAIN, DANNY PAUSED at the threshold of his home. After a year in Fox Cottage, he was back to stay along with the children. It was a bittersweet pull, this moment. Even when he wasn't living inside this house, Ellen's presence had made it home.

But he had the children with him again, and he would hope for Ellen's return.

"Pappy, open the door," Petey said.

Instead, he turned around and sat them down on the stoop. They burrowed into his sides when he wrapped his arms around them. He'd missed them, holy hell, had he missed them.

Around them, a low twilit sun caught at shadows and lost the fight with darkness. An orange glow settled over the countryside, deepening to red and purple and welcome night and welcome bedtime for all three of them. The fog had finally lifted.

"Kidlings." He cleared his throat. "You remember what we talked about—about Mam?"

"It will be okay, Da," Mandy said. "I know it will. You'll see."

He squeezed her, wishing with every particle of his being that she hadn't turned into a caretaker of adults.

Petey's voice was muffled against Danny's side. "Grey Man almost got her, didn't he?" He sniffled. "I'm scared he'll come back."

He was so close to the truth of it that Danny had to force himself to keep his arm and hand loose around his boy. Malcolm would never be seeing Lisfenora again and thank the gods of old for that.

"He won't be back. That I can promise. He's gone even though you'll always hear stories about him, like faerie tales, nothing more."

"You got him, didn't you?" Petey snaked his little arms around Danny's torso. "I knew you would."

Oh hell, this was beyond Danny, this impending sense of doom that he would both love too much like Seamus and love too little like Malcolm. He didn't know what the boundaries of fatherhood should be. He'd been a dad for nine years now and was just beginning to understand its ramifications.

"When are Gemma and Dermot coming back?" Mandy said.

"I'm afraid—" He stopped. He hadn't thought about Gemma now that Dermot was in for a legal roller-coaster ride. There was still more to investigate about his claim that he'd struggled with Toby, not hit him with intent. Benjy would have to review the case all over again. Seamus had corroborated that Toby had admired the cross, so he'd given it to him. So simple. A boy who longed to be the family savior.

He'd succeeded. But at a tragic cost.

"Dermot can't stay here anymore," Danny said.

"But, Gemma, what about Gemma?"

Good question. She would need to remain local to support Dermot, and it could be better for her to stay here than at Fox Cottage by herself. They could barter. Free room and board for help with the kids. And there was Marcus too; his own roller-coaster journey toward sobriety might be sticking at long last. Danny would have to see. He'd have to see about everything.

"We might want to consider Grandpap Marcus too," he said.

Petey clapped his approval.

"But what about Gemma?" Mandy said.

"We'll ask her first to help her out, and then we'll see about Grandpap. And the kittens too. I'll fetch them from Alan tomorrow. This will be our plan."

Petey clapped again. "We can help them all."

Sweet, sensitive boy, already knowing how little they could help Ellen.

"Oh, look." Mandy pointed toward the hedgerow near the front gate. "Can we help it too?"

Danny squinted. "I don't see anything."

Petey pointed too. "We have to help it."

Danny didn't need to see the sparrow to know this was what they spied in the grass. A flutter caught his eye and was gone again.

"It's flying!" Petey called.

"And that's just as it should be." Danny held their hands and stood. "Now, let's see what we've got in the freezer for dinner."

Mandy grabbed his house key and unlocked the door and ran inside before Danny had a chance to hesitate again. Petey stayed close. His tone was both hopeful and cautious. "I like being home and you do too, right, Da?"

"I do indeed. Home is the best place to be."

The talk continued after that September of the unaccountable fogs. Locals hunkered down as winter cold and rain settled in on them, and a new tale grew, a tale of Lost Boy, who'd come to right a wrong and ended up Grey Man's victim instead.

It may be true that on the morning of his death a stream of light found its way through the fog. And it may be that in a lucid moment he remembered Matthew 10:28: "And fear not them which kill the body, but are not able to kill the soul."

It may also be true that by the strength of his final thoughts, he vowed that the truth about John McIlvoy would become known. Somehow. He didn't know how. He didn't care. Before he died, he believed.

So, if there be a providence in the fall of a sparrow, Lost Boy was that sparrow and providence let him linger long enough to die in the arms of a lost man, one of Lisfenora's own, who had needed his own talisman.

Thereafter, Lisfenorans spread tales about strange sightings when the fogs rolled in. They argued about what the sparrow with the drooping wing meant, but all would agree that Grey Man who rolled in with the fog was better than a grey man living within their midst.

THE END

© James Titus

ABOUT THE AUTHOR

Lisa Alber is a Rosebud Award nominee for best first novel for *Kilmoon*, a Pushcart Prize nominee, and winner of an Elizabeth George Foundation grant and Walden Fellowship.

Before devoting herself to the fiction life, Lisa worked in Ecuador, Brazil, and New York City. Her various career choices included international finance, journalism, book publishing, and technical writing, with a minor stint as cocktail waitress.

Lisa lives in the Pacific Northwest with a tiny dog and a chubby cat. She's a member of Mystery Writers of America and Sisters in Crime. You can find Lisa at http://www.lisaalber.com.